PENGUIN BOOKS

THE GIRL WITH THE JADE GREEN EYES

John Boyd was born in 1919 and brought up in Atlanta, Georgia. He was commissioned into the U.S. Navy in 1940 and served in northern Russia, England, Japan, and the Philippines. He was the only junior officer mentioned in Samuel Eliot Morison's naval history of World War II. After Mr. Boyd's marriage in 1944 he received his degree in history and journalism at the University of Southern California. He is the author of nearly a dozen science-fiction novels, including *The Last Starship from Earth*, *The Pollinators of Eden*, and *The Rakehells of Heaven*, all published by Penguin Books. John Boyd lives with his wife in Los Angeles.

The Girl with the Jade Green Eyes

———— ✳ ————

John Boyd

PENGUIN BOOKS

Penguin Books Ltd, Harmondsworth,
Middlesex, England
Penguin Books, 625 Madison Avenue,
New York, New York 10022, U.S.A.
Penguin Books Australia Ltd, Ringwood,
Victoria, Australia
Penguin Books Canada Limited, 2801 John Street,
Markham, Ontario, Canada L3R 1B4
Penguin Books (N.Z.) Ltd, 182–190 Wairau Road,
Auckland 10, New Zealand

First published in the United States of America by
The Viking Press 1978
Published in Penguin Books 1979

LIBRARY OF CONGRESS CATALOGING IN PUBLICATION DATA
Upchurch, Boyd.
The girl with the jade green eyes.
I. Title.
PZ4.U63Gi 1979 [PS3571.P35] 813'.5'4 78-10590
ISBN 0 14 00.4996 7

Printed in the United States of America by
Offset Paperback Mfrs., Inc., Dallas, Pennsylvania
Set in Fototronic Trump

Acknowledgments
Norma Millay Ellis: From *Collected Poems* by Edna St. Vincent Millay,
Harper & Row. Copyright 1923, 1951 by Edna St. Vincent Millay
and Norma Millay Ellis.
Oxford University Press: From "Pied Beauty" by
Gerard Manley Hopkins.

to Mildred Klinger

The Girl with the Jade Green Eyes

Chapter One

———————— ✳ ————————

When that encounter looked forward to since the beginning of human speculation—the meeting of mankind with intelligent beings from outer space—occurred two years ago in a remote area of the Idaho Panhandle, the event was not marked in the heavens with strange lights or on earth with newspaper headlines. It began prosaically one Thursday morning in late May when Chief Ranger Peterson entered his office at the Selkirk Ranger Station to find Tom Breedlove, the station's junior ranger, already at his desk and writing a letter to his sister.

"What's on your work schedule today?" Peterson asked Breedlove.

"I'll be checking out the snow reports after I've finished this letter to Matty. She's graduating next month and wrote to ask me if she should go to college or go to work. I'm advising her to do what she thinks best."

"Delay the letter. I got a call from Jack Haney last night. He was measuring the snowpack on Hallman's Peak yester-

JOHN BOYD

day, and he swears he spotted campers below in Jones Meadow."

Breedlove swiveled his chair and looked toward Peterson in mild surprise. The Selkirk Wilderness Area, patrolled from the station, was almost three hundred square miles of granite crags jutting above heavily forested slopes. Bears, deer, and even a few mountain lions still roamed an area so rugged that lumbermen had never touched it. It was kept as a primitive area with few trails and those only for hikers. Jones Meadow was in the heart of the wilderness. Camping in the area was by permit only, and no permits would be issued until June.

"They didn't come through Porthill or Kootenai," Breedlove said. "Someone would have spotted them. If they came down from Canada, how did they get over the snow on Sawyer's Summit?"

"It's a mystery," Peterson admitted, "but we're not finding out sitting here, and I can't fly the copter up because I've used up May's allotment of gasoline. You'd better backpack to the meadow. If you start before lunch you'll get there before sundown. Take along extra rations. If they biked in, give me a call, and I'll fly in and confiscate the bikes, using June's gas ration. Take along a camping permit and issue it on the spot if they're afoot. And you might take along a special activities permit."

"If they're already there, why worry about permits?"

"I do things by the book."

"But why the special activities permit?"

"Haney got a look at them through his glasses. It was twilight and he couldn't see very well, but he swears the campers didn't have a stitch of clothes on."

Breedlove whistled. "They must be polar bears."

"Haney could be wrong, but I thought I'd tell you. With a nudist colony to look forward to, you might make it to the meadow by four o'clock."

2

He would not make it by four o'clock, although he left before lunch. At a flat-out walk, his long legs could carry his six-foot frame five miles an hour, but this was not a flat-out walk. It was climbing up and climbing down, and he had a winter's inactivity behind him.

Yet he enjoyed the exertions because he loved the forest. In his high-school and early-college years he had spent his summers camping on the Quinault Indian Reservation, where he had learned the Indians' lore and language and adopted some of their attitudes. The woods had lured him early and with such attraction he had not seriously dated a girl until he reached college, and she had been a botanist who shared his enthusiasm for growing things. Even then, the girl's tendency to classify and categorize had finally left him feeling ambivalent toward her. Breedlove was more than a nature lover; he was nature's lover.

Not that he didn't groan, sweat, and curse under the loads nature placed on his too-willing shoulders. The profanity found expression several times in the rough going over Barton's Pass on the trail to the meadow. Snowshoe trekking over the snowfield left him chilled and sweating in the rarefied air. He felt vastly relieved when he cleared the pass, stowed the snowshoes under an outcropping, and continued on down the needle-carpeted path.

Breedlove's concern over the park's intruders lay mostly in the possibility that they had biked into the area, portaging their vehicles over the snow on Sawyer's Summit. Trail bikes on the thin topsoil of the forest wore erosion patterns that could lead to ravines, dirtied streams, and toppled timber. He wasn't concerned about nudity among the unauthorized campers unless it indicated that they were freaked out. Then they would be in danger of freezing or starving.

The latter possibility generated a mild anxiety in Breedlove which spurred him northwestward along the

3

shoulder of a descending ridge. Shortly after five o'clock he climbed the ridge and followed a stream a mile or so onward to where it broke from the forest into a meadow flanked by mountain walls. Three streams joined here to form Jones Creek, which would eventually flow into the Priest River. In this season of melting snow the meadow was almost a morass, and the grass he stood on was wet.

Jones Meadow lay deserted in the slanting light, its thirty or so open acres bisected by its wide, shallow creek looping toward a shimmering green stand of aspen at the north end of the meadow. For a moment he stood admiring the scene, glad that he had been spared a possibly abrasive encounter with other human beings, yet regretting he had no one with whom to share the view, one of the few open vistas in the wilderness and a favorite of summer landscape painters.

Two weeks before, he had come here with a fish and game man, and as he surveyed the scene now, he got a vague feeling that something was askew, that there had been some minute alteration in the scenery that two weeks' growth of foliage could not account for. Shaking off the feeling, he splashed across a tributary stream and squashed over the grass toward a well-drained hummock which swelled from the meadow sixty yards east of the creek. After climbing onto the knoll, he slid the pack from his back, letting it drop to the dry turf, and saw at a glance that Haney's report had been accurate. Someone had been in the meadow.

Atop the mound the grass had been mowed in a circle ten yards in diameter, as if someone had tethered a sheep here and let it graze within the length of its tether. No ashes from a campfire were in the circle. Evidently the campers had been extremely neat. No litter or cycle tracks marred the grass. He saw no indications of a latrine until, scuffling the grass outside the circle, he came across a sheep's pellet.

4

He stopped to investigate, doubting the evidence.

Someone had brought a sheep to browse in the meadow, and it had cleared the top of the mound. Apparently the animal had been released to defecate outside the cropped circle, but it had been a very fastidious animal. It had dropped only a single pellet, and then moved a respectable distance away before dropping another.

Shaking his head in wonderment, he went back to his pack and took out the walkie-talkie. He called the base and Peterson acknowledged.

"Jones Meadow is all clear," he reported. "The campers were here, but they have gone. There's no litter or bike marks. There's evidence that the grass has been eaten, not smoked, and there's sheep droppings here almost as large as golf balls. I'll catch a fish and camp here tonight. I should be in around noon tomorrow. Ten-four and out."

He caught a trout, built a fire, and cooked supper. Afterward he unrolled his sleeping bag atop the mound and sat watching the sunset as he played his harmonica. The last notes he sent quavering through the gathering darkness were from "Love's Old Sweet Song." The stars were coming out. Beneath the spangled sky he crawled into his sleeping bag, and as usual when he slept in the open, he went immediately to sleep.

He awoke prematurely. The sun, still well below the eastern ridge, was striking the snows of Hallman's Peak, but he had not been awakened by the diffused light. Ground fog coiled around him. Across the meadow a bird trilled, its notes hanging in the air. Drowsily he closed his eyes, chiding himself for letting a natural sound awaken him, and he dozed again. From the edge of sleep he heard once more the bird's song, and this time it brought him starkly awake.

Out of the lilting, dipping harmonies of a mocking bird emerged the refrain from "Love's Old Sweet Song."

He sat up and looked around. Coiling and swirling around the hillock where he sat, the ground fog turned the mound into an island in a pond of mist. It was an unreal world, and the song bending around him was unreal to the point of enchantment. The song ceased, but the enchantment deepened. Dimly he discerned a movement in the fog down toward the creek. Wisps coiled and coalesced into an apparition moving toward him. The wraith materialized as a girl, gray emerging from grayness, moving toward him.

As she drew nearer he could distinguish her form clearly above the knee-deep fog. At first he thought she was naked and trailing the mists around her. He saw the inward curve of her hips and her wide-spaced, high-borne breasts. She moved with buoyant grace on lissome legs, her flesh gray with the silvery hue of birchbark. From her ease of movement, high breasts, and square shoulders he placed her age as approximately that of his sister—seventeen.

He remembered that Haney had reported several campers on the meadow, and he reached over and drew his walkie-talkie closer. If the lone, naked girl was a lure in a badger game, wariness was advisable, and the walkie-talkie would bring help. He did not like to think ill of a girl who moved so gracefully, but this one was an oddball. She had dyed her hair green.

On closer view he could see she wore a dress of sorts, a veil that covered but hardly concealed her, but despite the attractions revealed through her gown, his attention was drawn to her eyes. He could forgive her for dyeing her hair to match her eyes; they were a deep jade green, luminous and friendly and questioning, and they seemed to gather the light from the pale dawn. His grip on the portable radio relaxed. He could not think ill of a girl with such eyes.

Suddenly he wanted to believe in her hair too. Thick, luxuriant, and wavy, it looked as natural on her as clover in

6

a meadow, and it too, flowing almost to her shoulders, seemed to draw light from the dawn. Though the proof was not definitive, the green swash of her pubic hair beneath the transparent gown supported his sudden theory that the hair was genuine. He wanted to believe in her hair, to believe in her, although caution warned him she might belong to some cult whose leader had decreed that all hair must be dyed green.

Yet the girl approaching him followed no leader, he sensed. Her poised elegance, her grace, the warm but regal smile beneath her finely arched eyebrows bespoke the inner assurance of one born to command. In fact her regality denied her semi-nudity. Given dignity by her bearing, her rather absurd dress became an imperial robe.

In curiously unaccented words her voice fluted toward him. "Good-morning-sir. Did-you-enjoy-a-refreshing-and-wholesome-night's-rest?"

"Yes, ma'am," he said, reaching for his coat and donning it as he scrambled to his feet.

The title of respect came involuntarily to his lips despite her youth, and he scrambled to his feet because he felt it improper to address her from a sitting position. Despite its lack of intonation, her speech carried a sense of noblesse oblige that made her seem actually concerned over the quality of his night's rest. Hers was the manner of a queen inquiring into the welfare of a beloved subject.

"Excuse me, ma'am, but when I'm out like this I usually sleep with my trousers on."

He was mildly astonished to hear himself apologizing for his lack of nudity. Standing near her, he towered a foot above her, and she asked, "How tall are you?"

"Six feet."

"How tall am I?"

"Five feet."

His coat caught her eye. She reached over and fingered

the fabric of his cuff, looking up at him to say, "This is superb material. Was it a once-in-a-lifetime buy?"

"No, ma'am. It's government issue."

"What color is it?"

The sun had topped the rim of the ridge, so there could be no question about the color of his coat.

"Green," he answered. "The same as your hair and eyes."

"You have a superb head of hair," she said. "May I inspect its marvelous quality?"

He bent his head. She ran her fingers through his hair, fingering the strands, feeling their texture. "And what color is this?"

"Brown."

She cupped his chin to straighten his head and stroked her fingers over his cheeks. "It's growing out of your face."

Her speech rhythm was growing so natural he caught the astonishment in her voice.

"I haven't shaved yet, ma'am."

"May I watch you shave?"

"Certainly."

"What's the color of your eyes?"

"Blue."

She questioned him with a child's artlessness, but her green eyes, open, friendly, and curious, seemed to be listening too. It was as if she were looking into his eyes to watch the words form in his mind and eliciting from them all their shades of meaning. She was investigating him, and he was supposed to be investigating her. It was well that she was charming and regal and very different, but he had official responsibilities.

"My name is Thomas Breedlove, ma'am. I'm a forest ranger assigned to this area, and I've come—"

"What does 'Thomas Breedlove' mean?"

"It has no meaning. It's just a name."

"My name has a meaning. I'm Kyra. Do you see that tree there?"

She pointed to a willow in the bend of the creek. The sun was fast dissipating the ground fog, which hovered in a thin veil over the lowlands and the creek.

"The willow." He nodded.

She spoke with the sudden enthusiasm of a child revealing a secret to a special friend. "My name is Kyra Lavaslatta. *Kyra* means 'willow,' and *Lavaslatta* means 'far wandering' in my language."

What was her language? he wondered. Her name sounded Finnish.

"Are you from Finland, Kyra?"

"No."

"Where are you from?"

She glanced toward the eastern ridge, studying it, and for a moment he thought she might point to a rock or a tree. Weighing her answer carefully, she pointed toward the top of the ridge and said, "From there."

"From the other side of the mountain?" he asked.

"No. From the other side of the morning."

She answered with a guileless simplicity that convinced him she believed she was telling the truth. She might be an escapee from a mental hospital, he realized, who lived completely in a world of delusion, and compassion came to him with the realization.

"How did you get into these mountains, Kyra?"

"In a vehicle."

"What kind of vehicle?"

"I could tell you, but you wouldn't know."

She had dismissed his question. She turned her face from his and looked into the now bright morning. "Isn't the sky terrific. It's getting almost as blue as Breedlove's eyes."

She was being shyly evasive, but she was not avoiding

him. Apparently she wanted to visit a while, and he was not averse to her company. Out of regard for her shyness he would desist from any official questioning, he decided, but would ingratiate himself with her and let her reveal the truth about herself in her own way. If she was a mental case, eventually she would divulge enough information to permit him to take her into custody, and he was mindful that others were probably with her. So far Haney's report was proving accurate in detail, so the others must be secreted in the woods. Perhaps an entire ward had escaped.

"I'll shave now," he said to her. "Then I'll cook some coffee and bacon. Perhaps you'll join me for breakfast?"

"Terrific, Breedlove. Does your bacon have easternmost flavor at westernmost prices?"

He was bending to take his shaving gear from his pack when she asked about the bacon, and her phrase sounded weirdly familiar. Straightening, he asked, "Who taught you English?"

"I learned your rich and diversified language from Station KSPO."

There was a peculiar logic to what she said. She had been talking to him in the fervid language of television commercials.

"Come to the creek with me, and I'll show you how I shave. You must be a wizard at learning languages."

Walking beside him, she said, "It's easy. All beings who communicate are alive, so 'to be' is a key to language. Find it, and you can pair other concepts to it by a frequency of usage relationship. But I do have trouble with your color words. The television signal is very weak."

"It's the mountains around here," he said.

Vaguely he grasped the method she used for learning a language, and it had the same crazy logic as her clothes. It would be an easy way to learn if the learner had total recall and a memory bank as large as a computer's. To use such a method the green-eyed girl beside him would have to be the greatest linguistic genius on earth—if she was of earth.

He paused at his random qualification and dismissed it as an idea his own sanity would not let him accept. The girl was a kook, delightful, whimsical, and regal, but still a kook.

He found reason to shove the vagrant idea further behind him at creekside. If she was an inheritor of a technology more advanced than earth's, the supposition was belied by the intentness with which she watched him shave, as if a tool so simple as a razor and a lubricant such as shaving soap were marvelous inventions. But after he finished shaving and bent to brush his teeth, he found her intentness had another motive.

"You didn't cut yourself and say 'ouch'!"

In short, he had not followed the television commercial.

"Did you want me to?"

"I wanted to see the color of your blood."

"It's red, like the lettering on this toothpaste tube."

"I'm glad, Breedlove. Then we both breathe oxygen. You're my brother."

"Welcome to the family, Sister Kyra."

She laughed, a pleasant, tinkling sound. She seemed vastly reassured by the color of his blood.

At breakfast she was fascinated by the design of his spoon, holding it to look at it from various angles. Her sense of wonder was so great it communicated itself to him, and he remarked, "Kyra, you're the original 'child of the clear, unclouded brow and dreaming eyes of wonder.' "

"You've got a terrific phrase there, Breedlove."

"It's not mine. It's from a poet. Do you like poetry?"

A shadow flickered over her face as she answered, "We had poetry once, long ago, but the poets left us."

He wanted to ask where the poets had gone, but he did not wish to stir the grief he had seen in her eyes, and he was growing protective of her madness. On the other hand he admired her quickness and grace and remained always conscious of her dignity, despite her absurd dress, which almost totally revealed her nubile loveliness.

Her face enchanted him most. Though regal, it was a fine-tuned instrument for conveying the wide range of emotions that arose from her Cloud-Cuckoo-Land. The bone structure beneath the silvery gray skin was classic Swede—she could have been a young Garbo—and as they talked her charm wove a spell that made her odd coloring as unobtrusive as her semi-nudity. She ate only a slice of bacon and a slice of bread with a bit of jam and drank half a cup of coffee.

"If you don't eat more you'll be famished by noon."

"The sunlight feeds me, Breedlove," she said, fluffing her hair.

The charm of her wholly feminine gesture buffered the implications of what she said. She claimed the ability to photosynthesize light. If that was true, it would explain the green of her hair as chlorophyll. There was a scientific logic to her fantasies, and, playfully, he matched her zany logic with zaniness of his own.

"Maybe you're descended from a plant."

"Some believe so," she said. "Plants that lived on air."

"I'd have to agree." He smiled. "We call them aero-phytes, and among them is the world's most beautiful flower, the orchid. From the first time I saw you I felt you were the kissing cousin of an orchid."

Her eyes sparkled at his compliment, surprising him with her delight in flattery, but she could give as well as receive. "You must have sprung from the loins of a sturdy oak, Breedlove."

"Where did you see an oak around here?"

"I saw them on KSPO. We had them on Kanab."

"Kanab? Are you from Utah?"

"No. Kanab was the name of my world."

She was drifting into her mania, and he was intrigued by the novelty of her delusions. It was a pattern followed by many psychotics, he had read; outside the areas of their delusion they could be bright and sensible. Only when they moved into their illusionary world did their behavior grow strange, but they could become upset when their version of reality was derided. He decided to treat her imaginary world with gravity.

"What does the word *Kanab* mean?"

Seated on the grass before him, her legs crossed, she considered the question before answering hesitantly, "*Kanab* means 'mother,' but it means something more to us, perhaps 'queen-mother.' "

Suddenly she leaped to her feet and swirled before him. "What do you think of my dress, Breedlove? It's made from the sheerest of fabrics, laminated hydrogen plasma. Am I not the height of fashion?"

"Height of fashion" was a phrase plucked from a dress advertisement, he realized, but as she settled to the grass again as lightly as a falling thistle, she awaited his answer with girlish eagerness.

"It's beautiful. Laminated hydrogen beats nylon by a country mile. But earth women use dresses for conceal-ment as well as decoration. Your dress is very decorative but also very revealing."

"We used to decorate ourselves on Kanab, but we found it was too . . . provocative."

For the first time she groped for a word, to find the least offensive, he sensed, and not because her vocabulary faltered. Her vocabulary was excellent and apparently growing stronger by the minute. He didn't know precisely what hydrogen plasma might be. Probably it was a term learned from the early-morning science courses broadcast by KSPO.

"Actually you need to complete your ensemble with undies," he said, "to conceal your breasts and bottom."

"What are undies?"

He explained, and she sighed in genuine disappointment. "I feel bound enough with the dress alone. It's getting too warm in here."

Her madness and his common decency put a shield of propriety between them far stronger than her inadequate garment, and she seemed so vexed by the confinement of the dress, he invited her to take it off. Rising to her knees, she slithered from the garment in sinuous bendings and twistings, and she was totally unaware of the sensuality of her movements. Heaving a sigh of relief, she sat down in front of him as naked as a curd, folded the dress and laid it on the grass beside her.

Breedlove almost gasped his astonishment when he noticed a peculiarity of her anatomy that gave him the first inkling of evidence that she was not some mad waif wandering in the wilderness but exactly what she said she was, a girl from another planet.

Glancing over, she read the astonishment in his eyes incorrectly. "Breedlove, you do not consider me well formed and beautifully proportioned."

"Kyra, your body's beautiful, but—I hate to tell you this—you've got no bellybutton."

"What's a bellybutton?"

He unbuttoned his shirt, slipped up his undershirt, and exhibited his navel. The whorled bud of flesh struck her as humorous, and she laughed. "If that's all it is, I'm doing quite well without one."

Chagrined by their sudden focus on anatomy, he turned to another subject, asking, "What is it like on Kanab?"

"Oh, it was beautiful, Breedlove. Almost as beautiful as your own gorgeous planet, with mountains and snow and meadows with bright streams flowing to rivers which flowed to the sea."

The elation in her voice plummeted into sudden silence, and she added softly, "But that was long ago, long, long ago."

He could almost touch the sadness in her voice, but she was shaking off the mood. "My people worked by day and slept by night. At twilight they gathered to tell stories and pass on their knowledge to the young. We had but one creed, 'Love one another,' and we loved until the end. For men such as you death often came from too great a happiness, when they melted like snowflakes in the fires of life. But that was before the great sadness when the twilights grew too long."

"Why did you leave, Kyra?"

As her eyes and hair had seemed to absorb the dawn's earliest light, the sorrow in her face extracted sadness from the air they breathed, and the chill of her desolation infected him. He regretted his question as she looked away from him, out over the meadow, as if averting her eyes from some inner abyss of despair.

"Kanab is no more. Our sun grew pale, collapsed upon itself, and exploded."

Her palpable sorrow convinced Breedlove of the truth of what she said. His heart believed her, and with his knowledge came a great unease. Men had speculated that this might happen which was happening to him now, and he, a simple forest ranger, had become the first man to establish contact with an emissary of an alien species. Beyond his inner turmoil, overshadowing Kyra's sorrow, loomed the overwhelming question he knew he had to ask.

"Tell me, Kyra, out of all the planets in the universe, why did you choose to come to earth?"

Chapter Two

———————— ✷ ————————

"We came for help."

Her answer aroused his suspicion. It was not credible that one who traveled interstellar space should seek aid from a planet of toddlers only now making their first step into the solar system.

"You want our help?"

"There are only ten of us, and we are not gods but exiles. We heard radio noises from your planet and knew we'd find a civilization here. We seek a planet where we may renew our race, but we do not wish to usurp the dwelling place of other intelligent beings. But our fuel is exhausted. We need only a few gallons of water and a spoonful of fuel."

"What is your fuel?"

"It is a heavy metal that gives off heat from its own furnaces."

"You're probably looking for uranium 235."

"Two-three-five," she repeated, looking at him closely; then her face lighted up, and he could see a burden lift from her mind. "Yes, uranium. Could you give us a spoonful of uranium?"

She was asking for a spoonful of uranium as a neighbor might drop in to borrow a cup of sugar, and the absurdity of her request helped convince him of its authenticity.

"Uranium is controlled by the government. It's a very dangerous element. It's radioactive and has to be shielded with heavy lead whenever it's moved."

"I have a very light shield to carry it in."

"I'm sure the government would be interested in your shield, but the government guards the supply of uranium very carefully."

"Would you take me to your government?"

He laughed. "On earth, Kyra, there's a famous cartoon showing a being from another planet walking up to a grazing cow and saying, 'Take me to your leader.' I'm afraid that you've come to that cow."

She sensed the humor in the situation and repeated, "Breedlove, take me to your leader."

"There are so many leaders I don't know where to start. The topmost leader is the President of the United States, but two houses of Congress and a Supreme Court pass on most of what he does, and he doesn't ladle out spoonfuls of uranium. The agency in charge of uranium used to be the Atomic Energy Commission, but it has been divided into two separate agencies. Neither could act on your request without referring it to other interested agencies, such as the Department of Defense. . . ." As she listened, he wove his way through a maze of bureaucracies that might be concerned with her request. "The man who would know offhand which agency to take you to would have to be a lawyer specializing in political science."

"So there's nothing you can do?"

She spoke with a sympathy and understanding for his plight that made him more concerned with hers.

"There's something I can do. It's called 'passing the buck.' I can take you to my leader in the National Park Service and let him figure out what to do. Have you any written authorization from your planet's government to make the request?"

"My planet no longer exists," she reminded him.

"That's only a technicality," he told her. "The government needs documents. I'm not officially alive unless I produce a birth certificate and not dead until I have a death certificate."

He thought for a moment and said hopefully, "There may be another way. In my capacity as a civil servant I could act as an official witness to authenticate your arrival on earth, but to make the deposition I'd have to see the space vehicle you arrived in and officially attest to your need of radioactive uranium."

"I would take you inside the vehicle, Breedlove, because I trust you, but first I must ask you: How long will this take?"

"I'd hope to get it done within the next three weeks because, after that, this meadow will be swarming with campers and fishermen."

Her question had been voiced with concern, and his answer seemed to relieve her.

"It must not be much longer, or we may never leave."

"Would this environment be fatal?"

"No. Already my people love your planet, so beautiful and so like our own. It has given us hope. But we are people of light, Breedlove, and the day will soon come when the light from your sun will bid us to stay. This must not be."

The gravity of her manner disturbed him. Trying to cheer her, he said, "If you don't get away, there's an earth ritual I'd like to be the first to introduce to you. It's called 'courting.' Young men call on young women in their parlors with the intention of proposing marriage or a reasonable facsimile."

"Then I must show you my parlor." She smiled.

"First let me call my office. I'm expected back by noon."

"Can you spend another night on the mound and join my people in our twilight ceremony? It will teach you much about us."

"I'd be delighted. Was it your people who cropped the grass?"

"We ate it."

He had grown so accustomed to her oddities he only glanced around and commented, "I hope the wire grass didn't upset your stomachs, and you should leave enough for me to clean my pans."

He radioed Peterson and requested permission to stay overnight to conduct a survey of the trout population in Jones Creek. Peterson agreed and wished him luck.

"Thank you for being discreet, Breedlove."

"I want to keep you secret until we've made plans. If it became known you had landed here, there'd be claim jumpers all over the place, and I want to keep you for myself. You're my chance to go down in history. Now, take me to your leader."

"We have no leader, Breedlove. We are all as one."

"What do you know about the qualities of light, Breedlove?"

Her question came as they neared the aspen grove on the far side of the creek.

"Not much," he admitted. "I'm no scientist. But I read a lot. I just finished an article about lasers. A laser beams light amplified by the stimulated emission of radiation, but don't ask me what that means."

"Then maybe you can best understand when I tell you

that what you don't see before you is an optical illusion.''

Forty feet in diameter and over three hundred feet high, the Kanabian space vehicle rested on its base in the aspens barely four hundred yards from the hillock in the meadow. It was invisible and unrecordable on human instruments. It had destroyed three or four trees on landing, but even its self-made landing pad was invisible.

Kyra continued to explain the ship's properties in terms intelligible to a nonscientist.

"Light corpuscles travel halfway around the circumference of the craft and continue onward as rays so you can see behind it from any angle. Its invisibility protects us and keeps it from frightening animals. In nonmountainous areas it would be a hazard to low-flying aircraft, but birds sense it and fly around it because it alters the magnetic lines of a planet in its near vicinity.''

Leading him into the grove, she whistled three notes on an ascending scale. Before them in the shadowy forest he saw a swash of pale light grow visible, lengthen downward, and become a door opening to form a stepless ramp, resembling translucent ivory, leading into the spaceship. It was a gateway through nothingness leading into something. For a moment the sight disoriented his sense of reality, and he faltered in his stride. She reached over and took his hand lightly and said, ''Be careful going up. The ramp's slippery.''

Her touch and conversational tone steadied him. He followed her up the ramp, feeling massive and gross, a mortal invading a fairy dimension, but he was not alarmed, no more, he thought, than Aeneas following the Sibyl into Hades. When he stepped into the rotunda of the ship, he had lost his feeling of unreality completely to his sense of awe, but he remained alertly observant.

Centering the rotunda they stood within was a shallow concavity about four feet in diameter surrounding a man-

20

hole cover with an inset handle. A narrow ramp without a guardrail spiraled upward from the rotunda until it was lost in a pink haze of sunlight filtering through the skin of the ship. Anchored to the deck at the base of the ramp stood a padded couch, designed, he assumed, to absorb the G forces on its occupant at takeoff, but it was like none constructed for earth astronauts.

The gravity lounge had straps he assumed were safety belts, but the headrest and shoulder straps were at the foot of the couch, which was tilted at an acute angle. Three separate lines of tubes, red, yellow, and green, wound down from the bulkhead above to cluster at a terminal box above the couch. From the box itself, a single tube with the dimensions of a garden hose dangled from the terminal box, its knobbed head almost reaching the couch.

His observation of the peculiar gravity lounge took only seconds, and as his eyes traced the varicolored tubes upward he saw a woman descending the ramp.

This female, too, was nude and green-haired, but there her resemblance to Kyra ended. Barrel-torsoed, with a massive uplift of pectorals in the travesty of a bust, her gross-featured head was sunk into a wrestler's sloping shoulders. Advancing on him, she scowled, and began to hiss as she drew nearer.

She was the Gorgon of this fairyland. He cowered as she descended, fighting an impulse to flee even as he felt the beginnings of paralysis from the irrational, primordial terror the sight and sound of this creature aroused in him. Kyra fluted in the direction of the brute in a purring, lilting language, and the she-thing halted, her scowl relaxed, the hissing ceased; but the female remained standing above them, crouched in baleful alertness.

His terror subsided, but Breedlove felt inwardly weak and shaken as he struggled for lightness in a comment, "That must be Medusa."

"She's Myra. Her function is to guard the door, but you're safe. Just ignore her."

Above Myra he discerned a vanishing line of hatchlike doors opening onto the ramp. Trying to ignore the guardian, he said, "Why, you have only ten people in a ship that could carry hundreds."

"It's designed to be our first city when we find a planet to inhabit."

"Why so many tubes leading to the couch?"

"They lead from the couch," she said. "They're designed to relieve internal pressures on the occupant of the couch. The box is sort of a . . . medical device."

"Where are your other people?"

"In their compartments. They come out only for the twilight ceremony."

"Your constant traveling must get boring," he said with strained amiability, still conscious of the woman on the ramp.

"Oh, no. Below a certain temperature we fall asleep."

"Then you hibernate, your faculties grow dormant."

"Our faculties cease altogether," she said. "We die. At the speed of light, we become light. The ship flies itself from star to star, and whenever a star swings near, the ship slows, the star's light awakens us, and we scan its solar system for habitable planets. After liftoff the ship powers itself with free hydrogen from space, but even so our fuel decays, and we need its energy for landings and liftoffs."

She stepped into the concavity around the manhole cover and he followed, getting his back to Myra.

"We're standing above the engine room," Kyra said.

"The ramp elevated us only a few feet above the base," he commented. "It doesn't seem possible for such a small engine to lift such a mass."

"There's much volume here, Breedlove, but little weight. The ship's walls are thin so as to admit the light that feeds

22

us. The walls are thin and very strong. Here's the power plant."

Bending, she twisted the inset handle in the manhole cover, lifted the cover, and handed it to him. "Feel how light it is."

He hefted the cover in his hand, saying, "On earth we could use this for a toy called a Frisbee."

"It pleases me that you can think of such things, Breedlove, for it shows you have presence of mind. But this may surprise you. Here is our entire power plant."

She squatted on the rim of the hole, and he stooped beside her. Inside he saw a four-spoked wheel with a plastic ball in the center. Between the spokes were four flasks with tubes leading to the ball and coiling around the tube in which the ball rested. Below the entire assemblage, but considerably deeper than ten feet, he saw the roots of trees. The ship had dug down and was resting in its own excavation.

"It's magic," he said.

"Actually it's simple. Any technology is magic to a nontechnician. The wheel spins to stabilize the ship, superheated steam is vented against the ground to give the initial liftoff, and the heat comes from the fuel in the ball. Of course, the power of the steam is amplified by the forcer tubes there, which are pulsed by concentrated radioactive emissions."

"Steam? Just steam?"

"It's not just steam. You might call this a staser. You know what force a laser gives to light quanta. Imagine the force this gives to heavy atoms of oxygen and hydrogen. It's quite adequate for liftoff, and the force is not needed in a free fall."

She bent to unscrew the top hemisphere of the central ball, while continuing a casual lecture that was exploding new concepts into his untutored mind.

23

"Once we're under way, the hydrogen scoops bring fuel to the ball, which is ionized into a constant thrust that impels the ship into the speed of light. At that point, for us, time stands still, and that's why I'm younger than you are, Breedlove, although I was born thousands of years ago."

Inside the ball she unscrewed, in a maze of silvery pipes, nested a smaller ball, its dimensions between those of a tennis ball and a grapefruit. She lifted it aloft and said, "This is the core shield. With it, you could carry drops of liquid sun in your pocket."

She unscrewed the two halves of the ball and showed him a residue of grayish ash. "Once, if you had looked at this without protection, the results would have been more devastating than looking at Myra. Now, it's harmless and useless."

She spilled the ash through the spokes to the ground below and screwed the halves back together, holding aloft the small pink ball. "This is all the shield I'll need for my uranium."

She handed it to him to hold while she reinserted the manhole cover.

Tossing the ball in his palm, Breedlove said, "You'd better make yourself a woman's shoulder bag to carry this in or the first child who sees it might make off with your pretty pink ball. And we have another problem. I can attest to what you've shown and told me, but I'll not be able to explain anything when the technical people start asking questions. They'll never believe us."

Straightening, she said, "You believe me."

"Yes, but I trust you."

"And why do you trust me?"

She spoke in the manner of a schoolteacher probing the knowledge of her star pupil, and he groped for an answer to a suddenly difficult question. Finding none, he seized on a playful ambiguity. "Because you're so cute."

She had watched him seek an answer and she laughed at his evasion, but before he spoke he saw a premonitory play of mirth in her eyes. Again he had the impression that she interpreted his words before he voiced them. If she could read his mind, he thought, she had advanced beyond any conceivable level of mere technology.

"Breedlove, you are 'they.' If you believe me, they will also. I'll reveal enough to your technicians to persuade them I speak the truth, but no more. Knowledge acquired too soon can be dangerous. What I say is no reflection on you as a person. Your native intelligence is as great as mine. It is simply that I am more informed on methods. I can tell from your sun that your race is newly born, and adults have to protect children from their own folly. Now, what is a shoulder bag?"

He explained with gestures. Listening, she nodded, and asked, "Is pink a fashionable color?"

"I suppose so."

"I must make me a shoulder bag while you survey the trout population of Jones Creek."

"Will you join me for lunch at midday?"

"No, the sunlight feeds me, but we will all join you at twilight. Now begone, or I'll set Myra on you."

She was laughing as she spoke, ushering him toward the door, but even her playful mention of the sentry made him emerge from the spaceship with a feeling of relief.

Later, as he fished along the creek, Breedlove's mind entertained the implications of Kyra's arrival. In the past winter he had read the works of Father Teilhard de Chardin, and it occurred to him that this visitor to earth supported the Jesuit's hypothesis that mankind was evolving toward the Godhead. Her similarity to the human species indicated that the logic of evolution for higher species was cosmic, and it was benign; that her race had survived the ultimate holocaust, the death of its planet,

25

testified that her fellow mortals of earth held within themselves the key to practical immortality. Kyra synthesized religion and science.

Gradually he forced himself to grapple with the practical problems her appearance and her request for uranium would create. He foresaw no mass hysteria arising from the visit of such an appealing space pilgrim, but if her presence became publicly known, her progress would become as dignified as a traveling freak show, and he wanted his fellow human beings to be on their best behavior for this girl—he could not think of her as other than a girl—who combined regality with such airy grace.

Peterson would have to be informed of her presence because the chief ranger was the station's helicopter pilot. Peterson would see the reason for flying the girl to the Breedlove farm, near Spokane, and concealing her there. Once at the farm Kyra could borrow dresses from his sister, and his mother could find a wig to conceal her green hair.

He had misgivings about turning her over to the officials with a "take her, she's yours." Kyra trusted him. She had enlisted his aid, and she would need him to verify her story. Thinking the matter over, he saw instantly that no written deposition given by a man who lacked scientific credentials could begin to bridge this potential credibility gap, and that fact presented an opportunity. By insisting on oral reports only, he could let his sincerity be his credentials, and the need for his testimony would keep him close to Kyra.

He would not abandon her to officialdom.

His determination to stay by Kyra's side would probably be opposed by the bureaucrats, but he was a minor bureaucrat himself, and an idea was forming in his mind that might test the limits of bureaucratic procedures to the breaking point. If he could pull if off, he would stay with Kyra. Then there was the problem of his parents' reaction to Kyra. In what he assumed was the norm for mothers, his own mother had always been intensely interested in the girls he invited to his home, but she might have more than she could handle when a green-haired, green-eyed girl from another planet entered the Breedlove parlor. He had less concern for his father. With two volatile females in the house, the senior Breedlove had long ago learned the value of equanimity in emotional situations. He had no concern at all for the reactions of his sister, Matilda; she could handle anything.

As the day moved on, he let future problems hang and turned his thoughts to the exhibition he would prepare for the visitors who would join him at twilight. He would catch enough fish to feed them all, unpack his bag, set up a pup tent, and present them with the extra C rations he had brought. A hatchet, a fishing rod, and a pair of binoculars would not be the World's Fair, but it would give the Kanabians the idea of woodcraft.

By six the fish were caught and the exhibition readied. Stretched atop his sleeping bag, he lay watching the declining light over the snow peaks westward. The Kanabians were out of the grove and crossing the creek before he noticed them, approaching in a cluster grouped around Kyra. In the forefront was a girl who might have been Kyra's sister, though slightly taller and more slender. There were nine of them, eight females and a boy, all nude. Only Myra was absent, and Breedlove assumed that she had been left to guard the door. Or perhaps Kyra was being very diplomatic.

Breedlove took the boy to be the equivalent of a twelve-year-old on earth. Solidly built, his body gave promise of a powerful manhood, and he walked between two females, who held his hands rather tightly, Breedlove noticed. None of the females appeared to be over thirty, earth age, and they presented a wider variance in bodily form than an equivalent group of young earth women. The girl who was taller than Kyra was almost breastless, but most were heavy-bodied, and three thrust voluminous bosoms before them, breasts out of proportion to their torsos.

He stood as they neared the mound and called, "Citizens of Kanab, welcome to earth."

Kyra interpreted his greeting. In her language, "earth" emerged as *urritha*.

Ignoring the exhibits, the females broke from around Kyra, leaving her to hold the boy's hand, and gathered around Breedlove, moving in close to inspect him. It was a thorough inspection, at times embarrassing, yet weirdly sexless. There was nothing voluptuous in the press of these naked female bodies. They pummeled his buttocks, kneaded his muscles, and stroked his hair. Only the tall girl did not seem to regard him entirely as an object. She took his hand and rubbed it against her cheek, murmuring close to his ear, *"Cricket atelya."*

Escorting the boy around the milling females to the inanimate exhibit, Kyra smiled in amusement at the orgy of touching and sniffing and called out to him, "Take off your coat, Breedlove, and let them feel your fantastic muscles."

He squirmed from his coat and handed it to the tall girl, who folded it in her arms and brushed her cheek against its fabric. Others pinched him. One tried to pluck the hairs from his wrists, but there was nothing essentially feminine about their curiosity. In their faces he read admiration, delight, and—he could have sworn—the premonitory pride of ownership.

Kyra voiced their possessiveness, calling to him, "They want to take you with us, Breedlove, but first they'd like to see you with your clothes off."

"I've gone as far as I'm going, Kyra. Call them back."

Kyra spoke once, sharply, and the females fell away

reluctantly, moving toward the exhibits. The slender girl returned the coat, bending her knees in a dipping motion, in what he took to be a Kanabian curtsy, as she handed the garment to him. For a moment she stood facing him, hand on hips, and delivered her parting judgment, *"Cricket atelya."*

Kyra stood apart on the mound, her arm over the shoulder of the boy. With obvious understanding of their purpose, the boy had taken Breedlove's field glasses and was intently studying the rocky terrain to the southeast. The presence of the boy in the group aroused Breedlove's curiosity. A well-muscled man would have contributed more to the expedition, however sophisticated its technology.

He walked over to the pair and asked Kyra, "What's his name?"

"Karilet, which means 'big oak.' Usually we call him Crick."

Et at the end of a word apparently meant "big," he deduced, and the women had called him a Cricket. Whatever it was, he was a big Crick.

"What does *Crick* mean?"

"In a general way it means 'boy,' or 'little man.' In your scientific language it might mean more accurately a sperm bank."

In their language, then, he was a big sperm bank. The term was dehumanizing.

"What does *atelya* mean?"

" 'Gorgeous,' or 'fantastic,' or 'wow.' "

Then the inspection had not been as objective as he thought, he decided, looking at the boy now with an understanding of the child's future function in the group.

"Introduce me to him, Kyra."

Kyra took the binoculars from the boy's hands and turned his face to Breedlove, introducing the ranger as *urritha cricket Brrreeedlove*. In an instinctively male gesture, Breedlove extended his hand to the boy, who grabbed it in both his own and clung to it, looking up at Breedlove with a beginning hope, a longing, and finally a stark plea.

"He needs a father, Kyra. May I show him how to fish before sundown?"

"No. He must stay close to us."

The boy continued to cling to Breedlove's hand, and the ranger was loathe to disengage the child. Kyra called over to the tall girl, "Flurea," and the girl came. She tapped Crick's wrist, and he released Breedlove's hand. Flurea led him away.

Despite their meticulous cropping of the grass, the Kanabians were not herbivores. With delicate mincing bites they ate the trout he cooked, bones and all, flavoring it with sprigs of clover they plucked from the ground. They relished the cheese, jams, and jellies they found in the C rations. They only tasted the canned meat and gave Crick all the chocolate bars, which he loved, but they only tossed the candy casually toward the boy. He was watched, but he was not doted on.

After supper he gave them, through Kyra as interpreter, the standard park lecture on the geological formation of the area. They listened but asked no questions. Afterward he commented to Kyra about their lack of curiosity, at such a variance with her own, and she answered, "It is not their function to be curious. Besides, this is your planet, and they have the pride of the hungry poor who will not ogle diners at a feast to which they have not been invited."

The pathos inherent in her remark so stirred him he veered away from the subject to ask bluntly, "And what is your function?"

"At the moment," she said, "I function as a diplomat."

Her reference to the function of each individual and the

disparity in their shapes were altering his attitudes about evolution on Kanab. It had gone beyond earth evolution in producing differentiation and specialization. Or at least beyond the evolution of man and animals, he corrected himself. Such functional specialization did exist in some insect colonies on earth. Still, these people were far from being termites, and in time, perhaps, the social evolution of mankind would take a similar turn. There were signs of it already.

As twilight approached, the Kanabians sat in a circle atop the mound, clipping the grass with their fingernails and munching it as each in turn told a story. Without knowledge of the language, Breedlove was able to catch the moods of the speakers in the susurrations of their voices, which assumed the quality of the twilight, a wavering, evanescent ephemerality distilling the sadness of farewells. Seated beside Breedlove, Kyra whispered interpretations.

"The limbs of our trees grew long, writhing, with fronded tips imploring the sun to live. The tree trunks molded. Fungus grew. Our days were long twilights and our nights brittle with frost."

He had never felt himself particularly gifted with a visual imagination, but under the spell of the voices he could literally see the Rousseau-like landscape of the dying planet.

Another voice sent an iron clang of determination ringing through its melancholy. "Our great, green mother was dying, the cold ordered us to go, but the little mothers came with us to spread the web of life from star to star. Now we have seen magnificent earth with its promise of planets awaiting us, and we have touched the warm Breedlove, whose blood flows red as ours."

As each skald recited her version of the Kanabian saga, a listener might quietly detach herself from the circle and go into the bushes briefly to attend to natural functions, but otherwise each speaker received the rapt attention of minds which, it was growing clear to Breedlove, shared with human beings the ability to feel loneliness and sadness, the terrors of the void and the wanderer's longing for home. Yet each speaker ended on a note of affirmation, a reverence for life, and a faith that the wayfarers would survive. *Atelya urritha* was a promise to their faith and perhaps—as he soon surmised—more than a promise.

A group sing marked the finale of the ceremony. Kyra invited him to join hands with them for this ritual, saying, "I can't sing and interpret too, but if you listen closely you may grasp the meaning of some words from their sounds."

After the singing began, Breedlove had no need for an interpreter; Kanabian was indeed uniquely onomatopoetic. The song, apparently an Edda of sorts, narrated the tale of the group's exodus, and he could recognize the rising, then long-diminishing roar of a departing spaceship. Fluting vibrations from deep within the throats of the singers projected a sensation of blurring speed which grew into a sibilant keening, like a scream in the night, that conveyed the horror felt by sentient creatures hurled into darkness at fantastic accelerations they had not been created to endure.

He could not pinpoint when his understanding began, but at some time on the flight outward he became certain of the accuracy of the images he elicited from the melodious chant and aware, too, that his mind was opening into new dimensions. He felt the awesome loneliness of interstellar darkness, felt the slow awakening to the light of his own sun, saw the blue orb of Planet Earth, and swung in tightening orbits around the globe that had given him birth. His mind descended to the majesty of mountains, verdure, and running water.

Then his apocalypse began, a dual revelation of alternate futures as if envisioned separately and simultaneously by the twin lobes of his brain. On the one hand he saw a future for mankind leading to the stars, and on the other he witnessed a silent Armageddon in which the cities of men crumbled from the disintegration of unknown atomic pulsations. He saw the dreams of men dissolve into darkness and knew the abstract, detached terror of extinction.

Yet even as he witnessed these alternate futures his critical faculties remained alert, and he recognized that the choice of visions was mankind's own. Moreover, he was beginning to understand that there were factions in this group, that some were being swayed toward militant action, and Kyra, the magnanimous, was asking . . .

His visions were shattered as a tremor of tension jolted the group, tearing the hands from his own, and Breedlove looked around him as a sleeper awakened. The chanting had ceased with the dropping of the hands, and he heard a sound of scurrying from the bushes. He glanced toward the sound. With his boy's legs hurtling him away at a pace incredible in an earth child, Crick raced through the gloaming toward the tossed boulders at the mouth of a ravine to the southeast, but Flurea, fleeter of foot than Diana, had taken up pursuit. Halfway to the rocks, the chase ended. Flurea caught Crick's arm and swung him toward the group, dragging him stumbling and falling back to the mound. Around Breedlove the tension relaxed.

"Do you have a behavior problem with the boy?" he asked Kyra.

"Only in that he is a child who longs for a sunlit place to play, and space is cold and dark."

She spoke to the group sharply, and as one the people arose. Two of the heavy-bodied females went to take the boy, each grabbing him firmly by a hand. Docile, his face expressionless, Crick walked between them.

"Breedlove, we must go."

Forming around Kyra, the group moved toward the aspen

grove and into the gathering dusk. Breedlove watched them go, thinking, Flurea's function was to catch the boy and for that one purpose she had evolved into a runner. But the behavior of Crick aroused his more intense curiosity. With acumen remarkable in a child, he had studied the terrain with the binoculars before attempting escape, and if he could have reached the boulders and found a crevice narrow enough, he would have been lost to the group forever. Granted that space held terrors for a child, it was still strange that he should flee from his own kind to seek sanctuary on an alien planet.

A fully grown male would have made good the escape.

Turning to police the area, Breedlove was bothered by another incongruity. Kyra had told him the group had no leader, but when she spoke the others obeyed. Unless her definition of leadership was far more complex than his own, Kyra had lied to him.

Chapter Three

———— ✳ ————

On his second morning in the wilderness Breedlove slept until the sun had burned the ground fog from the meadow, and awakened to sit up and gaze around him as if striving to drive away his inner mists with the morning brightness. He felt as one awakening from a bad dream to find its images gone completely from his mind while its baneful aura still lingered. He assumed his subconscious was still roiled by yesterday evening's vision, and he solicited the serenity of the morning with the same reassuring observation with which, last night, he had invited sleep: if Kyra's power to convince others was as effective as with him, even if her techniques involved nothing more than hypnosis, she would get the uranium and be gone long before the summer solstice, leaving mankind to its future and unchallenged possession of the earth.

Fully awake now and, as he supposed, with his superego in control of his emotions, he could realize that Kyra's presence posed no threat to him personally. But then, there had been no threat as such in the vision he had seen, merely a choice of futures, and mankind had always had suicide as a choice.

He arose to roll his sleeping bag, tricing it without its poncho covering. The poncho's drape would be bulky and its Marine Corps mottlings were more functional than decorative, but it would conceal Kyra's nakedness. Yesterday he had been remiss in not impressing on her more forcefully the strength of earth's social taboo against nudity. This morning he would be introducing her to Peterson, who obeyed regulations, observed conventions, practiced decorum, and reverenced propriety. The chief ranger would have trouble enough adjusting to the girl's appearance and origins. Besides, Kyra was receptive and sensitive to human emotions. Peterson's embarrassment might shame her.

It was too early to call Peterson, who had not yet begun to monitor his radio. He shaved and ate breakfast and packed his gear and shortly after seven he sat on the knoll, waiting, when Kyra emerged from the aspens wearing only a pink shoulder bag. Stepping into the creek, she waded upstream, trailing her fingers in the water as she walked. Exuberant in the morning, she could have been Eve in a still-pristine Eden, and, watching her, Breedlove regretted that he was not a poet capable of enshrining the sight of her in memorable phrases. When she passed beneath the willow at the bend in the creek, she strode dappled by its shadows, reminding him of the line from Hopkins, "Glory be to God for dappled things."

It occurred to him that it was unlikely that she had heard any poetry over Station KSPO, and yesterday she had brightened with delight when he compared her to an orchid. He could pirate the deathless phrases of the poets and fling them at her, with variations to suit the circumstances, without fear of detection. When she emerged onto

the east bank of the creek and waved up to him, he arose
and waved back, calling down to her:

> "You walk in beauty, like the night
> Of cloudless climes and starry skies;
> And all that's best of silver and green
> Meet in your aspect and your eyes."

"Breedlove, you can't see green at night."

Drawing closer, she swirled before him, modeling her
bag by holding it to her hip. "Is my bag the height of
fashion?"

"It is. But I'm going to call my leader to come and get us
and take us to Spokane, and we'll need a dress to cover
you."

"Breedlove, is my body so uncomely you're ashamed of
me?"

Genuine hurt in her eyes brought his instant rebuttal.

"Absolutely not! It was once said of earth's first geome-
ter, 'Euclid alone has looked on Beauty bare.' That's no
longer true. Euclid and Breedlove alone have looked on
beauty bare. But it is a rigid custom on earth for women to
wear clothes in public, and I've got this little number
here"—he stooped and lifted the poncho—"that will get
you to my house and my sister's dresses. It will cover
enough of you to keep Ranger Peterson from going into
deep shock when he sees you."

"You didn't seem very shocked when you saw me."

There was a note of suspicion in her accusation.

"I know, but I'm young and resilient. Peterson is mature
and believes in custom and going by the book."

"And not as lusty," she added, amused now by his
obvious confusion. She took the proffered poncho and
slid her arms through the slits, looking down at its folds.

"I think I've known you long enough, Breedlove, to tell

you frankly this is not a gorgeous creation. If you will cut me a length of your rope, I think I can improve the drape."

He complied, and while she worked at the drape he radioed Peterson. "Pete, this is for your ears only, and I mean only your ears. A historical event has taken place in the meadow. You'd better draw on your June ration of gas to get the helicopter to the meadow as soon as possible. Come in from the south over Hallman's Peak and don't circle the meadow. Come straight down to where you'll see me signaling."

Apparently impressed by Breedlove's urgency, Peterson did not argue, saying only, "Wilco. Out."

"My leader is on his way," Breedlove said to the girl, who was dubiously holding the pink bag against the dull green and yellow of the poncho. "I plan to take you to my parents' farm and hide you there until Peterson contacts the authorities. I planned to tell you this last night, but you left in too much of a hurry."

"I know. My people were upset by Crick."

"I noticed they obey you promptly. I thought you said you were not their leader."

"I command, but I do not lead them. How do I look from the back?"

"*Atelya!* You'll have to help me convince Peterson you are what you say you are."

She swirled before him, spinning the poncho outward until centrifugal force canceled its purpose. "That's easy. We'll compare bellybuttons."

"No, not that!"

She laughed at his expression. Settling to the grass and pulling him down beside her, she said, "Now, Breedlove, tell me more about you earth people."

He was sitting cross-legged before her, telling her of the rivalries of nations and the origins of civilizations when they heard the helicopter and looked up to see it swinging from behind Hallman's Peak. Breedlove signaled Peterson to a landing on the mowed circle of the mound and moved Kyra away from the blast of the propellers.

When the blades ceased to spin, he led Kyra back as Peterson emerged from the craft, adjusting his hat to its proper angle before he swung his feet to the ground. He carried a metal-backed clipboard. Walking toward them, he glanced at Kyra, and his gait faltered, his face paled visibly. He stopped. He kept his eyes glued to her hair with frantic, despairing disbelief.

"Chief Ranger Peterson, may I present Miss Kyra Lavaslatta from the Planet Kanab?"

The historical moment was lost to Peterson, lost even to his hearing, Breedlove suspected, for the ranger was drifting into a peculiar form of shock. His voice sounded as if it came from some remote area of his throat, for his lips hardly moved.

"Miss, if you and Tom are conspiring to use government transportation . . ."

"Mr. Peterson, I'm from Kanab," Kyra said.

"I've been to Kanab, miss, and I've never met a Mormon girl with a Greek name who dyed her hair green."

"Pete, she's not from Kanab, Utah. She's from another planet."

"I heard you the first time, Tom." He seemed angry.

"Nine others from her party are nearby. They're all from outer space."

"Did you have them sign an unauthorized campers' release?"

"Pete, they can't sign anything in English."

"They can sign with an X. How does she speak English?"

"She listens to KSPO. Now, sit down, Pete, and think. Would a girl be dressed in a poncho if she were from this planet? If she were a nudist, she'd be nude. If she were a camper, she'd be wearing jeans. She'd not wear a poncho."

Peterson sank to the turf, dazed, asking, "Why not? If it rains here, it rains in outer space."

Peterson was fighting to accept the girl's origins, but he was losing the battle. He looked away and downward, as if his thoughts were focused on some peculiar personal problem that his mind recoiled from, and for a moment Breedlove feared he might be drifting into catatonia. Kyra must have feared the same. She stooped beside him, looking down at him with an expression of grave concern.

Suddenly she squatted on the grass in front of Peterson, gently removed the clipboard from his hands, handed it to Breedlove, and took both Peterson's hands in hers. She began to speak to him, but in her own language. Tentatively, at first probing and hesitant, she seemed to be questioning him. Then her voice grew more rhythmic, flowing in easy undulations, and she was singing, less a song than the rendition of a melody by the flow of air over her vocal cords. It was a wind song, a sound as pleasant as the hum of bees in the fields of summer, and Breedlove suspected it was a Kanabian lullaby.

Yet the singing was more significant than the sounds a mother makes to pacify a child. Over Breedlove's mind it cast visions of a green and pleasant land slowly yielding to the desolation of frost, and he could feel the despair in Kyra's voice. A counternote emerged, bringing intimations of hope, which swelled into an affirmation, and the wind rush of her coda brought again a sense of motion resumed through the far-flung glitter of stars.

Her singing ceased. She dropped the ranger's hands.

Peterson snapped from his stupor. His eyes focused on Kyra, and his voice was clear though apologetic. "I never doubted you, Kyra. I knew Breedlove wouldn't be calling me unless something big had happened. I didn't tell anybody you were here. Still, I'd appreciate it if you'd sign for your group. Where's my pad?"

Breedlove handed him the clipboard, and he took a pen from his pocket. "Sign here, Kyra."

She drew three characters at the bottom of the form. The lettering resembled Arabic script. She handed the pad to Breedlove, who took it and chided her. "You never sang like that to me."

"Pete had something in his mind blocking his belief in me," she said. "Now, you take the papers back to the helicopter. I want to speak to Pete alone for a moment."

Breedlove turned toward the helicopter, hearing Peterson say, "So, you're actually from outer space."

"It depends on your point of view," she said playfully. "To me you're from outer space."

Moving out of earshot, he returned the clipboard to the helicopter, wondering about the mental block that affected Peterson's belief in Kyra's origins and how the girl had discovered it so quickly. Despite her disclaimers she might well be a supermind, either that or a highly skilled diagnostician, but whatever else she might be she was certainly a superb singer of wordless songs and a genius at the art of persuasion.

Leaving Peterson to Kyra's ministrations, he pretended to check the cables on the voice amplifier attached to the far side of the helicopter and was not drawn back to the two until he smelled smoke. Peterson had regained his self-control. He was lounging on the grass, smoking a cigarette and showing Kyra photographs of his family.

"Tom, you can quit worrying," Peterson said as Breedlove walked up. "Kyra's told me all about her troubles. Of course, they're not solved yet. I'll fly her back to your folks, and that's when the situation starts getting hairy."

"You and I believe her," Breedlove said. "Somebody in the government with the authority to dispense the uranium will believe."

"If it were that simple I'd fly her over to Hanford and

41

pick up a cupful of the stuff, but she's an unregistered alien, and radioactive uranium is hemmed in by all kinds of restrictions, national and international."

"I figured we could pass her up the chain of command to the Secretary of Interior," Breedlove said.

"She isn't going up my chain of command," Peterson demurred. "I never told you why I resigned my Air Force commission. I just told the little lady and she suggested that I tell you, since now we're partners in the crime of believing. When I was a captain, which is as high as I got in rank, I flew wing tip to saucer's rim with a flying saucer in broad daylight in a flight from Laramie to Cheyenne. I waved at the pilot and he waved back, a little baldheaded guy as green as this lady's hair, and when I reached the base with my report I was sent to the wing's psychiatrist and held for observation. I wound up with a reprimand from my commanding officer for making flippant flight reports. I don't want another incident on my record, so I'm delegating you to stay with Kyra in Spokane until the authorities get there, and you can make all the reports."

"Will you certify my sanity?"

"I'll sign anything you type up, but I'm not guaranteeing I'll read it."

"What authority will you notify?"

"Immigration and Naturalization. It happens that the regional chief in Seattle's an old flying buddy of mine. Kyra's an unregistered alien, so she'd fall under his jurisdiction."

"Pete, we're not using our heads. Other bureaus hog the publicity picture. Why not get a little favorable publicity for the forestry service? You can take the credit and I'll take the risks if you'll make her a ward of the National Park Service and assign me duty as her escort and guardian. I can type the documents. This is no disrespect to Kyra, but the idea came to me yesterday that she is technically 'rare and exotic fauna,' and as such she is the responsibility of the Park Service."

"You're right," Peterson agreed. "By law I can appoint you her keeper while she's out of the park area. She's not only exotic fauna, she's a threatened species."

"What's exotic fauna?" Kyra asked.

"A rare and unusual animal," Breedlove said, breaking the news to her in a gentle tone.

"That's me, Breedlove." She beamed. "That's me exactly."

As a friend of John Breedlove, Tom's father, Peterson had visited the Breedlove farm before, but it was the first time he had spiraled down into the Breedlove feedlot in a helicopter without a prior notice of arrival. John Breedlove emerged from the barn as the machine landed, a look of wonderment on his face. His wonderment changed to an expression of vexation and mild reproof when he saw the trio approaching across the feedlot, stepping cautiously, and the barefooted, green-haired girl wearing only a poncho.

"That's my dad," Breedlove told Kyra.

As they approached closer, the senior Breedlove recovered and walked toward them, without greeting them, to complain, "Pete, if I'd known you were coming I would have gotten dressed for company, and, Tom, why did you bring the young lady through the cattle lot and her barefooted? Miss, I apologize for my son and my overalls."

"Don't apologize for your overalls, Mr. Breedlove, and look at this sack your son dropped me into."

"Why, miss, it's the most beautiful poncho I've ever

43

seen on a woman. It matches your hair."

"Dad, this is Kyra. She's a Kanabian from the Planet Kanab."

"Welcome to the farm, miss. I have many Canadian friends."

Breedlove was beginning to analyze the adjustments the human mind made to Kyra's presence, and he suspected that his father's misinterpretation of the word "Kanabian" was deliberate. John Breedlove extended his hand to Kyra, who took it and performed the peculiar knee-jerk curtsy Breedlove had first seen done by Flurea. By this time Breedlove's mother, drawn by the noise of the helicopter, had emerged from the kitchen of the house and was coming up the path. She was studying Kyra's face as she came, wiping her hands on her apron.

"Mother, I'd like for you to meet Kyra Lavaslatta from the Planet Kanab."

"Welcome to the farm, dear. Is Planetkanab in Saskatchewan?"

Mrs. Breedlove was eyeing Kyra's hair discreetly and suspiciously as she asked the question.

"It's nowhere, Mrs. Breedlove," Kyra answered. "Its sun blew up and destroyed it."

"How dreadful. But I'm glad you're safe."

"She's telling the truth, Mother. She's been traveling for thousands of years, earth time."

"Then you must be hungry. But we'll have lunch shortly."

"How was the weather on your planet, Kyra?" It was a farmer's question from the senior Breedlove, and Kyra answered graciously.

"Much like yours, but probably milder. My planet's axial tilt was not so great as yours."

The group moved toward the house, a white, two-story frame structure shaded by maple trees. His parents,

Breedlove realized, were clinging to the forms of polite hospitality just as Peterson had steadied himself with the ritual of official behavior, and they were adapting to the girl with more success than Peterson had managed, but they had no UFO sightings on their official records.

"John, I'd like to requisition about thirty gallons of gasoline," Peterson said.

"No problem, Pete. Kyra, have you really been traveling for thousands of years?"

"Yes and no, Mr. Breedlove. I've been traveling for thousands of years your time but only a few months my time."

"You certainly look young for your years," Mrs. Breedlove commented. "What is your beauty secret?"

"Speed, ma'am," Kyra said pleasantly, surprising Breedlove with her use of "ma'am." "The faster you go, the slower time becomes."

"You must have been traveling from east to west," Mrs. Breedlove said. "John and I left New York one morning just after breakfast and got to Spokane before lunch."

"Kyra's talking about relative time, Mother," Breedlove interjected.

"Oh, relative. You know, Tom, except for her coloring Kyra reminds me of your cousin Mary. If we had known you were coming, Kyra, we would have dressed for you."

"You look better than I do, Mrs. Breedlove. This is your son's idea of a fashionable creation."

"I'm sure that our daughter, Matilda, has clothes to fit you, and I have a new supply of panty hose."

Since his mother was larger than Kyra, Breedlove asked, "Will your panty hose fit her?"

"They're stretch-fits," his mother explained.

"But do stretch-fits shrink?"

"That's not your department, Tom," his mother answered, and turned to Kyra. "Matty has several bras. She's rehearsing her graduation ceremonies at school this morning, but I'm sure she'll not mind if I select one for you."

"Mother, I know she can't wear Matty's bras."

"Now, just how would you know that, Son?"

It was a question he left unanswered. His mother had old-fashioned ideas about behavior between the sexes.

They entered the kitchen, and Mrs. Breedlove said, "Come upstairs with me, Kyra, and we'll find you something to wear."

Peterson went to the living room to telephone Seattle. John Breedlove went upstairs to change for lunch, and Breedlove went into the sun parlor to type out orders detaching him to duty away from the Selkirk Ranger Station. Peterson's signature on his orders would be certification enough for his sanity, he realized, and the classification of Kyra as exotic fauna, while not compromising the Park Service, which dealt routinely in such matters, would offer later officials a credibility escape clause in dealing with the girl, in short, a convenient avenue along which the buck might be passed.

After typing the orders in quadruplicate, Breedlove took them to the living room, where Peterson, having completed his call to Seattle, sat talking with John Breedlove, who had rejoined his house guest.

"I'm not saying you have to hide her, John. Just cover her hair and don't talk about her after she's left here. Remember what happened when Orson Welles broadcast the invasion from Mars. I don't think the country would scare as easily today, but if word got out that a spaceship was parked there, the Selkirk Wilderness Area would be ruined. For all I know, women's groups might start lobbying to keep her on the planet, but Kyra wants her people off. If they stay here they'll become habituated to the climate, as she put it, and it will make it harder on them to leave. If that happens, there'll be hell to pay."

"I don't see why," John Breedlove demurred. "Apart from her hair she's like any other woman, a mite prettier than most and no doubt more intelligent, but such a friendly creature."

"You hit the nail on the head with the word 'creature.' She's not human, and we've got problems enough on this planet with the yellows, reds, browns, and blacks. Throw in a few silver-skinned green hairs and we've had it. Besides, they've evolved beyond human beings, and it's a law of evolution, she tells me, that the better-adapted species drive out the lesser-adapted. They can gather energy with only a minimal demand for vital minerals, and they don't really need shelter, since they can hibernate in extreme cold."

The extent of Peterson's knowledge amazed Breedlove. Kyra had not "told" him anything in the helicopter. He must have got the information during their private conversation on the meadow.

"What have you got for me, Tom?" Peterson turned to Breedlove.

"My orders. Sign here."

Peterson had recovered sufficiently to read the orders before he signed them. He signed and handed the original back to Breedlove, saying, "You'll be on a per diem, so watch your expenses."

"Yes, sir."

"In the morning the man from Immigration will come to take Kyra into custody. His name is Aloysius Kelly, and he's a nice guy, but he's something of a con artist. It'll be up to you to out-con him, because he might not like the idea of a man from the Park Service intruding on his turf. He might try to squeeze you out, but your authorization is as good as his. Visitors from other planets aren't covered by immigration regulations, and Kyra's not seeking citizenship. All she needs is a visitor's permit. She doesn't come under the Bill of Rights, but she does have rights as a threatened species, and that's where I'm concerned. Besides, you have another ace up your sleeve: you're the only human being who has seen the inside of her spaceship. Keep that ace hidden until you're ready to play it."

"Didn't you tell him she's from another planet?"

"Not over the telephone. All Kelly knows is that she's a VIP and an unregistered alien. You can fill in the details. I'll admit I'm passing the buck to you, but I have a feeling this is one buck everybody's going to be grabbing for. The best way to handle Al is to get him confused. He's an ex-military pilot and his mind works from a checkoff list. Throw him a few nonroutine ideas and he'll be asking you what to do. Now, John, I'd like to pay my respects to Kyra and your missus, get the gasoline, and get out of here."

Peterson did not have to leave the living room to pay his respects. In tight jeans with a tighter blue-denim shirt and loafers with bobby socks, Kyra danced into the room, leaping and pirouetting in a riotous display of controlled energy and grace, saying, "Breedlove, what would you and Euclid think of me now, with all my bare beauty covered?"

Entering behind her, Mrs. Breedlove whispered accusingly to her son, "She's wearing *my* bra, and I had to take it in only two notches."

He barely heard his mother's revelation. He was remembering Kyra's remark that the women of Kanab had discarded dresses as being too provocative. Not merely dresses, he amended. He had never before suspected to what heights of fashion a pair of jeans and a denim shirt could be exalted.

"Put one of my old Glenn Miller records on, Tom," John Breedlove said. "I'd like to teach this little girl to jitterbug."

"John," Mrs. Breedlove snapped, "aren't you supposed to get the gasoline for Pete?"

As he moved to do his father's bidding, it occurred to

Breedlove that although his mother was not his father's leader, she commanded, and his father obeyed. When the music began, John Breedlove and Peterson had gone. Kyra came and stood before him, saying, "Then, you teach me to jitterbug, Breedlove."

Embracing her, he swirled her onto the floor, feeling her lightness communicate itself to his movements, and he thought of Goethe who had written of "the eternal feminine." In the coquettish laughter of the green eyes beckoning him to dance, he had seen more than the eternal feminine, he had seen the universal feminine. Kyra's lure was cosmic.

Chapter Four

———— ✳ ————

At a lunch Peterson left too early to share, there were crosscurrents from which Breedlove was sure Kyra elicited subtle concepts of the human condition.

He knew his mother had accepted Kyra when she commented, "Your green hair looks perfectly natural, Kyra. It's becoming."

"I met a lady in Tacoma, once, with purple hair," John Breedlove volunteered. "After a while it began to look natural."

"John, what were you doing around a purple-haired woman in Tacoma long enough for her hair to look natural?"

"She was a saleslady, Ellen."

"Retail or wholesale?" Mrs. Breedlove inquired sweetly.

Breedlove saw Kyra's eyes reflect amusement at the jest. She could not have caught the double entendre, but in the exchange, he sensed, she elicited concepts of jealousy and possessiveness, and her own behavior was merging into human patterns rapidly. After observing the others, she handled her knife and fork with the ease of a girl from a finishing school.

After lunch she went to the kitchen to help Mrs. Breedlove bake a cake. Breedlove stayed as close to her as he could unobtrusively manage, to share her joy of discovery. A world was opening to the eyes of a very perspicacious child, and she greeted it with silent shouts of glee, finding marvels in the commonplace. The scent of vanilla enchanted her. She gazed with adoration on the shape of an egg. She marveled at the rise of beaten egg whites, was entranced by the lightness and whiteness of sifted flour, delighted in the whorls her ladle formed in the yolk-yellowed batter, whose smooth sweetness enthralled her tongue. The placing of the cake layers into the oven she saw as a solemn ritual.

After the cake went into the oven, Breedlove invited her into the living room to view the world's high fashions in *Harper's Bazaar* and *Vogue*. Sprawled on the living-room rug, she could not read the words, but she grew ecstatic over the pictures.

"Breedlove, would you buy me this gorgeous dress when we get to Seattle?"

He looked down at the illustration she pointed to, a line drawing of a two-piece dress with a boxy tunic that had jutting, padded shoulders with a flaring below-the-knees skirt. No descriptive copy extolled the features of the dress, just these words in bold type, "AN EXCLUSIVE POLINSKI CREATION, AT $720.00." Beneath the announcement in small type were listed the stores that carried the dress.

"Kyra, the dress costs seven hundred and twenty dollars, more money than I earn in a month. You pay twenty dollars for the material and seven hundred dollars for the name of a designer, Polinksi, you and I never heard before. Find something you like in Ohrbach's basement for twenty dollars, and I'll buy it for you."

"Is Polinski a height-of-fashion designer?"

"You'll have to ask my sister."

Through the window he saw the school bus stop at the end of the lane and excused himself. He walked out to meet his sister, ambling up the lane with her books dangling from a shoulder satchel, and when she saw him she ran to meet him, greeting him with a shy but happy embrace and an accusation, "You didn't answer my letter."

"When I got it, Peterson flew me home so we could explore your options without me having to write a book."

"You're too late. I've decided to go to nursing school."

"I'm glad that's settled. Now I have a surprise for you. I brought a guest home with me."

"Is he six foot two with eyes of blue?"

"It's a she, and she's wearing your jeans. I found her stark naked in the woods and Peterson flew her here."

"That's neat. Does she have a brother?"

"Ask her. She's got green hair, and it's natural."

"Is that what she told you?"

"Yes, and I believe her. Her name's Kyra Lavaslatta and she's from another planet."

"Fantastic!"

In the entrance hall Matilda laid her books on a table and walked into the living room, where Kyra was sprawled, looking at the illustrations.

"Kyra, this is my sister, Matilda. We call her Matty."

Kyra stood and said, "You're as gorgeous as Breedlove."

"Wow, where'd you get that green hair? It's crazy. And those jeans never looked like that on me."

"Do I look the height of fashion, Matty?"

"You look out of this world, which is where Tom tells me you're from. Were you really naked up there in the woods?"

"Until Breedlove rescued me."

"Way out! If I had your figure I'd go naked too. Why did you land on this crummy planet?"

"To get a spoonful of uranium."

"Uranium? This is getting crazier by the minute. Wait'll the kids at school hear about this. What planet are you from?"

"Kanab, but it is no more. Its sun exploded."

"Exploding suns. Fantastic. Did you get to watch it?"

"I could see it on my viewing screen. It was gorgeous. One moment the star was a black hole in space, then, wham, it was a huge blob of light, a bright, fantastic supernova."

"That must have been neat. Did you bring a brother with you to earth?"

"No."

Matilda's exuberance skidded to a halt against Kyra's flat negative, and the silence gave Breedlove the chance to speak.

"Matty, I don't want you telling the kids at school or anybody else about Kyra until the government makes the announcement. She's top secret, but she'll have to appear in public tomorrow, and I wonder if there's anything you can do about her hair and skin coloring."

"Easy. There's a terrific new hair rinse out called Silvery Platinum and a flesh-toned cosmetic the kids are using to cover their acne, but why fool with her skin? It'll match her platinum-blond hair. If you'll drive to the drugstore, I'll tell you what to get. And get some color film for the Polaroid. I'll take some before-and-after pictures for my scrapbook. And while you're gone I'll take Kyra horseback riding. Would you like that, Kyra?"

"Terrific!"

Bemused by the turn of events, Breedlove went about his chores, considering how Kyra had come in a starship from an abyss of space to find refuge in a farmhouse on an alien planet to confront a female of her own organic age who spoke the language the visitor had acquired in precisely the visitor's same breezy style. When he returned from the drugstore he took the afternoon paper from the porch into the living room. The girls were still out riding, but he had no reservations about their activity, since Matilda had lent Kyra a scarf to cover her hair and they would be riding on a stretch of desolate hills behind the farm. Matilda was an excellent horsewoman, and Kyra, with her agility, could easily be a rodeo rider.

He was reading the sports section when his mother came down from her afternoon nap to join him. She took the headlines and went to her favorite chair beside the window. Looking over, he noticed she was not reading but gazing out the window.

"What are you thinking about, Mother?"

"About the girl. She is strange."

"Do you mean 'stranger than strange'?"

"I suppose. She's very inquisitive about us, but she tells very little about herself or her own people or the way they lived. It's not that she's evasive. She's just not volunteering any information. She'll answer if you ask, and then fly off onto some other subject. I've learned very little about her family."

"She's sensitive," he said. "The subject's painful to her."

"She doesn't always sound sensitive. I asked her about wars on her planet and she said they used to have tribal fights. I asked her if they had peace treaties between the tribes like our Indians, and she said no, because they fought until one side was exterminated. She didn't seem one bit horrified. So I guess I did learn something about her family. They weren't exterminated; they were the exterminators."

"Why were you so interested in her family, Mother?"

"Because of you. I noticed how you looked at her at the table. I've never seen you so attentive before. You may be falling in love with her, and we know nothing at all about her family."

"You'll have to admit she's a very unusual woman," he said lightly. "In fact she's so different a human probably couldn't mate with her."

"She's not that different. I saw her upstairs. I can't understand why she has no navel. Of course, you've seen as much of her as I have, and no doubt you noticed she has no navel. She might be a test-tube baby."

"If she was, all her companions were also," he said. "But don't worry about any romance between us. As soon as she gets the uranium she's leaving earth."

"A woman's been known to change her mind."

"You don't seriously think we'd run off and get married?"

"That's one way she could get her citizen's papers, and she's a lot older than you. Older women can twist a young man around their fingers. Then what would my grandchildren be, piebald?"

"So you don't think your future daughter-in-law's family is acceptable?"

"She may be foreign royalty for all I know. Sometimes she behaves, well, queenly, as someone who expects to be treated as a lady of distinction. Sometimes I catch myself on the verge of calling her 'ma'am.' "

"Matty didn't defer to her," he pointed out. "Matty took to her like a lost puppy."

"I noticed." Mrs. Breedlove nodded. "Matty was very solicitous toward her, something Matty usually isn't. Maybe she'll make Matty her lady-in-waiting if she decides to reign on earth. She wouldn't have to wave any scepter to get your daddy to throw himself prostrate at her feet."

"Mother, you sound jealous."

"Maybe I am, Son," she admitted, turning her attention back to the newspaper, "or maybe I'm frightened."

Back from the ride, Kyra stayed in the kitchen to observe the icing of the cake, and Matilda reported on their activity to her brother, upstairs, where he was packing for Seattle.

"She rides like Lady Godiva, Tom, or at least the stallion must have thought so. It nickered and champed so much I thought it was going to climb into its saddle with her."

His sister left him to go down the hall to her room and pack for Kyra, but she returned at times to confer with him on some item of dress. She was sending Kyra to Seattle with a fully equipped wardrobe, minus bras. "She doesn't really need them, Tom. Mama's old-fashioned."

Mother might be old-fashioned, he observed to himself, but she was perceptive. Matilda acted the role of lady-in-waiting to the hilt, packing her favorite dresses and costume jewelry and attempting to coordinate the colors with silvery blond hair. Breedlove did not object to his sister's generosity; hopefully he would return the clothes within two weeks.

At dinner Kyra tactfully apportioned her attention between his father, mother, and sister, with occasional asides to keep the son from feeling neglected. As guest she guided the conversation, and he noticed that she did avoid discussing Kanab or space travel, but he felt uncertain about her motives for doing so. Her interest in things of the earth was lively and genuine. She seemed spontaneous and candid, and she could have been bored with marvels to them that were commonplaces to her. He would have found it dull to lecture on the internal-combustion engine to cavemen.

After dinner Breedlove posed her alone and with his family for her "before" pictures and for Matilda's scrapbook. She was photogenic and posed naturally, but no camera could have captured her personal magnetism. He made a snapshot of her for his billfold to show any doubting official he might encounter that her hair was naturally green.

Matilda asked her brother to leave the kitchen while she dyed Kyra's hair, because it made her nervous when people watched her work, and he joined his parents in the living room, where they listened to the evening news. It was difficult for him to be impressed by the day's events when he was already involved in the greatest news story in human history. He was more interested in the occasional progress bulletins Matilda came to the doorway to announce: "She's been given a shampoo, and I'm applying the dye." "I'm putting her hair in rollers." "She's under the dryer." "She's ready for combing out." "She's ready."

In the kitchen Kyra sat on a high stool, a plastic cape over her shoulders, and Matilda was putting a few finishing fluffs into her hair when the family filed in. Then the artist flung back the cape to reveal her creation and accept the compliments of her family. The father's praise was directed toward the subject, the mother's to the artist, and the son stood mute.

Silvery blond, he assumed, would appear as exotic to his eyes as green, but Kyra's hair looked natural. The color altered the hue of her complexion until it too appeared normal, although nothing could have been done to make her inconspicuous. Now framed by the platinum hair, her green eyes looked depthless, and they were focusing on him with growing trepidation as he stood silent.

"What's the word from Breedlove?"

"You look mystic, twice mystic," he said, trying to find the words to communicate his admiration. "Your beauty,

57

it's as near and shimmering as moonlight on Lake Chelan, yet as remote and as glittering as the Northern Lights. If I were king of earth, I'd make you queen, and you'd have a crown for your curls made of the stars."

He had blown the fragile moment sky-high, he thought, with his rococo metaphors. He should have tried Keats or Shelley. His voice had trembled when he spoke, he had given his mother more reason to be disturbed, and he had only confused Kyra, who was looking at Matilda questioningly.

"Translated that means you look smarmy and romantic."

"What's smarmy and romantic?"

"It's the dreamy feeling a boy and girl get when they fall in love," Matilda explained. "Usually it lasts for a week or two after they're married."

"Who told you that, young lady?" Mrs. Breedlove asked.

"My sex-education teacher."

"You'd better drop that course. Romance in marriage can last a lifetime, and don't you dare contradict me, John."

"Then romance has to do with marriage," Kyra said.

"Don't you have romance and marriage on your planet, dear?" Mrs. Breedlove asked, a slight strain in her voice.

Kyra deliberated for a moment before she answered, "After a fashion, yes. Our men were attracted to us, and they were self-sacrificing. But the custom of romance seems like a terrific idea. Does an earth girl have a wide choice of suitors?"

"A girl like Matty, no," Matilda answered. "A girl like Kyra, yes."

"Nonsense, Matty." Kyra turned to her. "You are charming."

Mrs. Breedlove would not be diverted. "Is there divorce on your planet?"

"There was no divorce on Kanab. When a man mated

with a woman on our planet it was forever, but there is no more Kanab."

She had answered with an almost painful hesitancy, and sensing that she was moved to sadness by her memories, Breedlove interjected a question, "Will the dye interfere with the light-absorption qualities of your hair?"

Looking sideways into the mirror Matilda held for her and fluffing her hair, Kyra answered absently, "Yes, but Matty tells me it will wash out, and in the interval my body will compensate. If I can find a place to sunbathe in Seattle, my pussy hair will spread like crabgrass."

A brittle silence fell over the kitchen. There was only one source from which the curious Kyra could have learned the taboo word. Mrs. Breedlove fixed accusing eyes on her daughter, who avoided the gaze by glancing with sprightly innocence toward her brother and saying, "Tom, I've made up my mind about a career. I'm going to become a beauty-school technician."

In a blue knit dress fitted snugly against her waist and revealing the lift and cleavage of her unhampered breasts, Kyra stood beside the green-uniformed Breedlove at eight-thirty the next morning, watching a long black limousine nose hesitantly into the lane and drive toward the Breedlove farm.

"Here comes Kelly," he said.

He walked onto the porch and watched the car approach. It pulled to a stop and a uniformed chauffeur emerged and opened the rear door. The man who got out wore a dark suit, white shirt, tie, a gray homburg, and carried an attaché case. Only one flaw marred the ambassadorial elegance of Kelly's arrival: the car bore the commercial license plate of a rented limousine.

About five feet ten inches tall, square-shouldered, chest thrust forward, Kelly swung up the steps with a quick, prancing stride, announcing himself as he came: "Aloysius Kelly, Immigration and Naturalization, Pacific Northwest."

"Thomas Breedlove, Forest Ranger, the Selkirk Station, Idaho."

They shook hands. About fifty, Kelly was red-haired with an Irishman's pinched nose, watery blue eyes, and square jaw. Pale freckles spanned the bridge of his nose and clustered under his eyes. His square, broad shoulders and spread-leg stance projected aggressiveness.

"Peterson tells me you're holding a very important unregistered female alien for my eyes only. What's her status or rank in the country of her origin?"

"I've made no determination of her rank, Mr. Kelly. For all I know she may be an empress. She's from another planet."

Kelly threw a searching glance at Breedlove and asked, "Has Peterson been seeing his little green men again?"

"Step into the house, Mr. Kelly, and judge for yourself. She's waiting in the living room. I can certify she landed here from an alien planet."

Kelly, who had started into the house, stopped. "Who's certifying you?"

"I think the matter will become academic once you've met the lady."

Kelly continued into the house and into the living room. He stepped through the door and stopped. Kyra stood at the window looking out. Her profile was starkly outlined in the eastern light.

"Jesus," Kelly said, "is *she* stacked!"

"Careful, Mr. Kelly. She understands English."

"If this lass is only a wetback from Mexico, I forgive Peterson. If she walked in from Canada, I forgive Peterson. If he claims she comes from the dark side of the moon . . ."

"Peterson has nothing to do with authenticating her origins. I'm here to do that."

Kelly's voice paused when Breedlove broke into his slow, chanting monologue, but obviously he did not hear the ranger, for he resumed where he had left off. ". . . then I forgive Peterson. Those breasts exonerate Peterson. Ranger Breedlove, I'm a married man and reasonably faithful to my wife, but I travel a lot and I get opportunities and what's a man to do when something like this stands before him, spit in her eye?"

"Snap out of it, Kelly! You've got business to attend to."

Kelly shook his head, like a fighter shaking off a jolting punch, and stepped forward, all smiles and affability, his officiousness shucked like a cloak at the door, ignoring Breedlove's presence.

"Miss Kyra Lavaslatta, I'm Aloysius Kelly, Chief of Immigration and Naturalization, Pacific Northwest, but just call me Al. Please be seated, Miss Lavaslatta; I have a few questions to ask."

She sat on the sofa. Kelly pulled a chair before her, crossed his legs, and using his kneecap as a desk, opened his attaché case. He took out a form, uncapped a pen, and looked across at her. The forms in his hand seemed to stabilize him, as similar forms had steadied Peterson.

"Give me your last name, first name, and middle initial."

"Lavaslatta, Kyra. No middle initial."

"How do you spell it?"

"I don't know. Spell it for him, Breedlove."

Breedlove spelled her name, and Kelly wrote it down in block letters.

"What is the country of your origin?"

"I come from a planet my people called Kanab."

"Where is Kanab located?"

"Nowhere. It is gone."

"Well, let's just enter 'Nowhere.' " Kelly's officiousness was returning, but now briskly cordial. "Where was your former planet located?"

"Without a star chart I can only say somewhere in space."

"Very well, we'll just put 'Somewhere.' Where is your closest living relative?"

"She would have to be at least five hundred light years away."

" 'Closest living relative, five hundred light years away.' " Kelly addressed himself briskly as he wrote. "What is your political affiliation?"

"Political affiliation?"

"What philosophy of government do you embrace?"

"I believe in the sisterhood of all living creatures."

" 'The sisterhood of all living creatures.' That's a new one on me, but different strokes for different folks."

It was a long form, but Kelly was extremely helpful. In fact, he became hopelessly involved in a series of questions he himself answered. The questionnaire would have defied interpretation by any immigration clerk, and it was compromising Kelly as hopelessly as the UFO had compromised Peterson, but Breedlove did not interrupt the man. It was his method of coming to grips with the reality of Kyra.

He finished the form, signed it, and handed it across to Kyra. "Write your signature below mine. You may keep the original for your files."

She signed in Kanabian script, tore off the top sheet, and handed it to Breedlove. "File this for me, very carefully."

Her accent on "very carefully" alerted Breedlove to the importance of the document, an importance he was already aware of. He folded it and put it in the envelope with his orders from Peterson. As Kelly started to return his copies to the attaché case, he paused and took a second look at the form. He looked up at Breedlove.

"Ranger Breedlove, this is a rather unusual document. I think you should witness it."

"No, sir. I can't certify it. I doubt if it's verifiable even by Kyra. What I suggest instead is that we sit down and discuss the ramifications of Miss Lavaslatta's arrival."

Surprisingly Kelly did not seem aggrieved at Breedlove's refusal. Instead, he nodded judiciously. "I'm sure you're right. That other descent from heaven had far-reaching consequences. No sacrilege intended, miss. We're got a problem, Breedlove: who's going to believe this? You wouldn't have a spot of whisky around the house, would you, Tom?"

"Name your poison, Al."

Kelly took two fingers of bourbon, neat, in one swallow, and looked around him dazedly, but the whisky braced him. His sense of reality was returning, Breedlove knew, when he muttered to no one in particular, "Peterson passed the buck."

For a long moment he stared at the far wall as if analyzing the wallpaper. Finally his eyes swung back to the girl. "I knew you were from another planet, Kyra, when I walked into the room."

With a soft fluttering in her voice, Kyra asked, "How did you know I was from another planet, Al?"

"Because there's never been anything as beautiful as you on God's green earth."

Emotion gave Kelly's cliché a wild, piercing Celtic beauty. Kyra's green eyes drew in the light from the room and sent it out again in glitterings, and she smiled on Kelly. With that smile Breedlove knew Kelly was hooked. He moved to take command of the situation, seating himself beside Kyra.

"Al, we're faced with a situation unique in human history. Kyra and her small band of exiles are looking for a planet with an oxygen environment. She landed on earth because her fuel source decayed in flight, and she needs a new supply of uranium 235."

"That brings the Atomic Energy Commission into the picture."

"Definitely, which means she'll need authentication that the fuel is not to be used for military purposes. In turn, this means her identity has to be established beyond question. I can speak for the Department of Interior because any evidence I have is not hearsay. I inspected her space vehicle."

"But you're a ranger. You have no security rating."

"No, but I have the original data that's to be classified."

Kelly smiled, his old, officious smile. "I'm prepared to take your deposition, Ranger Breedlove, and relieve you of custody of the immigrant."

"You don't have the security clearance to accept my testimony, Mr. Kelly, so I'm not yielding custody. I'm going with her."

"Any person in this country without identification papers and no proof of citizenship falls under the custodial control of the Immigration and Naturalization Service."

He arose and turned to Kyra. "I didn't want to put this to you so bluntly, miss, but you're under arrest. Get your things together. We're going to Seattle."

Kelly had drawn the bureaucratic battle lines, but he had drawn them in the wrong place.

"Sit down, Al. She's going nowhere without me. From the nature of the form you've filled out and signed, I judge you incapable of taking sole control of an endangered species of park fauna previously entrusted to the park ranger who discovered it. Kyra's not a person. She's an unclassified member of the animal kingdom, maybe. Even her animality is in doubt."

Chapter Five

———— ✳ ————

Incredulity spread over Kelly's face, but not confusion. "She may not be a member of the family Hominidae," he snapped, "but it's plain she belongs to the class Mammalia, even if you don't often find the likes of her outside Italy."

"Her breast development merely demonstrates that nature works from universal patterns. In Africa, Asia, or on the Planet Kanab, form follows function."

"No, Breedlove," Kyra interjected, "function follows form."

Breedlove took her interruption in stride. "Which proves the point I'm trying to make. There's disagreement all around. Kyra may not be an animal at all. She may descend from an air-nourished plant. The natural color of her hair is green—here, look at this snapshot I took last night. . . . Her hair is green because it is capable of photosynthesizing sunlight, a characteristic exclusive to plants on earth. Kyra gets part of her nourishment from sunlight."

"Now who's crazy?"

"You'll notice I'm telling you this, Kelly. I'm not writing

it down. I'll leave the biological depositions to the biologists. They'll have to depose as to whether she's plant or animal, but in either event her habitat is the Selkirk Wilderness Area, which puts her under my jurisdiction, and, flora or fauna, she's threatened with extinction. She stays in my custody."

"She's an unregistered alien."

Kelly was clinging to his one certitude with a weakening grip, and Breedlove began to pry his fingers loose.

"Even that's open to question. As a representative of a foreign power, protocol places her under the jurisdiction of the State Department."

"Oh, no! Not another bureau."

"All she needs is a visitor's permit you're empowered to grant under your own cognizance. I'm willing to let your quarantine doctors determine her biological status, and you can share in the announcement of her arrival on earth, but I'm claiming joint jurisdiction until her status is determined."

Kelly was confused. Breedlove's tone became authoritative.

"The big problem is to get her the uranium. Before that, I have been given authority to see she's properly housed, fed, and clothed."

"Look, Tom," Kelly said, "it's Sunday. It'll be late afternoon before we get her to Seattle. The medical examiners won't schedule her before Monday morning. For security reasons she'd better stay at my house. I have a wife and two daughters—"

"Not a chance, Al. I'll see that she's registered in a hotel at Park's expense. This is for your sake, Al. Kyra has a very unsettling influence on men's wives."

Kelly glanced wistfully at Kyra and nodded. "I understand. I'm willing to go along with you, Tom, for visiting rights after she's cleared quarantine. But as long as we're going to cooperate, why don't you show good faith and give me back my Alien Registration Form."

"Certainly, Al." Breedlove removed the paper and handed it to him. "Now come meet my family. They've all been sworn to secrecy, and they want to tell Kyra goodbye."

On the local flight to Seattle, which touched down at Tacoma, Breedlove was mostly left alone to doze intermittently and awaken to strange confusions. Kyra wanted a window seat, and the two men wanted her there to guard her from casual conversations with people in the aisle. Kelly shouldered past Breedlove to take the middle seat beside her, saying, "You'll have her all this evening. I want her for the flight."

She had brought along the fashion magazine, which lay unopened in her lap as she studied the landscape below, asking "Al" about landmarks and place names. In less than five minutes she had been calling Peterson "Pete," yet she always called him the formal "Breedlove." Now she sat huddled with the solicitous Irishman, and for all the attention he was getting Breedlove could have been in North Dakota.

A vague hurt roiled him, like none he had felt since high school, when he had blurted out an invitation to the girl he wanted to take to the prom and found her already promised to a football star. Stretched out on the seat, a pillow under his head, he regurgitated the sour aftertaste of adolescent rejections and tried to ignore the chatter beside him. He feigned sleep so successfully he dozed until he was aroused by a new note of excitement in Kyra's voice.

Apparently they were flying over clouds, for Kyra's attention had turned to the magazine on her lap, and she was showing Al the Polinski Creation.

"I see it's sold in Seattle," Al was saying, "at Mason's department store. If the Jolly Green Giant will let me have you for lunch after you're out of quarantine, I'll take you shopping. Maybe I'll buy you that fantastic creation."

"Terrific, Al. I'd love you to death for that little number."

Breedlove was twice disturbed. A married man such as Kelly on a government employee's salary would not be buying a girl a $720 dress for altruistic reasons, and nice girls did not accept such expensive gifts from married men. Kyra would have to be lectured discreetly on this subject.

On the ground in Seattle, Breedlove was brought back into the party when Kyra took his arm possessively on the way to baggage pickup and asked, "Does my Jolly Green Giant feel refreshed after his wholesome rest on the plane?"

He didn't particularly care for Al's cute expression, but his only indication of disapproval was in the restraint of his smile.

Kelly drove them to the Federal Building in his 1973 Plymouth coupé he had left at the airport. At his office he called the medical facility at the Navy base and arranged with the duty officer for Kyra to report Monday at 0800 for her physical examination. At the same time he arranged for Breedlove to escort her onto the base and to the sick bay. He called a family motel near Lake Washington to reserve two suites for them, then he carefully filled in a new Alien Registration Form, with Breedlove's assistance, which the ranger witnessed.

Since the offices were closed for Sunday, Kelly had no secretary, and it took the two men almost an hour to fill out the form. Once during the session Kyra excused herself to go to the women's lounge, and Kelly took advantage of her absence to advise Breedlove: "Tom, you strike me as a sensible young man, not one to go overboard with the hanky-panky, but remember, Kyra has not passed quarantine yet. As pretty as she is, she might be carrying some exotic disease fatal to human beings."

Breedlove accepted the advice, but he was not deluded. He had the definite impression that if Kyra had any communicable diseases, Kelly wanted to be the first to catch them.

After signing the forms, Kyra was a registered resident of the U.S.A., whatever else her status, and Kelly wasn't done. He took them to the basement garage and assigned Breedlove a Lincoln automobile usually reserved for visiting dignitaries. As he drove the car from the basement with Kyra beside him, Breedlove felt life within him turning to a pleasant tension it had not achieved since the strings snapped in the high-school-prom debacle. He was looking forward with a teen-ager's enthusiasm to a night on the town with the prettiest girl in the school.

The motel where Kelly reserved their rooms was a two-story Spanish-mission-style structure built around a swimming pool in its completely enclosed quadrangle. One of a California-based chain, the motel retained a California flavor even to two artificial palm trees overhanging the pool. After they checked in, Breedlove, mindful of Kyra's love of twilights, suggested they drive to the campus of the University of Washington to watch the sunset.

On the campus few students were abroad on a Sunday afternoon, and he took her on a tour, showing her the various buildings where his classes had been, talking of professors and of student escapades. Passing the library, she remarked, "You must teach me to read, Breedlove."

She listened to his stories with a grave serenity so different from her usual animation that he asked, "Why are you so pensive, Kyra?"

69

"You are remembering an old happiness, and such memories are sacred. Breedlove, I wish I could have shared your happiness."

Her vivacity revived near the stadium. A group of young athletes emerged from the field house, four whites and three blacks, and as they approached Breedlove and Kyra the emanations of their libidos seemed to crest ahead of them. Coming closer, they moved from the path politely to skirt the ranger and the girl, but once past they looked back and whistled their admiration.

"They approve of you, Kyra."

"You earth men come in all sizes, shapes, and colors, and there are so many of you."

A boy and girl passed, holding hands and oblivious of all save themselves. The couple elicited Kyra's first question of the outing, "Did you have a sweetheart when you were here?"

He told her of the botany student he had courted and the ambiguous end of the affair.

"Did you suffer pangs of unrequited love, Breedlove?"

"No, I've only been panged twice in my romantic career, and the first was the worst."

Suddenly to his surprise he was telling her of the senior prom and about the shyness that kept him from asking the girl of his choice to the dance until it was too late.

She listened with absurd gentleness, as a mother might listen to some tale of a childish wrong, and said, "Poor Breedlove, too shy to make out."

"You learned that expression from Matilda."

"Yes. She has a tremendous vocabulary."

As twilight drew closer he walked with her to a bench beneath a spreading tree, and they sat in silence as the shadows deepened around them. The old brick buildings grew more scarlet in the dying light.

"What a beautiful planet."

A sadness in her voice transmitted her desolation to him and her wistful longing for home. Above them pale stars were beginning to flicker, and he thought with a feeling of dread of their boundless reaches awaiting her. Reaching out, he took her hand in a gesture of human concern and said, "Kyra, even if it means the personal end of me, I wish you would stay."

"It would never mean the personal end of you, and if I could not return your love for me I would stay."

She clung to his hand, and her words, though paradoxical, held connotations of a truth he was only beginning to admit to himself.

"Are you speaking of your capability to feel love, or are you making a more . . . personal statement?"

"I speak of both, but for you my feeling is private. You have always been my lover, Breedlove, and you will always be my lover. I am the summer and you are the flower."

Moved by the quiet dignity and conviction in her voice, he asked, not in doubt but in curiosity, "How do you know I love you?"

"You tell me in a language without words."

It could be that she was confessing that she could read his mind, and he said, "I'd like to explore that remark over dinner with you tonight at the Space Needle Restaurant."

She dropped his hand. The vivacious, bantering girl had returned. "There's nothing more to say, Breedlove. I know when your second pangs of love struck—while you were faking a snooze on the airplane."

"But you weren't even looking at me."

"I saw your leg muscles tense up."

For her first night out on earth, Kyra chose a dress on which Matilda had penned a note, "For dinner and cocktails. Wear with pearl choker." Burgundy-colored velvet underlaid an outer skirt of voile, which flared from her waist to slightly below her knees. Crimped and sitting snugly, the tight, high waist forced her wide-cleft breasts upward to swell above the low arc of her neckline. Around her neck three strands of pearls gleamed to match the highlights of her hair.

He felt clumsy and earth-bound around her and drew comfort from the knowledge that her aura of femininity and lightness would have made the most epicene escort appear graceless. His self-consciousness left him, however, when they followed the headwaiter to a booth in the soaring restaurant. He became both anonymous and proud, for her entrance was a royal progress drawing all eyes from him.

Her hair caught the attention of the diners, her eyes, luminous in the glow of the table lamps, held it; and her swaying walk drew the gazes after her. They were seated and he ordered martinis. The drinks came, he toasted her, and she lifted her glass in abstract acknowledgment of his salute. The panorama of city and harbor lights held her enthralled.

She tasted the drink, then sipped it, and continued to gaze in wonderment at the lights. Her enchantment communicated itself to him, and he sat in silence, covertly watching her as she watched the slowly revolving landscape.

"Weren't there city lights on Kanab?"

"None like yours. We lived in tribal communities which followed the springs and autumns from one hemisphere to the other, sowing in one and reaping in the other."

"You were migrant farmers, then?"

"We didn't plow or tend herds. The continents of Kanab were vast arboreal parks. We tended our forests and they fed us."

Distracted by the lights, she gave only partial attention to his questions, answering with no trace of the melancholy that memory sometimes stirred in her.

"What did you fly in?"

"Vehicles that could hover, as your helicopters. Entire families moved in them. But they were made in parts and easily assembled, so there was no need for great manufacturing centers. . . . Oh, it was a joy to be soaring over the great forests, to settle and plant and prune. We ate only nuts and fruits. We became a race of vegetarians."

"You seem to enjoy the meat you've eaten here."

"In the early days we were meat eaters. It's surprising how appetites hang on. Tonight I'd like a thick, juicy steak, rare."

"If you had no herds, where'd you get meat?"

"From other tribes. In ancient times, when the planet grew too crowded and the forests could not support us all, we fought over territory. After we learned to fly and developed seasonal methods of birth control, we reverted to a vegetable diet."

"You mean the victors ate the vanquished in your tribal wars?"

He knew the answer from his mother, but he wished to judge her attitude for himself. She answered easily, "Of course. Otherwise the flesh would have been wasted."

"That's cannibalism."

"Don't sound so shocked. If you have a name for it, you've done it. You'd make a terrific pot roast, Breedlove."

Her attention was focusing on him now. He called the waiter and ordered a Châteaubriand, rare.

"What was this seasonal birth control?" he asked.

"Our biological urges were controlled by the angle of our sun. When the planet's tilt brought deep summer, our mating season began, so we tricked nature by flying to the winter hemisphere. . . . Tell me, Breedlove, why is such a handsome man as you shy around women?"

"I don't know." He shrugged. "I don't understand them, or maybe they don't understand me. I was born too gentle in an age in which even the women have macho."

"What's macho?"

"Hubristic masculinity."

She cocked her head and studied him intently. "Maybe women don't understand you because you use such big words."

"Could be." He laughed. "I was never good at small talk."

"You don't seem tongue-tied around me."

"This is not small talk. Besides, when I'm with a highly intelligent woman I feel relaxed. Even so, I don't seem to have scored with you. I noticed you were calling Peterson 'Pete' and Kelly 'Al,' but you never call me 'Tom.' "

"On my planet, Breedlove, when a girl calls a boy by his family name it's to honor him. It's her way of telling him he would be acceptable as the father of her race."

The complaint had flown from his martini, and he regretted its juvenility the moment he uttered it, but her words reshaped his mood.

"Would that be possible with us? After all, we're of different species."

"We'll let your doctors give their opinion tomorrow, but if I had another martini I might be willing to try tonight."

"Then, by all means, let's have another martini."

"Not with the fate of the world in the balance, my dear. Besides, your wordless words are getting too saucy."

It was a delightful evening. From his loosened tongue extravagant compliments flowed. Her eyes glittered to his witty and flirtatious small talk, and she was not the passive recipient of his unleashed social charms. As if atoning for all the proms he had missed, she lent an appreciative ear to his conversation. The steak pleased her. She never once referred to him as a Jolly Green Giant. Their talk, however, concerned only the customs and traditions of earth.

When the hour grew late, he drove her back to the motel, and as he stood in the doorway of her suite he gave her his final lecture on the customs of earth.

"When a man takes a woman to dinner, it's the custom for her to award him with a good-night kiss."

"What's a good-night kiss?"

"It's best defined by demonstration. Put your arms around me and tilt your face."

He was being more playful than ardent. When his arms went around her he intended to give her only a brotherly kiss, educational for her and historically significant for mankind, but Kyra's intuition immediately grasped the romantic symbolism of the gesture. Her lips clung to his as if she sipped the nectar of his admiration. Feeling the warmth of her arms around him, the play of her fingers on the nape of his neck, the thrust of her upturned breasts and the inward arc of her thighs against his palm, he forgot the historical implications of his act and pressed her closer. Even as she yielded easily to his strength she bound him closer with her lightness.

It was a woman not of earth but desirable above all women of earth who pressed herself to him, frankly reveling in the sensuality of their embrace, but a blitheness in her voluptuosity gave it the innocence of a kitten at play and aroused his protectiveness. His delight in her nearness further annulled his desire; she stirred him, but to a wild imagery. From her lips he sipped an elixir of springtime compounded of the fragrance of violets and bird song, the blossoms of trees and the hum of bees, all of spring's bright cornucopia dissolved in a distillate of sunlight. Drunk on her lightness, he felt his psyche levitate and begin to soar in tightening circles toward a beckoning, dazzling sun.

She pushed him away.

"That's a terrific custom, Breedlove. Now, first thing in

the morning, I want you to teach me to read.''

Smiling, she closed the door.

In his own room Breedlove sat on the edge of his bed wondering about her. As the Pied Piper had led the children of Hamelin to the mountain cave, she had led him to the gates of Wonderland, and, as the Piper had done to a little lame boy in the legend, she had closed him out. For one shimmering moment he had experienced an unforgettable view, but of what? Of an ideal romance? Of a perfect woman? Had she lured him to the gates with the beckonings of an unearthly feminine appeal, or had she used necromancy? Whatever his vision had been, he knew that Kyra had cast her spell around him, that he would never again walk completely free of her brightness and wonder, that he on honey-dew had fed and drunk the milk of Paradise.

Chapter Six

———— ✳︎ ————

Over orange juice Monday morning in the motel dining room, Breedlove read Kyra a caption beneath a photograph in a copy of an outdoorsman's magazine he had bought in the lobby, pointing out each syllable in the words he read. She listened, her eyes registering the open and relaxed fixity he had first noticed on Jones Meadow, and then she asked him to write her name in English script. She copied his scribbling once, and he considered her handwriting superior to his.

When breakfast came, her attention shifted to the pancakes he ordered. She questioned him about the milling of grain. With the authority of a wheat farmer's son, he discussed the processing of flour and the history of pancakes. When he had finished his dissertation, she glanced back at the magazine and asked, "What's a falcon?"

She had read the word in the magazine, and it led him into a discussion of birds of prey. After coffee, while the waitress totaled their check, she said, "Test my reading, Breedlove."

Haltingly she read a caption under the photograph of a hunting dog she pronounced "set-ter," and asked his assistance on two words, but it was an exceptional demonstration of intellectual ability, and he complimented her.

"It's not my intelligence," she said, "but the techniques of concentration I've learned."

He could not accept her demurral fully, although he realized she was not a superbeing. On the drive to the Navy base she grew edgy with apprehensions, which she evinced in purely human terms; she sat on the edge of the seat, grew silent, moved her hands around, and finally got snappish. She wore Matilda's jeans, loafers, and denim shirt with her own shoulder bag, which contained a few dollars and change. Some instinct for caution had made Breedlove insist that she leave the pink container in his custody.

Soon it would no longer be his responsibility to convince anyone that Kyra belonged to a species alien to earth—the medical examiners would prove that—but he would have to make the preliminary announcements to the authorities, and he was concerned about first reactions to Kyra. So far they had ranged from polite befuddlement to semihysteria, but he had counted on Kyra to help soften the shock of her strangeness, and now she herself was upset.

She had landed on earth with the attitude of a motorist pulling into a filling station, figuring to fuel up and be on her way, but the man at the pump had referred her to a credit manager in the office, and now she was being led to a washroom where she would be stripped, pummeled, and probed. And stuck. He had forgotten to warn her about the needles.

"They'll stick you with a needle to get a blood sample," he said, "but it's not painful."

"If it's not painful, why are you warning me?"

He shook his head resignedly. "You're just too logical for

a female, on earth or anywhere else."

"My, how superior we feel this morning," she snapped. "Our hubristic masculinity is breaking out all over."

At the gate he was directed to the sick bay, and his tension grew as they walked from the parking lot toward the entrance. Navy doctors would handle the quarantine procedures. The Navy was under the Department of Defense, which had more clout than Interior and Justice combined. The wolves of Defense would come howling down on Kyra for one reason—her brain held secrets undreamed of by earth's military scientists.

Kyra could be declared a top-secret archive, and he had no security rating. His stride faltered, and Kyra took his arm, saying, "Steady, Breedlove, I'm the one that's getting the needle."

"I was thinking more of hooks. When Defense gets you, it might want all of you, and I've got to find some hook to hang onto you with. Listen, keep your timid, frightened manner and let me do the talking. When you see me push, you pull."

"What do you have in mind?"

"I don't know. I'll play it by ear."

"You'll think of something. You're resourceful, for a man."

The Navy clinic was housed in two long, gray, one-story frame buildings that bisected each other at right angles. Ushering Kyra into the lobby, Breedlove whiffed the miasma of disinfectants, antiseptics, anaesthesia, urea, and human misery from a corridor that seemed to dwindle interminably into the distance. At the reception desk he started to introduce himself, but the nurse on duty, seeing his uniform, said, "You're Ranger Breedlove with Mr. Kelly's patient. Won't you be seated? Chief Pharmacist Pilsudski will be with you in a moment."

The receptionist cast no covert glances at Kyra as she

seated herself beside Breedlove on a bench against the wall, and the nurse's lack of curiosity indicated to him that Kelly had not prepared anyone in the clinic for Kyra's strangeness. He hoped Chief Pilsudski proved emotionally stable, for the chief would be the first to know.

Breedlove was answering Kyra's question about the nurse's uniform when a door opening down the hall drew his attention to a woman who emerged. She wore a Navy uniform, with a skirt short enough to reveal well-muscled but shapely legs that matched her stocky torso, and he deduced from her straight-line approach toward them that she was Chief Pilsudski.

About forty, her broad, Slavic face seemed to be formed for smiling, and she exuded an air of maternal warmth, strength, and serenity. Her sandy hair, tinged with beginning gray, gave her a look of distinction. Though cool and appraising, her gray eyes were friendly. Breedlove guessed she had been put in charge of admissions because of her ability to calm entering patients and reassure anxious relatives.

"Ranger Breedlove, if you and Miss Lavaslatta will follow me, we'll have the quarantine forms made out in a jiffy."

They followed her down the hall to a door marked ADMISSIONS, and Breedlove was beginning to feel confidence in her. From her name and facial structure, he assumed her antecedents were Eastern European. From her broad, muscular body, he deduced she came from peasant stock, solid, enduring, and imperturbable. And she was a woman. So far women seemed to adjust to the idea of Kyra more easily than men.

"Chief Pilsudski," he said, "I think I should warn—"

"Just call me Chief, or Anna, if you prefer. Strangers often call me 'Pilsener,' and some of the doctors try to get away with 'Suds.' My dearly beloved late husband left me with a rather beery name."

"Chief, I don't think Mr. Kelly spoke to you in detail about Miss Lavaslatta—"

"Oh, we're aware she's a very important person. If Miss Lavaslatta's quarantine has to be extended, she'll occupy the VIP's quarters."

"Extended? How long can quarantines be extended?"

"By law up to forty days, but the law's rarely observed nowadays, with the new techniques for uncovering diseases."

She turned to Kyra.

"Your examining physician will be Doctor Condon. His Navy rank is commander. He should have you through quickly."

"Chief," Breedlove interjected, "Kyra's more than a 'very important person.' She has no living relatives on earth."

"Poor dear. An orphan."

"I'm her guardian in a manner of speaking—"

"Then you'll have to sign a release deposing that you are her guardian, and she'll have to witness your signature."

Pilsudski reached into her desk for another form.

"Of course," she continued, "you realize it's a routine legal form which releases the Navy from any liability in a malpractice suit brought against the examining physician. It doesn't release the physician of responsibility, but there's very little danger of malpractice in a physical examination."

She handed the form across the desk to him with her pen. He immediately saw an opportunity to bind Kyra to him with hoops of paper stronger than steel. Once signed, witnessed, and recorded, documents assumed their own inviolability only lengthy court procedures might challenge. He signed and handed the form to Kyra, who signed it. The chief witnessed their signatures, appended her serial number, time-stamped the document, and put it in a manila folder.

"You were saying Kyra has no relatives."

"Not on earth, Chief Anna. Kyra's a visitor from the now extinct planet of Kanab. She has come to petition the U.S.A. for enough uranium 235 to power her journey onward into space. For reasons I can't go into, her quarantine must be expedited. I know this may be hard for you to accept, but I think the proof of what I say will be evident to any doctor."

"I don't find it hard to accept at all." Chief Pilsudski smiled. "I knew Kyra didn't get those beautiful green eyes anywhere on earth, and with so many stars in the sky it's incredible to me that we earth folks haven't been visited before."

Suddenly a look of dismay clouded her eyes, and Breedlove tensed slightly, but the chief continued in a speculative tone: "Unfortunately my security rating doesn't clear me for restricted data concerning space exploration. I have a clearance for classified medical intelligence only, so I may be violating Navy regulations by asking Kyra questions."

"Chief, how could the Navy possibly issue directives about interviewing visitors from space, since it's never been done before. You're establishing the precedents, here and now, for others to follow."

"Of course, you're right," the chief said, still retaining her composure in the face of Kyra's origins. "There can be no regulations concerning that which never happened. I'll go right ahead with the forms."

Again Breedlove observed the steadying effect of routine on the human nervous system. Chief Pilsudski questioned Kyra calmly as she went through the form, skipping only one question, "Proof of Alien's Birth in Country of Origin?" Kyra signed it; Breedlove, as her guardian, attested to her signature; and the chief witnessed it. For a moment she sat considering the form, tapping her forehead with her pen.

"I do wish you had brought along a birth certificate, Kyra." She eyed Kyra's shoulder bag as if expecting Kyra to rummage through it and come up with a birth certificate. "Don't you have any evidence of your birth on Kanab?"

Kyra thought for a moment and said, "Yes, Anna, I have."

She stood to unbutton her shirt and jeans. Thinking she intended to flash the true green of her hair, Breedlove averted his eyes and heard Kyra say, "Look, Anna. No bellybutton."

"This is most curious," the chief said. "You have no navel but you have breasts, so you must be a mammal, but what happened to your umbilicus?"

The chief had asked herself the question, and her eyes groped for an answer, rolling around for a moment until the whites were visible in odd places. Slowly she rose and leaned over the desk toward Kyra, asking in a sharp, accusatory tone, "Kyra, where is your bellybutton?"

"I have none, Anna." Kyra's voice assumed its fluting, soothing tone.

Chief Anna Pilsudski was beyond being soothed. A harpy was emerging from the woman of distinction, but the wild words that poured from her were not directed solely or even mainly to Kyra. They were breast-beating imprecations against a malevolent fate.

"What's a mammal without an umbilicus? Only kangaroos have teats without bellybuttons. What are you, a wallaby? If you're a marsupial, where's your pouch? You've got to be from Australia. All strange things come out of Australia: koalas, platypuses, Evonne Goolagong, wombats, dingos, and the flat-faced swagman I married the first time. Don't you deny it, young lady. You're a dinko from the Outback!"

She scooped the forms from her desk, clutched them to her bosom, and plunged head first through the swinging doors marked PRIVATE, screaming, "Doooctor!"

"Well, this should forewarn Doctor Condon that you're a very unusual person," Breedlove said to Kyra.

"Breedlove, I've always known I was an unusual person, but it never frightened me before." Tears were forming in her eyes. "What's a dinko from the Outback?"

"I've never heard the expression before."

He could sympathize with Kyra, so tiny and appealing, who had come so far to suffer these indignities, but he reserved a portion of his compassion for the quivering chief pharmacist, who had hurled herself through the swinging door. Anna Pilsudski had conducted herself in the highest traditions of the Navy up to the very threshold of credulity, and she might have carried on had it not been for the happenstance that her first husband was a flat-faced swagman from the Outback.

After an interminable two minutes the doors swung outward and a tall man in a smock, with coarse salt-and-pepper hair and the cragged features of an Abraham Lincoln, shouldered his way into the office, reading the forms Anna had completed with an abstract and faintly skeptical air. Glancing at Breedlove and Kyra, he smiled the confident smile of a man in control of the situation, laid the papers on the desk, and came to stand beside Kyra. He cupped her chin in his palm and looked down into her eyes. When he spoke his voice was low, friendly, and reassuring.

"So, this is the unnaveled young lady who reduces our Suds to foam and gives to airy nothing the name of Kanab. The Girl with the Jade Green Eyes. Welcome to earth, Kyra Lavaslatta."

He took his hand from Kyra's chin and extended it in greeting to Breedlove. "And you're her guardian."

"Yes, I'm Breedlove. If it's possible I'd like to wait while you examine her. I'm driving her."

Condon turned back to the desk and picked up the papers, looking at them now without skepticism.

"If half what Pilsudski has written is true, she may have to remain here overnight. We'll take very good care of her. I wouldn't advise you to wait. You can telephone her around 1700, and if she's staying overnight the operator will give you her extension."

Breedlove nodded and turned to Kyra. "I'll leave, then. You can call me if you're released early, and I can get down within half an hour. Go with the doctor now and be brave."

He felt no irony in telling the being who had dared the perils of space to be brave, for she was frightened. As she stood to go, she reached out and took his hand and squeezed it in a gesture of sadness and regret. She took her bag and moved toward the swinging doors Condon held open for her. As she entered she cast a wistful look toward Breedlove before the doors swung shut behind her.

He returned to loneliness at the motel. Telling the desk clerk he was expecting a call, he sat in the lobby and penned a report to Peterson and a letter to his family. In the letter he described his sadness over having to tell her good-bye with such graphic power that it occurred to him that he might objectify his emotions, and in a measure purge them, by writing a poem to Kyra in language simple enough to match her budding literary skills but poignant enough to capture his feelings. Besides, it was something to do.

For over an hour he tried to write her the poem, but the words he found were too heavy-footed to bear such delicate freight and the meter was atrocious. Still, the idea was too good to let drop. In his frustration he decided on an expediency. Coming from an alien culture, Kyra would not be able to recognize a plagiarized source, and an appropriate, pirated poem—he had just the poem he could quote from memory—would give her a relic to take with her to the stars. Thousands of years from now, earth time, on some far-distant planet, she might gather her grandchildren around her to read to them, in his own English tongue, the tribute a long-dead earth man once penned to her beauty.

The image was so compelling Breedlove decided to use the motel's stationery as a curio to enchant her grandchildren further, and he wrote beneath the motel's letterhead the title he had chosen for Kyra's poem, "To One in Quarantine."

> Thou wast all that to me, Kyra,
>   For which my soul did pine—
> A green island in the Sound, Kyra,
>   Mount Rainier and a shrine,
> All intermingled with fairy fruits and flowers,
>   And all the flowers were mine.
>
> Now all my days are trances,
>   And all my nightly dreams
> Are where thy green eye glances,
>   And where thy footstep gleams—
> In what sidereal dances,
>   By what galactic streams?

He looked upon his handiwork and was pleased; Kyra did not know Edgar Allan Poe from little green apples.

By 1:15 p.m. (1315 Kyra's time) he was dawdling over coffee in the dining room when a voice page sent him quickly to the telephone—but the caller was Kelly.

"I've been euchred out of a lunch date with Kyra. The Navy has taken over. Condon called Houston to fly in a

NASA expert in space medicine, and he won't be in until tomorrow."

"How did you learn this?"

"Immigration's got informants over there, and quarantine is supposed to be my operation. By the way, would you get the Lincoln back to the car pool on the double."

"I'll bring it as soon as I get a call from Kyra."

"Forget it. They're holding her incommunicado."

A disturbed Breedlove hung up, then did what any concerned friend of a patient would have done: he called the patient's doctor. He had only a brief wait before Condon answered.

"Doctor, I'm inquiring about Kyra."

"She's doing as well as can be expected."

"I'm concerned about her time of release. I have to be away for a couple of hours, but I don't want to be out when she calls."

"You'll have time to drive to Vancouver."

"Would I be able to speak to her now for a moment?"

"No. She's busy. Call her back after five."

Condon hung up. His words substantiated Kelly generally, but it remained to be seen if Kyra was being held incommunicado. If the Department of Defense tried to keep her from communicating with her guardian, a whole new ball game would begin. Defense's only argument for holding her would be for reasons of national security, and that argument had become suspect in the eyes of the public. With his photographs of Kyra, his letter of authorization, and his eyewitness's account of her arrival on earth, he possessed the equivalent of the Pentagon Papers. The newspapers would love the story.

Breedlove returned Kelly's car to the pool, walked down the street to a rental agency, and rented a less pretentious vehicle. He drove back to the motel and at 5:05 called the operator at the clinic. She gave him the private number of the VIP suite and he dialed the number. A recording of a woman's voice answered. "We are sorry, but this number is temporarily disconnected."

He could not argue with a recording, but he feared the number had not been temporarily disconnected, that Kyra was vanishing into the vast anonymity of the Department of Defense. He next called Peterson at Selkirk. Within the Department of Interior, chief rangers held positions analogous to those of ship captains in shipping firms. They were not of the hierarchy, but they were deferred to as the men who got the work done. Peterson listened as Breedlove described the situation. His answer was temporizing, soothing, encouraging.

"Frankly, Tom, I think you're getting emotionally involved. Blackmailing Defense is an irrational move. Maybe the telephone *is* out of order. I'll call Washington in the morning. There are a few legalities in our favor. Sit tight and I'll call you back at nine tomorrow."

"Sitting tight" was easier advised than performed. At 6:30 Breedlove called Kyra's number and the recording answered. From 7:30 until 9:30 he called at quarter-hour intervals, and the recording continued to answer.

At 9:45 his telephone rang. Like the sound of many waters, Kyra's voice rippled over the line. "Breedlove, what the hell does *Veni, vidi, vici* mean?"

"That's Latin for 'I came, I saw, I conquered.' "

"They've got a terrific library here, and I'm learning to read, but I came a cropper in that one. Who speaks Latin?"

"Nobody. It's a dead language. Where are you calling from?"

"From a telephone booth behind the sick bay. You only gave me two dimes and I've used one already."

"I gave you two quarters. You can get anyone to change them for five dimes."

"Breedlove, you never cease to amaze me."

"How's your examination coming?"

"*Veni, vidi, vici.* Every doctor on the base has come to pay me homage, and nobody around here worries about my nakedness. What have you been doing all day?"

"Moping around. Pining for you. I wrote you the first poem I've written to a girl since high school."

"Read it to me, Breedlove, with expression."

"I was hoping to give it to you."

"Don't leave me dangling. Read it now, Breedlove."

He read the poem with expression.

For a moment she was silent, and when she spoke she seemed genuinely thrilled. "It's darling, Breedlove. I'll treasure this little poem forever."

"But I haven't given it to you."

"You have, Breedlove, It's engraved on my heart. Shall I read it back to you, word for word?"

"No. I'm acquainted with your memory. Did they give you any idea how long you'll be there?"

"Nobody knows. Some doctors are coming in tomorrow to ask me about Kanab. Everyone here is very nice, but you know, Breedlove, underneath they're afraid of me. I know Myra scared hell out of you, but anyone who's not afraid of Myra is an idiot. With all these big men around they're afraid of *me*."

"They're afraid you might bring diseases to the planet no one has ever heard of."

"They shouldn't judge me by their Neanderthal standards. I know about diseases and take preventive measures. Anyway, if they were afraid of diseases they'd put me behind glass."

"Where'd you learn the word 'Neanderthal'?"

"I've been in the library since chow. If I couldn't learn something about the planet in three hours, I'd be stupid."

His heart sank. If she was already reading books on

anthropology, it was only a matter of time before she came across an anthology containing Poe's "To One in Paradise."

"You ought to find lots about uranium in the library. Get the books on chemistry and physics."

"I've read a few already. Look, I'd better hang up. If the nurse comes and finds me out of my room, she'll get worried."

"Doesn't she know you're calling me?"

"No. I went out the window. The telephone in my room isn't working. They're setting up something that'll hook me into the command network, a man told me."

Then the recording had not been wrong, he realized, but he still did not know what the Navy's policy would be regarding her private calls.

"If I haven't called you by seven tomorrow, if you're still there, slip out the window and call me. If they try to hold you incommunicado, I'll start pushing to get access to you."

"Don't worry, Breedlove. I've got a few tricks to play."

She hung up, and for the first time since she had passed through the swinging doors he felt optimistic. Peterson was right. His plan to blackmail Defense had been wild. And he didn't need Interior's help. He had his personal *deus ex machina*, Kyra, who would drop down to lift him over his problems.

Clasping his hands behind his neck he lay back on the bed, remembering the musical lilt of her voice. She had the most *non sequitur* mind he had ever encountered, leaping forward and back, keeping to no agenda, yet her observations revealed strong deductive powers. As she said, if the doctors had feared disease, they would have kept her isolated, but if they didn't fear disease, what did they fear? And who were the doctors coming to question her? Of course the interviewers did not have to mean medical doctors. That was it.

She was no longer in quarantine. She was being held for interrogation. Experts were coming to question her, anthropologists, sociologists, zoologists, awaiting their turns to question her. She might be there for weeks while the planet tilted toward the solstice, when the instincts of her species, commanded by the sun, would bind them forever to an earth they could not share with others.

Yet, strangely, it was not genocide for his own species that fretted most strongly at his mind. In the long hours she would be forced to spend in the library, she would run across the poems of Poe, and his fraudulence would be revealed. A remorse all out of proportion to his transgression filled him with a bleak despair, and when he arose to undress for sleep, sleep did not come easily. For almost an hour he tossed and turned, tortured by symptoms he did not recognize, because he had never before suffered the disease.

In the morning he slept late and was emerging from the shower when Peterson's call came.

"A lawyer by the name of Abe Cohen will call on you around noon. He couldn't be sure of the exact time, because Abe's a very busy man, but he's on retainer with Interior and happens to be an expert in immigration problems. Also he's worked in Washington and knows interdepartmental procedures. Tell him your story and let him take it from there. He's not there to make waves, but the fact that he can won't go unnoticed. He'll see that Kyra's out of quarantine in a reasonable time, and he'll see that you sit in on any conferences involving her. Meanwhile, take a cold shower and try to forget the girl."

Cohen arrived before noon and telephoned Breedlove from the lobby. Breedlove went out to meet him, and the man he found waiting had none of the poised tension Breedlove expected in a dynamic Washington lawyer. About sixty, Cohen had a soft voice and softer manner.

Thin gray hair receded from his high forehead. Large brown eyes and age-slackened jowls gave him a faint resemblance to a cocker spaniel. His thin frame was stooped, and he walked with a sidling motion. At Cohen's suggestion—he feared being overheard—they returned to Breedlove's room.

"I've come at the request of Interior, Mr. Breedlove, to look out for the interests of the young lady. There might be a tendency to exhibit her as a talking simian when in fact, under provisions of the immigration code, she might qualify as a head of state entitled to a grant of privilege by the State Department. At the moment I'm not looking forward to any request so ambitious, but it offers a line of attack.

"The de facto situs of her space vehicle is important. If it is in fact in the state of Idaho, she might be covered by provisions of Idaho's Good Samaritan Law. Then we could quote a few state ordinances in her support."

"Her ship's a good twenty miles south of the Canadian border," Breedlove assured him, "and thirty miles east of the Washington line."

Breedlove motioned Cohen to a chair and settled himself on the edge of the bed.

"I'm here in her interest," Cohen said, "but I'm still mindful of my own reputation. I wish to be sure I'm not perpetuating some hoax."

"You don't have to worry about that, Mr. Cohen. She took me inside her spaceship. It's real."

"Yet we have to admit, Mr. Breedlove, there's room even here for skepticism. As the Devil's Advocate, I must ask you, have you ever taken any hallucinatory drugs?"

"Never."

"Then there's the possibility of false memories implanted through hypnotic suggestion. Did you bring any item or artifact with you when you exited from her spaceship?"

"No. I went fishing."

"Then, actually, we lack all but subjective evidence when it comes to your testimony."

Breedlove saw that Cohen was moving to establish the credibility of Kyra's chief witness, and his gentle manner softened the incisiveness of his interrogation. He was beginning to understand and respect Abe Cohen.

"I have before-and-after Polaroid shots of Kyra taken when her hair was its original green and later after it was dyed platinum. But I suppose those could be faked."

"Hardly," Cohen said. "It's difficult to fake a Polaroid shot."

He showed the photographs to the attorney, who took them to the window to study them under various angles of light, then handed them back to Breedlove with his verdict. "They're not faked. She appears very human, and very attractive. Now, let's take your step-by-step story of how you met her and how you became convinced she was not a fraud."

Breedlove told the story of his encounter with Kyra. He could not be sure the lawyer believed everything, but Cohen did not seem to disbelieve him, either. In his polite manner Cohen cross-questioned him, taking an occasional note. Breedlove was finishing the tale when the telephone rang.

A woman's voice inquired, "Ranger Thomas Breedlove?"

"Yes."

"Admiral Harper's office calling. The admiral would like to see you without delay. It's concerning the fair visitor. If you do not have transportation, a car will be dispatched to your motel immediately."

"I have a car. Where's the admiral's office?"

"Room 812, Federal Building. When may the admiral expect you?"

"I haven't had lunch."

93

"The admiral invites you to lunch with him in the commissary at 1300."

"Accepted," Breedlove said tersely, taking his cue from the voice.

Breedlove hung up and turned back to Cohen. "We're getting action. That was Admiral Harper's office. He wants to see me, whoever he is."

"He's Naval Intelligence," Cohen said, glancing at his watch. "It's twelve-fifteen, and it's not kosher to keep an admiral waiting. You can finish the story on the way to your car."

With quaint, old-world gallantry Cohen held Breedlove's jacket for him and, with his slue-footed walk, went with Breedlove to the parking lot as the ranger continued his tale. The lawyer smiled when Breedlove described Pilsudski's reaction to Kyra's absent navel.

At the car Cohen gave Breedlove his card.

"Call me if you need me. Admiral Harper should give you some idea of the official attitude, and if it's hard line, if it looks like they're going to hold Kyra for more than a couple of days, I can start making legal noises."

"Would my rights as her guardian hold in court?"

"Definitely. It was sagacious of you to sign those papers."

He held the door open for Breedlove, saw that it was locked when closed, and said, "If Harper tries to tell you that the Bill of Rights does not apply to nonhuman aliens, you tell him Abe Cohen has a different opinion."

Chapter Seven

———————————— ✳ ————————————

Admiral Jonathan Harper was a vegetarian. He ordered soyburger for lunch.

Cohen had suggested cocker spaniels and Levantine warmth. There had been human softness in his eyes and manner. Tall, lean, ramrod straight, Harper's florid features, topped by well-groomed white hair, suggested New England birches and Maine frost. His eyes were a wintry blue. Though his manners were gracious, his demeanor projected power and authority.

He apologized for the tape recorder beside his salad plate. "I don't approve of these infernal machines, but you'll be talking to others after lunch, and this one will spare you repetition. You're my guest. If you prefer the repetition to the recorder, I'll turn it off."

"No problem," Breedlove said. "Leave it on."

"I met Kyra this morning, a very impressive young she-thing if you consider a life span of a few thousand years as being young. She's charming, and she has a high opinion of you."

"It's a mutual trust, Admiral. I believe she's here for exactly the reason given, to get fuel for her space vehicle."

"We'd all like to believe that."

"Don't you, personally?"

"I can't permit myself the luxury of personal opinions."

By the snap in his voice the admiral dismissed such speculations. In the military hierarchy, Breedlove knew, admirals were royalty, and it was not good form to question royalty; but Breedlove was not in the military, and the admiral had said this was a social conversation.

"Then what is your official attitude?"

"The official attitude is still being formulated," Harper said. "No doubt it will hold that Kyra's a danger to the planet. That she's a charming female does nothing to abate the danger." Here the hint of a smile played over the admiral's face. "Heightens it, in fact. Except for very limited breeding purposes, men have been eliminated from her social order."

"She told you that?"

"With amused candor. And, I might add, she looked at me with a certain avidity when she spoke."

"It was her sense of humor," Breedlove said.

"I hope that's all it was."

"If not, then all the more reason to get her off the earth."

"Superficially, yes." The admiral nodded. "But with the capabilities of a space vehicle immune to detection and with fissionable material aboard, she's more a threat off the earth than on."

"Not with the small amount of uranium she needs."

"You're probably correct," the admiral agreed, "but we have to hypothecate the more dreadful possibilities. With only the added intelligence it took to invent a bow and arrow, Cro-Magnon man eliminated Neanderthal man. Imagine what Kyra could do with her technology."

"But the dreadful assumptions aren't logical in the light of her behavior."

"Logic's a process of human minds, Breedlove, and Kyra's superhuman. . . . I'm not saying we won't give her the uranium, but we have to analyze the comparative risks, and it will be a while before we make our recommendations to the Atomic Energy Commission."

"Time is her problem, Admiral."

"We're aware of this. Our recommendation is being formulated with all due haste. That's why you're here—to help us decide."

"It seems to me we have no choice but to grant her request."

"Negative," Harper snapped. "We have options. She could be retained on earth in protective custody indefinitely."

"That would be illegal," Breedlove said, and there was an edge to his voice. "Abe Cohen would have something to say about that."

"Then we have legal but more drastic options, fail safe and, in the end perhaps, more humane." He was cutting his salad with the side of his fork when he added, "A formal declaration of war on Kanab would solve the legal problems very nicely."

Harper's passive, uninflected tone of voice when he advanced the proposal was more chilling to Breedlove than regret or even vehemence could have made it. Suddenly and incongruously he recalled that Adolf Hitler had been a vegetarian also.

"That would only be giving legal sanction to murder."

"Not murder," the admiral demurred. " 'Slaughter' is the better term. It's done in stockyards every day for far less urgent reasons, as we vegetarians know. Remember, we're not dealing in human beings."

He paused to taste the soyburger patty, focusing on his palate with the detached concentration of a wine taster, and delivered his verdict, "Excellent!"

Not to be put off by the epicurean interruption, Breedlove continued his attack. "Admiral, the beasts we slaughter in stockyards are dumb brutes."

"Don't tell that to an animal trainer. The beasts have a different order of intelligence, as do the Kanabians. But extermination of the visitors, if not a likely alternative, must remain our option, and you can help us here. You're the only human being on earth who can pinpoint the space vehicle on a military map of the area."

"It will be a cold day in hell before I do that!"

For a moment the admiral's gaze seemed to soften as he looked up from the patty, and he said, "Welcome to the loneliness of command, Breedlove."

"With all respect for the gravity of the problem as you see it, Admiral, I suggest that it's a criminal perversion of the Good Samaritan doctrine to even consider destroying that gallant band."

Harper took no umbrage from Breedlove's remarks.

"Yours might be my own personal opinion, but above my personal wishes stands my duty to my country; above that my duty to mankind."

"It's precisely my duty to mankind that I'm thinking about," Breedlove said, and even as he spoke he realized he was not thinking exclusively about his duty to mankind. Much of his concern was for Kyra, and a little of his loyalty to her was in atonement. In a manner of speaking, he had betrayed her already by trying to palm off Poe's poem to her as his own—it was an intellectual and cultural betrayal—and many a cock would crow before he betrayed her twice. No argument of this gold-striped merchant of death would go undisputed.

"Remember, this is a social conversation, Breedlove," the

admiral said placatingly, "and my reasons for mentioning the military contingencies are to give you time to think over the problems. You're not under oath, and you won't be at 1400 when I'm asking you to address a group of concerned scientists in the ready room. I'm confident you're a patriotic citizen who'll cooperate when the need arises, and besides, I'm sure as a ranger you'll want to minimize any damage to the park area that high explosives might incur."

Arguing with Harper was futile, Breedlove decided. The man reflected nothing but official policy, and the policy was hard line.

"I'd like to talk to Abe Cohen about these matters, Admiral."

"Leave his number with my secretary, and she'll have Cohen proceed over without delay."

"I'll be honest, Admiral, I don't like the drift of this conversation. I have confidence in Kyra. I trust that her reason for being here is precisely as she claims. I believe she's been honest with me all the way."

Harper arched an eyebrow over his lifted cup of coffee.

"Has she? Did she mention to you that she's been in constant communication with her space vehicle since she left it, that she's probably getting directives from that source?"

The question felt like a fist slamming into Breedlove's stomach, and there was no way he could conceal his shock and consternation. "No, sir."

"X-rays revealed an implant in her skull above her left ear with filaments from the bug leading to her tympanic membrane. Our experts have determined that it's a minutely transistorized ultra-high-frequency radio receiver, but she refuses to answer any questions regarding the device."

"Kyra never mentioned it to me."

It was a painful admission for Breedlove to voice, and Harper nodded tactfully. "Come with me to my office, and I'll show you the evidence."

When they entered the admiral's suite on the eighth floor, a Wave lieutenant at a desk near the entrance to the admiral's private office stood up as the admiral approached. Breedlove could hear her heels click as she snapped to attention and extended three telephone slips for Harper to take.

"Belay those calls," Harper snapped. "Call this number and get Attorney Cohen here without delay. Then bring me the file on our visitor."

Click, the Wave reached for the telephone. Click-click, she was dialing. As the admiral held open his private door for Breedlove to enter, he commented proudly, "I run a taut ship. Everything's done by the numbers."

The admiral's private office featured a window opening onto a view of the harbor. Height-shortened freighters lay at the docks below. The Bremerton ferry had left its Seattle slip and was scrawling its wake across the sound. Waving a hand toward the view, the admiral said, "This is the closest I've been to the ocean in two years, and I get homesick for the wheel's kick and the wind's song."

"What was your last command at sea, Admiral?"

"A guided-missile cruiser . . . Be seated, Breedlove. By showing you Kyra's X-ray negatives, I'm paying out the slack on the security lines, but I'm doing it because I like the cut of your jib and I think you're tacking against the wind with our fair visitor, the Navy's code name for Kyra. Incidentally, our astronomers determined that her sun lay in the general direction of the Pleiades. A classified program, such as Project Fair Visitor, is compartmentalized. Each operative functions on a 'need to know' basis. Security clearances run from 1-A to 3-B, and your classification is 3-B—you know the fair visitor is on the planet, and that's all you need to know, but as an eyewitness to her arrival you are yourself classified information."

With a half-smile Harper raised his hand. "Ranger Thomas Breedlove, I hereby classify you a top-secret document. You're on file for all qualified personnel who wish to share your information."

"How will I know who's qualified?"

"Your contact will tell you, and you'll be meeting him shortly."

"Who is coordinating the project?" Breedlove asked, thinking more in terms of government bureaus than of individuals.

"Only the chief coordinator knows that, because he's the only person who needs to know."

Two sharp raps came on the door and the Wave lieutenant entered, bringing a red manila folder. As if on parade she paced across the room, came to a heel-clicking halt before Harper's desk, laid the folder before him, about-faced, and paraded out of the office. The bulk of the folder amazed Breedlove. Yesterday he had left Kyra without a driver's license, and today her dossier was already as thick as a small town's telephone book.

Harper drew an X-ray negative from the file and handed it to Breedlove. "Here's the item she won't talk about."

Looking at Kyra's skull, the seat of her wit and wisdom, revealed in such dull shades of gray struck him as almost obscene. Showing brightly on the film, slightly above and behind the ear orifice, were the implanted metal object and its trailing filaments.

"Proof of perfidy," Harper said, and his tone sounded gloating.

"Not at all," Breedlove snapped. "Maybe the device is classified 1-A under Kanabian security regulations, and we have no clearance."

Harper's face went cold, and he snapped the folder shut.

"Let's go to the ready room, Breedlove."

Down the hall from the admiral's office, the ready room was designed to resemble the pilots' briefing room on an aircraft carrier. Leather upholstered chairs were anchored to the deck. The walls were painted gray, and at one end of the room stood a lectern on a dais before a blackboard. Three men were already seated on the front row of chairs. Each man had brought a tape recorder, and there was a mike on the lectern with a recorder.

Harper introduced the three early arrivals to Breedlove. The gray-haired man with the unlit pipe in his mouth nearest the window was Dr. Hargrove, an anthropologist. Next to him, black-bearded, young, and muscular, sat Dr. Teach, sociologist. Finally came Dr. Upton, short, rotund, a blond fuzz of close-cropped hair on his ball-like head. Upton wore thick glasses that magnified his pale blue eyes until they appeared huge and protuberant. He was an entomologist. Breedlove wondered what an entomologist was doing here, but apparently the Navy was covering all bases with Project Fair Visitor.

"These gentlemen, and others who will be arriving, interrogated Kyra this morning, briefly since her time is limited, and they're seeking substantiation of their interviews and additional information from your account of your relationship with Kyra."

Three other scientists entered as Harper spoke, but he ignored them. "You commence the lecture promptly at 1400. Latecomers will be required to play back the log tape. Tomorrow morning's debriefing will commence at 0900. Please report five minutes early, Ranger Breedlove, to test the recording equipment."

The admiral had issued an order, and Breedlove nodded, feeling suddenly optimistic. He had been given a chance to enter a plea for kindness and generosity toward Kyra and her people before an influential group of civilians, and if he could convey to these scientists a fraction of his own regard for Kyra, they might thwart any military solution of the threat her presence hypothetically posed to earth.

"Gentlemen," the admiral addressed a group, now swollen to eight men, "the smoking lamp is out, I repeat, out!"

He nodded to Breedlove and stepped back to stand behind the speaker. Hargrove laid down his pipe. It was exactly 1400 by the chronometer on the bulkhead. Admiral Harper ran a taut ship.

Breedlove began at the beginning, opening his talk with the report of the nude campers in Jones Meadow and of his setting out to investigate. He knew he was speaking for history, and he wanted all the facts in order and as accurate as his memory could make them. As a storyteller, he realized he was being somewhat pedestrian, and his listeners did appear to be fidgety until he told of Kyra drifting out of the mists. Now they were leaning forward, as rapt as children attending a favorite fairy tale, and he knew what had generated the intensity of their interest: Kyra. Her presence lay over them all as invisible but as obvious as the scent of perfume.

With twelve men present, Breedlove figured he had his full audience of the men who had interviewed Kyra before noon today, but there was no interruption from his listeners until he mentioned Kyra's claim that her dress was made of hydrogen plasma. The remark brought a disdainful snort from someone in the back row, and the snort brought an extemporaneous rebuttal from a physicist from the University of Oregon who rose to his feet and began to rattle off the mathematic formulae for interlocking nuclei of stripped hydrogen atoms. Breedlove had lost the floor until the admiral stepped to the lectern, gaveled for silence, and barked, "Gentlemen, postpone all disputation until after the debriefing."

Breedlove continued, growing more and more aware of the blue eyes of Upton, who was asking no questions at all but listening so intently his ears seemed to be cupping forward. Those blue, floating orbs, magnified and detached by the thick lenses, grew hypnotic and disturbing. Breedlove talked on, trying to keep his gaze from drifting back to Upton, and he was losing his peculiar battle with the entomologist when the thirteenth man stalked into the room.

The man entered to no welcoming nods or hand waves from colleagues who recognized him. With a pacing stride he walked down the side aisle to the rear of the room and stood looking over the group with cold, expressionless eyes. He was tall, whipcord lean, dressed in black with a long deacon's coat and a vest. His face was long, square-jawed, with an Indian's high cheekbones and hooked nose. For a moment he stood, his gray eyes moving over the group from an immobile face, his legs spread slightly in a gunfighter's stance. The black suit, the long, impassive face, and, above all, the cold and deadly eyes brought a menace into the room.

The stranger was out of his habitat in Seattle, Breedlove sensed. He should have been stalking down the street of a west Texas town, his thumbs hooked into a gunbelt, advancing toward some ultimate shoot-out. Finally, jack-knifing his legs, he settled into a chair, pulled a cigar from a coat pocket, a kitchen match from his vest, and struck the match with his thumbnail. He lifted the light to his cigar.

From behind Breedlove Admiral Harper called, "The smoking lamp is out, Mr. Slade."

"Up yours, Harper," Slade answered, loud and clear. "The smoking lamp is lit."

"Gentlemen, the smoking lamp is lit," the admiral said. "Doctor Hargrove, would you open the window, please."

A pleasant murmur ran through the room as the scientists reached for cigarettes or tobacco pouches, and suddenly Breedlove, though a nonsmoker, found himself liking the mysterious and malevolent Mr. Slade. Even Dr. Upton became animated, asking a question about the interior of the space vehicle Breedlove had been describing.

"Did the hatch covers opening onto the spiral ramp differ in size?"

"They seemed to me to be out of line, or staggered," Breedlove answered carefully, "but the appearance might have been caused by their different sizes."

Upton was scribbling notes now, and the compelling eyes were lowered, but he raised them shortly to inquire, "Did you notice if the jams and jellies in the C rations were particularly favored by the Kanabians?"

"Yes, they were."

Moving on to a description of the twilight ceremony, he tried to convey the home longing and the sadness of exile he had felt in the singing of the group, but he refrained from mentioning the peculiar vision he had experienced during the session. There was the matter of his credibility, and these men were mostly interested in objective facts.

"This singing," Upton said, "was it performed with a vibrating sound from deep within their throats?"

"Yes. It was similar to a cat's purr, but louder and more rhythmical."

"Or like the drone of swarming bees!" It was not a question from Upton but an exclamation, voiced with a sense of discovery.

Breedlove felt it was an accurate metaphor and said so. At this point Dr. Teach asked Upton a question in a low voice, and Upton almost screeched, "Socially functional structural differentiation." Teach laughed with a scorn that brought a buzz of low-voice argumentation from Upton until Harper intervened to permit Breedlove to resume his account.

He related an edited version of his dinner conversation with Kyra in Seattle and gave a sanitized account of their good-night kiss.

"While you were kissing," the man called Slade asked, "did she make any sexual advances?"

From his question the black-garbed poseur would be a psychiatrist, Breedlove assumed.

"None whatsoever."

"Ranger, would you recognize a sexual advance if you saw one?"

It was an outright jibe not worth an answer, and Breedlove could not have given one over the laughter. He was beginning to lose confidence in these men, not in their expertise but in their wisdom and maturity. Yet for Kyra's sake he finished his talk with a plea.

"Gentlemen, Kyra and her small band of exiles come in peace and wish to leave in peace. To me it's obvious that the risks we incur from granting her request for a small amount of uranium is less than the risk we incur by denying her, yet I have already heard arguments to the contrary. This is a moment of grave crisis for Kyra Lavaslatta. For humanity it is the ultimate crisis. If we fail these pilgrims we will have destroyed ourselves so completely it will matter no longer whether she stays to eliminate a lesser breed or is herself exterminated, for by our acts we would have abandoned those qualities which distinguish us from brutes and forfeited forever the Biblical status which once put us only a little lower than the angels."

To his surprise, a smattering of applause greeted his words, and his opinion of the group rose slightly. It mounted another notch when Upton stood to address the group in a shrill but certain voice: "I don't know where the rest of you stand, but I can say, before I feed the data to the computer, let's give the female anything she wants and get her off the planet, fast."

Clutching his note pad and tape recorder to his chest, Upton scurried from the room.

Someone in a back row called, "Teach, did Upton give you any idea what he's up to?"

"He's invading my turf with some fuzzy idea about the social organization of the Kanabians," Teach answered. "He thinks the study of insects qualifies him as a sociologist."

"There's no social organization there," someone volunteered. "It's an anarchic matriarchy."

"Not anarchic," Hargrove demurred. "Highly stratified but not anarchic. Her state withered away, and her people have achieved the ultimate synthesis of law and order."

"Kannerer, how long before her profile emerges?"

"Maybe a week," a swarthy man answered. "Her Gestalt's a humdinger."

"That'll be drawing heavily on her limited time."

"Can't be helped. She's mid-Victorian about sex, so we have to approach those areas by indirection."

Breedlove was eager for them to pursue this subject further, but Harper tapped his shoulder. "Breedlove, I'd like for you to meet your contact, Richard Turpin, a gifted member of the intelligence community. . . . Gentlemen, please do not discuss this subject across departmental lines. The debriefing is over."

With the babble of voices continuing unabated behind him, Breedlove turned to shake hands with a blond, blue-eyed man of about thirty who had the high cheekbones and slab jaws of an Oklahoman. "Pleased to meet you, Mr. Turpin."

"Call me Dick, Tom. We'll be seeing lots of each other." The trace of a drawl supported Breedlove's estimate of Turpin's origins.

"Dick Turpin," Breedlove commented. "A famous name in the annals of crime."

"Glad you've heard of me. I'm not Mr. Hoover, but I've solved my share of crimes."

"Then you're with the FBI."

"Was," Turpin corrected. "I'm now with the Special Security Squad."

"Excuse me, Breedlove." Harper tapped his shoulder again. "Attorney Cohen's waiting to see you in the passageway, and he's getting impatient."

"Show him in."

"He's not cleared for the ready room. . . . Gentlemen, the debriefing is over, repeat, over."

"Excuse me, Dick," Breedlove said, "I've got to see my lawyer."

"You can't be excused, Tom. We'll see your lawyer."

Not wishing to see his relationship with his contact begin on a note of acrimony, Breedlove said, "Then come along, Dick."

They walked into a corridor filled with people, mostly women, who awaited the men inside. Glancing over the people, Breedlove could not see Cohen, but Turpin called, "Hi ya, Abe! Here's your client."

A tall, well-tailored man with an attaché case moved toward them with the straight-line precision of a Manhattanite. The hand he extended to Breedlove was cordial, but his voice was exasperated. "My office relayed your call to me. I had to cancel a hearing to get here, then Harper keeps me cooling my heels for ten minutes. Glad to meet you, Ranger Breedlove. I'm Abe Cohen."

Chapter Eight

❋

"You're not the Abe Cohen who gave me your card this morning."

"Nevertheless, I'm Abe Cohen."

"What did the other Abe Cohen look like?" Turpin asked.

"About sixty, with drooping jowls, receding gray hair, and large brown eyes."

"This is a matter for Ben Slade," Turpin said. "Excuse me."

He turned and went back into the ready room.

"What's going on here, Ranger?" Cohen asked.

"It's top secret. I don't think I'm supposed to talk to you without Turpin listening in."

"Nonsense. The lawyer-client relationship antedates security regulations by a few hundred years. From what Peterson tells me, you've some sort of jurisdictional problem with a woman you're trying to palm off as exotic fauna. It sounds less like a legal problem than a psychiatric problem."

109

"It's real. Kyra Lavaslatta, a girl from another planet, landed a spaceship in the Selkirk Area. I brought her to Seattle to get radioactive uranium enough to power her liftoff."

"The uranium would be handled by the AEC. If she's an emissary and her papers are in order, she's under the jurisdiction of the State Department. If her papers aren't in order, she's a matter for Immigration."

"We know that, Mr. Cohen, but we were hoping—"

"Hoping I'd find a loophole! It follows."

"That's not all. The military wants me to pinpoint the location of the spaceship, possibly to destroy it, and I don't want to tell them."

"If you're not under oath you don't have to tell them anything, and if all this is so hush-hush they won't subpoena you. A subpoena would take a court order. But if she has no fuel for a liftoff, why is the military concerned?"

"They're afraid she might lift off and return and attack the planet with eight other women and a boy."

"Preposterous, but typical," Cohen snapped. "There's a peculiar angle to this case: the penalty for illegal entry is expulsion from the country, which is precisely what the alien wishes, and the expelling country must provide the means of transportation, which in this case is uranium. Illegal aliens do have some rights, you know."

He was beginning to sound very similar to the first Abe Cohen, Breedlove thought, as he continued: "The main problem here is that the dispensation of enriched uranium is outside the national parameters under the terms of the Nonproliferation Treaty. It would have to meet the approval of the signatory powers, but that shouldn't take more than two or three months."

"That is the problem, Mr. Cohen. She's got to be off the planet by June twentieth, and don't ask me why. Couldn't we go straight to the President?"

"Certainly, but he has no authority to act unilaterally on the matter. The man to expedite any transfer is the Chairman of the Joint Atomic Energy Committee, but he could not act without the Atomic Energy Committee's recommendation."

"Where have all our leaders gone?"

"Gone to committees, every one," Cohen said.

"But what about the girl? Does she have to be held in custody?"

"There are no procedural grounds for her retention *in situ*, and of course we could spring her with a mere threat of habeas corpus. But she'd have to remain in protective custody, which is another kettle of fish."

"That's where we need your help."

"You have it. I'm on retainer with Interior. This is an interesting legal problem, and one without precedent. It might enable me to establish a rule, the Cohen Rule for Interstellar Immigrants. Now it's obvious we're going to have to put our minds to the establishment of space law."

Cohen stuck out his hand, this time in farewell. "You already have my card so keep in touch. I'll talk to the girl."

With a quick, pumping handshake, Cohen was gone—a very busy man indeed. Breedlove felt as confident in the lawyer as he had in the first Abe Cohen, although to this Abe Cohen Kyra was only an interesting legal problem. Every man Breedlove had talked to so far had looked at Kyra from a particular angle of vision. No one saw her steadily and saw her whole. No one seemed to grasp the simple morality of her plight: she was a pilgrim dying of thirst in a land overflowing with water.

But Cohen II had shown him the face of the enemy, the formless indecisiveness of interlocking committees. By the time Kyra's simple request had worked its way through the committees concerned, the nose of her spaceship would be under twenty feet of snow.

"Where's Cohen?"

The question came from Turpin. He had returned, bringing Slade, who stood listening, a hawklike intentness to his hooded gaze.

"He couldn't wait."

"Did you tell him about our visitor?"

"Cohen's clean." It was Slade who dismissed Turpin's question. "Leastways, *that* Cohen is. About this other Cohen, son"—he turned to Breedlove, who wondered if the term "son" was used fatherly or as a contraction—"did he have a face like a beagle hound and sidle along like a land crab?"

"That's the man."

Slade's eyes narrowed, and he spat one word, "Ajax!"

"You know him, then," Breedlove said.

"Israeli agent." Slade nodded. "Former member of the Irgun. Deadly little bastard. What'd you tell him?"

Breedlove looked at Turpin, and Turpin read his expression.

"You can talk to Ben Slade, Tom. He's the ranking member of the local intelligence community, sort of a godfather of The Family. He's in charge of overseas security and cleared for all information."

"I told him what I told them in there, but he didn't interrupt me. How did he get onto me so quickly?"

"You and Kelly left a mile-wide trail from Spokane, and Kelly has a permanent tail."

"We're not at war with Israel," Breedlove said. "Does it matter if an Israeli knows about Kyra?"

"The smaller countries are the more dangerous. They try harder," Slade said. "Was there anything in Kyra's room that she brought from her planet?"

"Nothing. Her clothes belong to my sister, and she took her bag with her."

"No documents?"

"Well, I showed Cohen . . . Ajax her photographs, a couple of before-and-after shots of her hair coloring."

"Let us see them," Slade said.

Breedlove took out his billfold, but the photographs were gone. He stood looking at his wallet in stupefied amazement until Slade spoke, in what sounded to Breedlove like a tone of apology: "Ajax was an honor graduate of the Buenos Aires school for pickpockets. Now, if we find Kyra's room ransacked, I'll know he searched it and found nothing. It's his *modus operandi.* When Ajax finds what he wants, he leaves the room in apple-pie order. There was nothing in your room?"

Beginning a shrug of negation, Breedlove suddenly remembered the radiation shield in his suitcase. If the pink ball was missing, that could mean trouble, but he was dubious about letting these men in on the secret. He trusted them less than he had trusted the first Abe Cohen.

"No documents of any kind," he finally said.

"We'll tail you back to the motel and check out your rooms," Slade said. "We'll be seeing a lot of each other, boy, because you need guidance. In matters of security you're the biggest American leak since the Johnstown flood."

Flanked by the security agents, Breedlove walked to the elevator. Since the interview with Chief Pilsudski, he realized, his sense of reality had been disintegrating. Dr. Condon had steadied it slightly, but Admiral Harper had canted it further. Slade and Turpin, two burlesque spooks from a spy melodrama, were the most bizarre distortions yet, and nothing they said in the elevator helped enhance their reality.

"What's your cover for this operation, Ben?"

"No cover, Dick. I'm out in the open: Ben Slade. I want them to know I'm here to give them a diversionary target. They'll know they'll have to get me before they take her."

"Why should anyone want to take her?" Breedlove asked.

"Her technological savvy," Slade said.

"She couldn't have a detailed knowledge of her technology."

"She doesn't need detailed knowledge. Her brains are an archive of concepts we never dreamed of. She's an adventure into the possible who can point out areas of exploration that won't lead us down blind alleys. Take her invisible spaceship. If Ghana had that secret, Ghana could conquer the world; and if she landed in Ghana, they'd get the secret. I know. I set up the operation in Ghana."

"Torture?"

"We prefer to call it 'forcibly elicited information,'" Slade said. "One of the reasons I'm here is to see that none of my tricks are used on the visitor."

"Tell that to Admiral Harper," Breedlove said.

"Forget him," Slade snapped. "I got the drift of what you were saying in the ready room, and my only worry about Harper is his vote on the committee. He's an over-the-hill theoretician."

Slade was bringing Breedlove's sense of reality slightly back into focus until, in the parking lot, Turpin blurred it more. "I'll drive ahead of you, Breedlove, and Slade will drive behind."

"Why the convoy?"

"If you're stopped by a traffic cop, we don't want you spilling any more secrets while he's writing your ticket."

When he pulled into the motel parking lot, the acuteness of perception that had let Breedlove spot something amiss in the aspen grove on Jones Meadow told him this scene, too, was slightly askew. Glancing around, he analyzed the flaw. No campers or big cars were parked in the lot. All were sedans, medium-sized, with conservative paint, not a racing stripe or Volkswagen among them.

At the desk he got the keys to both rooms and escorted

the two security agents first to Kyra's room. Inside, her dresses were tossed on the bed and floor, drawers had been pulled from the dresser and tossed aside. A flung sheet of motel stationery hung atop a drapery rod.

"He found nothing," Turpin said.

"Why did he have to do this?" Breedlove asked.

"It's his *modus operandi*," Slade said. "We call him Ajax because he hits the room like a white tornado. Clean it up, Turpin, while Tom and I check his room."

The offhand order was Breedlove's first indication that Slade was Turpin's superior in whatever chain of command the two operated within.

In Breedlove's room the same tornado had struck, but with a difference. His suitcase had been emptied, the contents dumped on the floor, and the pink sphere was missing. Without it, it would take a four-hundred-pound lead box to get the uranium to Kyra's ship, and if she did not have a replacement aboard she might be grounded.

"Nothing's missing," Slade said.

"Yes. A little pink exercise ball about the size of a grapefruit."

"Is that it on the bedspread?"

Breedlove looked to where Slade pointed. His frantic gaze had missed the ball, whose color merged with the bedspread's.

"That's it," he said casually, and began to repack his bag.

Slade tossed it in his hand. "There's no weight."

"It's hollow. Fill it with sand and it weighs about ten pounds."

"Clever gadget," Slade commented, unscrewing the sphere and looking inside. He screwed the hemispheres together and tossed the ball to Breedlove, who stowed it in his suitcase.

As Breedlove worked, Slade walked to the window and

stood looking out on the parking lot. Disgusted with the chaos in the room, Breedlove said, "Mr. Slade, this is unreal."

"At first it always seems so, but after you've been in this trade awhile, it's reality that becomes unreal. You know, son"—his voice grew gentle and ruminative—"you learn to like being out in the cold. If I had to come in and take a desk job, I'd die."

Suddenly he slapped a thigh with his hand and said, "By god, I'll do it. I'll use the purloined-letter technique with Kyra. They'll know she was here, so they'll figure she's gone. If the technique worked for your pink ball, it should work for her. But these outside rooms are too vulnerable. I'll move her upstairs into the bridal suite that faces the patio. It has two bedrooms."

"You think bringing her back here will fool Ajax?"

"Not Ajax. He won't be around any more."

"Mr. Slade, if you'll excuse me, I'd like to take a shower."

Slade glanced at his watch. "Sure, but telephone Kyra first. She'll be expecting your call. If you're eating in the motel dining room, rap on 110 as you come by. I'll join you."

"You and your people have taken over this motel. Right?"

"Since check-out time, two this afternoon," Slade admitted. "We'll all be staying here, and that includes you. You'll be moving into the bridal suite with Kyra, but you'll sleep alone."

"That's generous of you, Mr. Slade."

"Don't thank me. Thank your raising. You're the last Victorian. We can trust you, and we'll need an inside bodyguard for Kyra. There'll be a man coming after her who'll make Ajax look like an amateur."

Alone in the room Breedlove felt enheartened by the speed with which the government had moved to protect Kyra. If such dispatch was shown all along the line, there was a chance she would get the uranium in time. Turning to the telephone, he decided not to disturb her with the news about Ajax.

When her number rang, the telephone was answered by a male voice. "Major Laudermilk, here."

"My name's Breedlove. I'd like to speak to our visitor."

"I'm permitted to put your call through, sir, but under the provisions of the Right to Privacy Law I must warn you that this line is being monitored."

After a second ringing Kyra's voice came on the line, "Kyra, here."

Apparently she had learned her telephone etiquette from the mysterious major, he thought, and said, "Breedlove."

"Breedlove! How nice to hear your voice, and how lovely it's going to be to talk in basic English again. All day they've been grilling me, giving me the third degree. I don't mind the engineers and mathematicians, but the psychologists are after me all the time about my sex life. Do they think I was running a cathouse in a spaceship?"

She had not learned "cathouse" from him, he observed to himself, and said, "Of course not, Kyra. I talked to some of the experts who interviewed you, and they have a high opinion of your morals and honesty."

He realized his remark about honesty was a subconscious reproof of Kyra. Anxiety feelings were crystallizing around his knowledge of the implant in her skull. But she rambled breathlessly on: "All I've done all day is talk, talk, talk, with only a few minutes off to rest my jaws. You know, I'm surrounded by a palace guard with my lord high chamberlain screening my telephone calls. But I got your name put on the preferred list— Oh, I must tell you, they have this thing called a post exchange, but they wouldn't let me go there to shop. They brought over a slew of dresses for me to select from, and I can tell you there were no

Polinski Creations in the lot. I managed to select some outfits that Gravy thinks are very fetching. You'll be having dinner with me tomorrow in the queen's suite—"

"The queen's suite?"

"That's Gravy's new name for the VIP quarters. . . . I've got this beautiful little number I'll wear for you at dinner. My rooms are very nice, but they're still a brig. Breedlove, when are you going to get me out of this chickenshit outfit?"

"Before you learn to swear like a sailor, I hope. . . . But what's this about me having dinner with you?"

"Oh, that! I must tell you. You said for me to push while you pulled. Well, I'm pushing. I have this little doohickey behind my ear, and it's got them all worried. I told Doctor Condon I wouldn't tell anybody but you what it is, and I wouldn't tell you except over the dinner table. That shaped them up! I've got all kinds of little secrets in reserve, and if I'm not out of here pretty soon I'm going to quit talking at all unless they let you spend the night with me, and *that'll* give those nosy psychologists something to talk about. By the way, well, not 'by the way.' I don't want to sound too casual. I've written you a little poem in answer to the one you wrote for me. Would you like to hear it, with expression?"

"Hear it! I'd like to write it down. Damn the monitor and full speed ahead."

In a clear, exquisitely expressive voice, she announced, "The name of my poem is 'To Breedlove,' and here it goes:

> *Breedlove, thy beauty is to me*
> *Like those Kanabian barks of yore,*
> *That gently, o'er the perfumed sea,*
> *The weary, way-worn Kyra bore*
> *From her own native shore.*"

"Enough," he cried. "So you've discovered Poe?"

"Is that a famous poem?" Her voice was suspicious.

"It's Poe's 'To Helen.' "

"That Gravy! I should have known. He's such a joker. I told him about my poem from you, and he wrote this one for me to give to you. He said you'd love it."

"Who is 'Gravy'?"

"Major Graves Laudermilk, the Army officer in charge of my security detail. . . . Now, what would you like for dinner tomorrow night, a nice, rare, juicy filet mignon?"

Despite his elation over their dinner date, when he hung up, Breedlove was concerned about the Army officer in Kyra's entourage who read poetry and had recognized the true author of Breedlove's poem. Apparently Laudermilk was discreet, and for that Breedlove was grateful, but what was an Army major doing at a Navy establishment?

Turpin had joined Slade in room 110, and the three went together to the dining room. The diners in the room were all young men, none wore long hair or beards, and all looked physically fit.

"You ought to have more women and older men in your group," Breedlove commented to Slade. "Your security slip is showing."

"You're learning, boy. Beginning to think like us."

"I might take that as a compliment if I knew who you were."

"This is my outfit, the Special Security Squad, here to protect Kyra. All the men you see in here, even the dining-room help, are hand-picked specialists drawn from every branch of the services."

"Something's becoming clear. I wondered why an Army officer had the security detail on a Navy base."

"That's Laudermilk," Slade said. "A good man."

Turpin's reaction to Slade's remark was quick and

sounded alarmed. "You've got the Champ guarding the girl?"

"Yep."

"Who's guarding the Champ?"

"By special directive from the Army," Slade said, "the visitor had been declared 'off-limits' to Major Laudermilk."

"The Army must be very trusting," Turpin said.

Turpin's dubiety tantalized Breedlove, but he was afraid to ask for clarification lest the question make his personal concern too obvious. He would bide his time, he decided, before attempting to learn more about Major Laudermilk.

They gave their order to a waitress who came over the moment they were seated at their table. The dining room had never provided such service before. Their drinks were served with a flourish, and, later, their dinner was brought promptly after Slade nodded to the waitress.

Dinner was preceded by an unusual ceremony. Turpin asked their indulgence while he said grace over the meal. For Breedlove, asking the blessing was not an unusual occurrence at home, but this was the first time he had ever done it in a public restaurant. Slade added an "Amen" to Turpin's short but gracious prayer.

Breedlove was taken by a curiosity so strong it tempted him to risk a personal question of Turpin. "How do you justify your possibly ungentle profession by your certainly gentle religion?"

"It's a misconception to think of Jesus as a doormat. He was the Christ Militant and leader of the Church Triumphant, bringing to his chosen ones 'not peace but the sword'."

Breedlove dropped the subject quickly. Strange lights were beginning to glow in Turpin's eyes.

Slade lead the table talk thereafter. He was a man with a

strange ambition: he wanted the government to establish a paramilitary, informal task force for carrying out undeclared wars, and he wanted to be its leader.

"How would you use it?" Breedlove asked.

"To cut red tape. The nation's choking on red tape. People are supposed to be disgusted with the government because it's grown too unwieldy for their needs, but the government is too unwieldy for the government's needs. If a President wants to declare war he has to get the consent of Congress, and the congressmen have to sound out their constituents, and by the time all that goes down, the tactical strike opportunity is long gone. With my group, if the President doesn't like an election in, say, Ecuador, he can call me and say, 'Ben, go take care of it for me.' In ten years I could have the whole Third World solidly democratic."

Turpin contributed little to the table talk. Either he had little to contribute or he was cowed by Slade's rank or reputation in the intelligence community, either of which, Breedlove deduced, was formidable. There were many covert glances thrown at Slade's table, and the waitresses hovered attentively near. But with all the attention Slade was perceptive of others. Once he remarked, "Something's bugging you, Breedlove."

Major Laudermilk was bugging Breedlove, a fact he did not choose to admit, but he had an alternate bug at hand.

"Harper wants me to give him the coordinates of Kyra's spaceship on a military map, apparently with the intention of zeroing in artillery at some later date. I don't want to rat on Kyra and her people."

"No problem. Lie to him. Give him the wrong coordinates. You can't be prosecuted for not being able to read a military map." Suddenly his eyes narrowed. He was thinking. "Tell Kyra about Harper's request, at your dinner tomorrow night, and let me know what she says."

"I don't want to give her a bad impression of human beings."

"She'll find out about us sooner or later. Her hearing before the AEC is coming up next week, and everybody's cards will be on the table."

He was surprised that Slade knew of his dinner with Kyra, but he was more pleasantly surprised to learn about the hearings.

"You think it will be that soon?"

"It will be sooner if I can get the 'aye' votes lined up faster."

The finality of Slade's answer brought a silence to the table. Turpin was reaching for the check when Breedlove asked casually, "Why do they call Major Laudermilk 'the Champ'?"

"That is some story," Turpin said. "Tell him about Laudermilk, Ben."

Turpin sounded like a child asking for his favorite bedtime story, and Slade was accommodating. "Why do they call Major Laudermilk 'the Champ'?" he repeated slowly.

It was not a real question the way Slade asked it; it was a prologue. He threw his shoulders slightly forward in a pose handed down from the generations when storytellers hunched forward over western campfires, and the simple gesture threw an expectant hush over the table. Despite himself, Breedlove found himself leaning forward to listen.

"Major Graves Paige Laudermilk—the Paige is always spelled with an *i*—is the most unforgettable character I have ever known," Slade began, "but this is one character who'll never make the pages of the *Reader's Digest*."

Chapter Nine

———————— ✳ ————————

"If this nation possessed a Samurai class, the Laudermilks would be it. The first Laudermilk to be killed in the service of his country was Corporal Jebediah Ezekiel Laudermilk of the colonial militia, slain at Quebec during the French and Indian Wars. Of eight Americans killed in the defense of Ticonderoga, one was Captain Hannibal Laudermilk. Mrs. Letitia Laudermilk, of Baltimore, inspired the famous Civil War song, 'She Had Two Sons.' One of those sons was killed while with Pickett at Gettysburg; he wore a suit of gray. The other died at Allatoona Pass; he wore a suit of blue. Apropos of music, 'Taps' is the family's theme song and the muffled drum its traditional instrument. Our Champ's grandfather died at Belleau Wood and his father on the banks of the Oder in World War II. No male Laudermilk lives to be over thirty-five."

Slade paused for a moment of reverence, not only from the listeners at the table but from the gathered waitresses, and driven by anxiety, Breedlove asked, "Were they champions at dying young?"

With the éclat of a born storyteller, Slade waved the interruption aside and continued: "The Laudermilk clan would have never accepted the slogan, 'Make love, not war.' Laudermilks make love *and* war. Our Champ's father, Major Robert E. Lee Laudermilk, earned for himself, before that final, fatal skirmish, the title, The Uncrowned Prince of the European Theater of Operations. When he was laid to rest at the American cemetery outside of Liège, Belgium, women mourners gathered from all over Europe, and the flowers they laid on his grave reached the dimensions of a haystack after a wet growing and dry harvest season. Yet his son, Major Graves Paige Laudermilk, claims that his father was only a Lothario, junior grade."

Slade paused again to let the enormity of the son's charge sink into listeners augmented now by the diners at adjoining tables, and Breedlove lacked the brashness to interrupt. These pauses were for dramatic effect.

"They're a fecund tribe, the Laudermilks; have to be to keep the line alive. When the Champ was a field officer in Vietnam, his company led the Army with a kill ratio of twenty-to-one, but the Champ had to be ordered home. For every Vietcong he killed in the bush, he sired two in the villages. He was a threat to the Army's genocide policy."

Another brief pause, and the question was wrenched from Breedlove's lips, "Is he a champion stud?"

Again ignoring the question, the raconteur set his own pace: "Laudermilk is one of the Army's top linguists. It is said he can learn a language overnight, which he usually does. He is fluent in the vernacular of twenty-seven languages. Beginning with short words and pungent phrases, he works his way up, following, as he says, the evolutionary patterns of a language from its root sources. His definition of 'root' may be open to question, but no one can argue his choice of teachers."

Then he would be a dilettante of languages, not a champion linguist, Breedlove realized, and the realization again brought a question to his lips, "But why is he called the Champ?"

This time, Slade yielded.

"Laudermilk is the statistical world champion of the international boudoir. He has had recorded affairs with women of 360 ethnic groups and 820 nationalities. Each liaison is attested by a Certificate of Consummation signed and dated by his participating partner. He seeks to leave behind him a record that can never be broken, but, to date, there's something missing from Laudermilk's rolls. He's never known an Uzbekistanian maiden. The Uzbeks, a mixture of Tartar and Mongol, form a distinct ethnic group. Of course, the Champ has had many Tartars and more Mongols than Genghis Khan, but never an Uzbek. Personally, I think he'll make it. The word's out that after this assignment he's being sent to Tashkent, the capital of the Uzbek Republic. There, after having tasted the nectar of every earthly flower, our major will die with honor, his work on earth done."

Now Slade paused on a note of sadness so certain and profound Breedlove asked, "Does Laudermilk suffer a terminal disease?"

"No." Slade shook his head. "Only one Laudermilk ever died a natural death. In 1816 Lieutenant Ethan Allen Laudermilk succumbed to premature satyriasis, a young soldier who faded away. Laudermilks die violently in love or war. No, it's that though born soldiers, all of them, with the capacity for high rank, fate has willed that no Laudermilk shall ever go higher than major. Our Champ is driven by his mortality. He knows he has another appointment in Tashkent he must keep, for he's due for promotion to lieutenant colonel in August. After Tashkent, the world may someday see his equal but never his superior; Major Graves Paige Laudermilk will have known all the women of the world."

On a reverent hush the tale ended, and the listeners sat or stood in silence, wrapping the mantle of a legend around their thoughts. An ominous realization clouded Breedlove's mind: Laudermilk did not need the women of the world to set an untouchable record. He could do it with the woman who affectionately called him "Gravy." For the man who had possessed the pearls of earth, the maiden from another planet would crown his family jewels.

Seeking a flaw in Slade's tale to help him brand it as an exaggeration, Breedlove said, "If all the Laudermilks die so young, how is the dynasty maintained?"

"Early marriages, most of them shotgun ceremonies." Slade slapped his hands together and said, "All right, boys, let's repair to the bar and bend an elbow."

After two hours in the cocktail lounge devoted to reminiscing, mostly by Slade, Breedlove went to his room to be alone and to sort out his impressions of the two men whose lives were suddenly intertwined with his own and Kyra's. Turpin was ten years younger than Slade, less forcible, and seemingly the product of a more authoritarian discipline; he was a Christian soldier with a gung-ho attitude toward the FBI. Slade's expressed attitude toward the FBI and CIA was that which a city dog holds for a fireplug. Breedlove had guessed right about his birthplace: he was a Texan, "Born, jerked up, and jacked off in Waco."

At Texas A & M he had been dismissed from the ROTC because of drunkenness. After graduation he became a ranch hand, ironworker, oil-field roughneck, deck hand on a shrimp boat, and eventually joined the Texas Rangers, from where he went to the CIA. Now he was on permanently detached duty for "that pussy outfit." The cold stare and overwhelming sense of menace he turned off and on at will were dramatic projections he had developed as a bill collector in Dallas. Yet this actor-spy, who preferred to be out in the cold without an overcoat, had written four western romances under the name of Belle Star Dalton. Slade was easily the most incredible character Breedlove had met until he met Slade's most unforgettable character, Major Graves Paige Laudermilk.

After a night's sleep and a full day's debriefing by another group of experts at the Federal Building, Breedlove drove to the Navy base through the gathering twilight, feeling more in touch with reality. He had not talked to Turpin and Slade all day, and away from the influence of the two-man incredibility gap, he felt he should let nothing Slade had said influence his opinion of a person, namely Major Laudermilk.

Initially Breedlove complimented himself on his withheld judgment. When he entered the Navy clinic, he spotted Laudermilk behind the desk formerly occupied by the receptionist, but there was a nameplate on the desk now, with Laudermilk's name and rank, and an Army sergeant manned a field gray telephone switchboard behind him. The man behind the nameplate appeared to be no more libidinous than anyone else his age, about thirty-five. He was clean-cut with wavy blond hair, blue eyes, and teeth that flashed when he smiled. He wore a tailored uniform with two rows of campaign ribbons above his left breast.

When Breedlove introduced himself, the major rose to shake hands, speaking easily: "Breedlove, that's an interesting family name. It has quite a history. Ben Slade tells me you're part of our team."

"I'm still not sure why," Breedlove admitted, "or what position I play."

"I can guess why. Whoever's directing the operation wanted to balance the security types around Kyra with a wholesome American to make it easier to gain her alliance for the U.S.A. I know what position you play. Slade's got external security, Turpin has domestic, and I have military. You'll be our D'Artagnan, her personal bodyguard, and her cover story. Sign the log, and I'll take you to our visitor."

Breedlove signed in. Without the ribbons and brass buttons, he decided, Laudermilk would have been a run-of-the-mill Lothario. As they walked down the hall together, Breedlove, feeling more congenial toward a man who had already done him a favor, asked, "What's the history of the Breedlove name?"

"Many English names reflect an occupation or a residence," Laudermilk said. "Churchill originally designated a family that lived on a hill by a church. Early Smiths were ironmongers, early Wainwrights were wagon makers. 'Breedlove' comes from feudal England. When the lord of the manor found himself unable to sire a son, a calamity in the days of primogeniture, he went among his vassals and chose a youth for whom the lady of the manor was not likely to form any lasting affection. He would be installed in the manor, temporarily, as a 'breed lord' and assigned a room near the lady's bedchamber. He would be fed a diet of oysters and granted the lady's favors under the strict supervision of her lord. Since the lady of the manor referred to her husband as 'M'lord love,' the breeder was referred to as 'M'breed love.' Once the serf fulfilled his function and was lucky enough to be allowed to return to the village instead of being taken to the chopping block, the villagers referred to him, perhaps contemptuously, more likely enviously, as 'M'breed love.' So, in a sense, the name was pejorative."

The story was all poppycock, Breedlove recognized, but

it did reveal Laudermilk's interest in the language. "I wondered why I liked oysters," he said, "but I'm sorry the name's pejorative."

· "Take heart. You could have been named Ramsbotham."

Two nurses were approaching down the long corridor. Both were dressed in white with the pipings of Health, Education and Welfare on their collars. The acoustics were such Breedlove heard one of them say excitedly, "Even the Islets of Langerhan ovulate, Sally said. Imagine that, fertile insulin."

Breedlove would have liked to listen to the rest of their conversation, but the nurses saw the two men and the conversation ended abruptly. They passed in silence, but Breedlove's sidelong glance detected the sidelong glances they threw at Laudermilk.

"You impressed the young ladies, Major."

"Not me. Our uniforms," Laudermilk said, magnanimously including the green-clad Breedlove. "We could peel off these uniforms, hang them in a hotel lobby, and sit there unnoticed in the buff while the uniforms made out with passing ladies."

They turned into another hall. At the far end stood a sentry guarding a door. Laudermilk was modest, Breedlove decided, he was obviously well read, and he was discreet.

"I want to thank you, Major, for not telling Kyra who wrote my poem to her."

"I'd never rat on another man, Breedlove. Besides, I've used the trick myself. But let me give you a tip, Byron's more potent than Poe. If you really want to make out, quote Byron. Ah, now there was a man who knew how to use a clubfoot."

The last remark cried for elucidation, but they were at Kyra's door. The sentry snapped to attention.

"As you were, soldier," the major said, and rapped three

times on the door. Then he opened it and stood on the threshold. Over his shoulder Breedlove saw Kyra, dressed in green and seated on a divan, look up from a book she was reading.

"*Kaleema Kyra*," Laudermilk said, his voice a throaty purr, "*marina abel marlon etrovna Breedlove. Navy elosa perrain commemora marlon, atelya kaleema.*"

The major's fluent use of Kanabian brought a sinking to the heart of the man behind him. If Laudermilk had learned Kyra's language overnight, he no longer needed Tashkent to become the romantic champion of the world. He was already sex king of the universe.

The major stepped aside, motioned Breedlove in, and closed the door, shutting Breedlove and Kyra alone in the room. Despair wafted from Breedlove's mind. Floating toward him, trailing a diaphanous gown, the faultless female spread her arms to greet him. Embracing her, he lifted her from the floor, swinging her around him and chanting, " 'There be none of Beauty's daughters with a magic like thee.' "

After the Byronic greeting and his fulsome compliments on her dress, Kyra gave him a tour of her quarters. The Navy had extended her full honors in what she called her "brig." Her living room featured a teak coffee table piled high with books, devoted mainly to science and history, he noticed. Her "wardroom" held a table set for two with candles, and her bedroom held a queen-sized bed. She had developed a penchant for Navy expressions as well as Navy nomenclature. During the tour he mentioned that Kanab had been located in the direction of the Pleiades by earth's astronomers.

"That's a crock! I located it for them on a star chart."

Not sure she knew what a crock was, he skirted her comment by saying, "Anyway, it's a romantic area to be from. The Pleiades are supposed to be seven sisters. According to myth, one of them, Merope, was an earth goddess who fell in love with a mortal. For her sin she was exiled among the stars and is there still, weeping for her mortal lover."

"Breedlove, that's astronomical data a girl can appreciate."

"I'd like to be the mortal lover Merope returned to, but after hearing your chamberlain call you a gorgeous *kaleema*, I fear the goddess might have found another love."

"Breedlove, you sound like your mother."

She led him back to the living room, seated him on the sofa, and stood above him, hand on hips, looking down at him with fondness touched by concern. " 'Why so pale and wan, fond lover?' "

She had quoted a Cavalier poet, another indication of Laudermilk's influence.

"I've spent a long day extolling your wit and wisdom to men more interested in your femur and the articulation of your knee joint."

"Gravy says they're shaping me up to ship me out."

The reference to Laudermilk irritated him, and he said, "Gravy's another one more interested in your parts than in your whole."

"I got the opposite impression." She laughed and sat beside him. "Quit being moony. If I took a mortal lover, everyone in the hospital would know it right away."

"What did he mean when he called you *kaleema?*"

"Oh, that! I've been teaching him protocol. He wants to learn the Kanabian language of state."

"Then, *kaleema* must mean 'your highness.' "

"Not exactly," Kyra said thoughtfully. "In your language, *kaleema* would mean 'the lady of the manor.' "

"Laudermilk set me up to ask you that question," he said, groaning in self-disgust. Then he told her of Laudermilk's contrived explanation of the history of his name.

"Gravy has a terrific sense of humor." She smiled. "When he announced you from the doorway, he said that the Navy had finally let my privy councilor out of the privy."

"You couldn't help but be charmed by such a witty man."

"Personally Gravy's a darling, but on Kanab we consider warriors as the vestigial remnant of a society of brutes. They're lowest in a caste society."

"They still have power on earth, and I've got to talk to you about them. There's an expression 'Business before pleasure,' and I want to get this subject out of the way before we speak of lighter matters. I'll begin by asking if you've met a man called Slade."

"Ben? Of course. He's a warrior who dislikes uniforms. If they don't get me out of committee fast enough, he wants to organize a little army to liberate me. He says I'll be his Joan of Arc."

"That's Ben, all right. He's a fantasist, but he has clout in the real world. He wanted me to tell you that Admiral Harper's trying to get me to pinpoint the location of your spaceship. Harper's up to no good, but if I refuse to tell him under oath, he might be able to put me in jail."

"Then, you tell him exactly what he wants to know."

"But Harper's a military man, and the military men on this planet could blast your ship to smithereens."

She shook her head in disagreement and said slowly, "Ben asked you to tell me this because Ben walks one way and looks another. He himself hinted to me of this danger, and I laughed at his fears. He thinks I will be truthful with you. He does not believe I speak only the truth or remain silent. So I will tell you, Breedlove, it is not your military caste I fear but the slowness of your committees. If I am held beyond my time, millennia-old urges of my nature will command me to stay. Earth cannot hold me hostage. If I cannot leave of my own free will, earth will become my hostage."

She took his hand, as if to reassure him, and said, "My ship can defend itself. True, it cannot rise without a propellant, but it converts the sunlight to its defense. It could destroy mankind. This is not a threat, and certainly it does not apply to you. Far from harming you, I would grant you an immortality of sorts. You would become the Lord Breedlove of my manor, but your grandchildren would see the last of the race of men."

Her words were gentle. They held both a threat and a promise, and he was more interested in the promise.

"Could you wave a wand and make me immortal?"

"No, you would wave the wand, and the immortality I give you could be given to you by any woman of your race. Now the lady of the manor has spoken. I hear my steward arriving. Let us lay aside the business of state and go to chow."

He arose at her imperial bidding, wondering and curious. From her remark he gathered that she was promising him genetic immortality if she was compelled to remain on earth, and by implication she was informing him that she could mate with a member of a different species. Somehow, despite the apocalyptic vision he had seen in the meadow, the idea was potentially attractive. To be the father of a new race.

Particularly with Kyra as the race mother. Her effervescence charmed him. Her lightness and wit delighted him. But beneath her shimmering, girlish vivacity beckoned a woman, more heavy-bodied and fecund, who exerted a compelling allure. That woman anchored Kyra's lightness and gave her grace notes deeper tones.

In the wardroom the steward had lighted the candles and

turned off the overhead. The light played over the snowy napery, the silverware, the translucent china.

"Look, Breedlove. This beats sucking paste from a tube."

The woman he had sensed momentarily was gone, and the laughing girl had returned. It was better this way. He was more at ease with the girl, and he could trip lightly into areas where a more deliberate pace might have alarmed her.

Helping her to be seated, he said, "I'd like to seat you this way for the next ten thousand years, but, if not, I'd be perfectly willing to fly away with you and suck on a tube of paste."

"Breedlove, Myra would have you in the tube. But we promised to speak only pleasantries at dinner, and I have the ideal subject for light comedy: earth scientists I have met."

As the mess attendant moved silently in the background, she gave imitations of her interrogators so accurate he recognized many of them from his debriefing sessions. Her mimicry fascinated him, but she ventured no information on the subjects they had questioned her about. It was as if she had been coached on his "need to know" and was avoiding areas off-limits to his knowledge.

"Meeting all those experts must be interesting."

"It's tedious," she admitted. "Here I am, surrounded by old men and parking lots. Out there is water, trees, mountains, a great blue sky. I'd rather run naked through the woods or go swimming in the sound."

"Do you swim?"

"Superbly. I'm so buoyant."

"Father and I own a cabin on a lake near Mount Rainier. Pine trees scent the air, and a mountain stream tumbles by within sound of the cabin."

"Could we go there after they let me out?"

"Certainly. We could live there if you're stranded on earth. You'd be happy in the green summers with birds and chipmunks for company. You could let your hair grow green again, run naked through the forest, and go swimming in the lake."

She was leaning forward, intent on his words. "How would you earn your living?"

"I'd open a general store in the village. Supporting you would be easy. With you around, I wouldn't need a television set, even, for entertainment. I'd grow for you an acre of the sweetest, most succulent alfalfa you ever tasted and store enough in the barn for winter. I'd set up a beehive to provide you with fresh honey, and you could lie on the beach of the lake, storing up sunlight while I tended store."

As his mind grew engrossed with the vision, her eyes glowed with the shared fantasy.

"When I came home at night, we'd always dine by candlelight and we could swap stories about what happened to us during the day. Your wit would make the most trivial happening an event."

"Breedlove," she asked anxiously, "would you be happy with a woman who knows more than you do?"

"I'd sip your knowledge as a bee sips nectar. And as men go, I'm not without some intelligence. I could write you sonnets. You'd be happy with me. Each morning would be a fresh awakening to a fresh earth, and each twilight would be a separate peace."

"That I know I'd love!"

"I can even keep house. All the rangers' wives at Selkirk agree I keep the neatest cabin. And we'd have children, a green-haired girl for me and a blue-eyed boy for you."

"Could we have an apple tree, Breedlove?"

"Several. Winesaps and Golden Delicious, for blossoms in the spring and fruit in the fall. In winter I'd teach you to ski on the slopes and skate on the pond. We'd snowshoe through the forest. There's a grandeur to a snowbound forest, and the sunlight's never wasted when it shines on snow. And we'd teach our children to skate on the pond."

"I can hear our children laughing, Breedlove."

It was then he asked her, "Could we have children?"

"Dozens, in all varieties," she answered blithely. "Why stop at two?"

"Any number and style would be welcome. I could add rooms to the cabin."

"Oh, being married to you would be fun. You give me the feeling of forests already, and to live with you among the trees would be heavenly. When you came home at night the cabin would be spotless. Does our cabin have a fireplace?"

"A huge one."

"Terrific. In winter I'd have a fire blazing, and when my big, handsome husband came through the door, he would lift me and whirl . . ."

Her voice trailed into silence. The wardroom seemed to darken as the light went out of her eyes. She no longer looked at him but through him with a weird fixity of gaze, and a mood as palpable as another presence entered the room with them. Frozen by a horror beyond terror, she stared through him into an abyss. He could feel the void arcing beyond the end of worlds and filled with a loneliness and a sadness as poignant as the weeping of lost children.

Speaking softly, as a man awakening a sleepwalker, he asked, "Kyra, what's wrong?" He was trying to draw her back from the precipice with his voice, and he saw her eyes struggle to regain focus.

She shuddered, and now she was looking at him again. Her voice trembled slightly, and she said, "It's gone."

"What was it?"

"I suffered a . . . slight dislocation. In my tongue it's called a *frilling*. Sitting here, imagining that we loved in the manner of earth, I felt the premonitory mating pangs of my own species."

"But there was fear in your eyes."

"Not fear alone. With us, love is the agony of the incomplete, a yearning for fulfillment, and it begins in a desolation of the spirit. Nature prepares my body to accept such longings when my time comes, and I am readied for my season by the swelling sun. The urge itself commences when the declining sun reminds us that all who live must die, that fresh generations are waiting to be born, and that the old must prepare for the new. Tonight my biological clock ticked prematurely." She forced a wan smile. "You tilted the planet for me, Breedlove, and you did it while we were on its dark side."

"Your agony I could feel—"

"You are so sensitive to my feelings, Breedlove, I've noticed before, and I think I've been given a clue to our understanding. . . ."

For once he would not let her divert him from a subject. Still shaken and frightened for her, he grew blunt. "You're right, I am sensitive to your feelings, and you were more than frightened, you were terrified. Why were you so afraid?"

Her poise crumbled. Her body slumped. For a moment she was on the verge of tears, a frightened child asking not for his aid but for comfort, wanting to lean on his strength, and in her vulnerability she was overwhelmingly appealing. The little girl in her compelled his devotion more profoundly than the siren he had sensed in her earlier.

"I was afraid for you. Breedlove, no matter how much you romanticize me, I'm no damned wand-waving goddess. There's lots I don't know about this planet and more I don't know about me. For one thing, earth's axial tilt is greater than that my body evolved from, and what will all the extra sunlight do to me? The life force is as much a mystery to me as to you. When I felt the *frilling* begin, I was petrified by the fear that it might be my true summons, and before it, my darling, we would have been as helpless as if before a hurricane. I would have been rapacious, and you couldn't have resisted me."

Because she was frightened and concerned for him, she was open to him as never before, he realized. And she had revealed more about her biological urges and about her feelings toward him. She had called him "darling" with a tenderness that signified the term was not chosen because of her faulty knowledge of English. He wanted to prolong the moment and its openness. He wanted to explore her definition of love as "the agony of the incomplete" and to learn more about her mating cycle. Above all, he wanted to put his arms around her and assure her he had no fear of her amorous rapacity.

Yet at the moment it was Breedlove who evaded intimacies with decorum and sought conversational diversions. Kyra's emotional storm had battered her defenses. Her wariness was weakened. In response to a show of his affection she might confide in him as an earth girl to her lover, and her quarters were surely wired, their words being recorded. He would not be an unwitting agent of electronic eavesdroppers or help earth's manipulators gain an advantage over her.

His suspicions gave him a logical diversion, and he said, "I couldn't resist you in a light breeze. You don't need a hurricane. And there's something else bugging me, or rather bugging Admiral Harper. What's the purpose of the implant in your skull?"

"Its main purpose was to get you invited here to dinner. It's an acoustic converter I haven't needed on earth. It permits me to communicate with any intelligent species which vocalizes at a higher frequency than that which you and I use."

"Harper thought it was something that kept you in communication with your spaceship."

"He would." She laughed, her composure regained. "He's a suspicious old bastard. Actually it has a limited use as a homing device in fog or darkness when I'm in the sound range of a howler on my ship. . . . Isn't this a delicious dessert?"

The steward had served them baklava, a Greek pastry steeped in honey.

"Somebody around here is very solicitous of your comfort, I see. They're learning your tastes."

"I think they've learned a lot from you," Kyra said, surprising him with her knowledge. "Ben was telling me that there was something in your psychological profile that made it easy for my security project director to get you free and unsupervised entry into my presence. He tells me you and I are going to share a bridal suite."

"The suite's got two bedrooms," Breedlove said, "so the setup is less intimate than Slade might lead you to believe. But what's this about my psychological profile? I haven't talked to any shrinks except those I've lectured to at the debriefings. How could Slade know anything about me I haven't told him?"

"Oh, you know Ben," she said. "He won't tell you but a little bit at a time. He claims you don't need to know, but what he's really doing is making your curiosity get up on its hind legs and beg for his tidbits. But he did finally tell me I'll be rejoining you after tomorrow's examinations. My hearing before the Atomic Energy commissioner is Tuesday."

"Why not Monday?" he asked.

"Monday is the Memorial Day holiday," she answered.

He had failed to remember the holiday because he was wondering about Slade's possession of his profile, where it had come from, who had evaluated it, and how it had provided him with a free entry into Kyra's boudoir.

Chapter Ten

Slade was waiting in Breedlove's room when the ranger returned, and Slade's debriefing procedure was to rub his hands together expectantly, grin, and say, "Okay, Breedlove, tell me all about it."

Breedlove hung his coat in the closet, straightened its drape on the hanger, removed his tie and hung it in the closet, unbuttoned his shirt, and said, "I know you've got top clearance, Slade, but this report is on my own 'need-to-know' basis which I call tit for tat. If you want the details of my wild evening with Kyra, you've first got to tell me what it was in my profile that earned me the right to share her living quarters?"

"Boy howdy, this is going to be fun. I know more about you, son, than your mother knows, which is a break for her. You'll remember you took a placement test for your ranger's job. It was comprehensive enough to draw up your profile from. Naturally when you showed up here, I ran a make on you, and the psychologist who wrote you up should have been jailed for purveying hard-core pornography. One interesting little kink of yours is that you have Oedipal fixations on trees. Seems your mother put your crib under one when you were a baby, and you thought the tree was your mammy. There's many a lumberjack who identifies his father with a tree and goes around axing his old man down, but you're the first man in the history of psychological testing with strong Oedipal longings toward trees. Boy, you're a knothole Casanova if there ever was one!"

Slade took such obvious relish in detailing a profile as unlikely as Laudermilk's history of the Breedlove name that Breedlove could not restrain a smile of sympathetic glee.

"When I spotted your little kink," Slade continued, "I wanted to check it against a bend in Kyra's chart. I fed the two profiles into a dating computer, and when the kinks connected with the transistors, the computer shook, rattled, and rolled. It's a perfect blend of compatibilities. Kyra has an Electra complex toward trees. To top it off, you both observe a code of sexual ethics that went out of style in 1889. For reasons you don't need to know, we have to protect our heroine from 'a fate worse than death,' and you've got just the right morality for the job. Also, her high regard for you might affect her political judgment of the United States, and, if it comes down to it, leave her feeling kindlier toward all the earth."

"Well, thanks for reposing special trust and confidence in my discriminating libido, Slade, but we may have a problem." He told of Kyra's remarks about the defensive capabilities of her spaceship, and Slade listened intently, dropping his burlesqued role of the uproarious Texan as quickly as he had donned it.

"She could still be bluffing," he mused aloud, "but I don't think so. Anyhow, it doesn't matter to you and me, since we want what she wants. But she's wrong if she thinks we're not aware of her threat to the planet. I am. Now, what's this thing behind her ear?"

"Oh, that. It's just a simple device that permits her to hear and interpret high-frequency sounds."

"You think that's simple?" Slade's question did not demand an answer. He was thinking. Then he whistled, low and thoughtfully, slapped his thigh in agreement with some inner argument, and stood up, saying with a note of exultation, "Boy, we don't have to worry about the Navy's vote any more. Our little lady's given us a chance to grab Harper by the whingding."

He turned from the room so excited and preoccupied with his plans he forgot to tell Breedlove good night.

On Friday morning, at the Federal Building, Breedlove lectured the scientists who had interrogated Kyra Thursday afternoon. After lunch he was walking back to the ready room when Harper stopped him in the passageway. "There'll be no afternoon session, Ranger Breedlove."

"What happened to my Friday-morning group?"

"That's a national security matter."

Vaguely curious about the cancellation, Breedlove drove back to the motel, and when he pulled into the parking lot he saw immediately that the lot was almost empty. The explanation came when he got to the desk and found a note from Slade.

> Breedlove, I'm gone. Your baggage has been transferred to the bridal suite. You sleep in the ready room and give Kyra the recovery room. See you Tuesday.
>
> B.S.

He had not noticed before how appropriate Slade's initials were, and he knew when he read the note that he would not see Slade Tuesday. Slade used cover stories as a conditioned reflex, and the only thing one could be sure of about a cover story was that it was not true. Also Slade's absence explained why there had been no afternoon lecture to Kyra's interviewers—there had been no Friday interviews. Kyra had left Seattle and her entire security force had gone with her, with one exception, Breedlove.

He went upstairs to inspect his new lodgings and found them rather unusual for a family motel. The suite held two bedrooms separated by a spacious living room containing in addition to the standard furnishings a small open-leaf table for intimate dining and a sparsely stocked bookshelf. The living room opened onto a balcony directly above the swimming pool. Flanking and overarching the balcony, the artificial coconut palms gave a tropical touch to the scene.

He easily determined from Slade's title, "the ready room," which of the two bedrooms was his. It had red carpets, orange walls, and purple drapes. Long, phallicized bedlamps on two-ball bases flanked the king-sized bed, and a bifurcated rump pillow of hymen pink lay atop the purple bedspread. A huge mirror was anchored to the ceiling above the bed. Kyra's bedroom was more tastefully decorated, and her bathroom was entered through a large dressing room.

As it developed, he would have almost six days to grow inured to the bedroom's ghastliness, and each day added an increment to his loneliness and anxiety in the semi-deserted building. Each day of Kyra's absence postponed her hearing, and he could sense the solstice rushing down on the northern hemisphere like an express train.

He augmented the collection of books on the shelf by shopping at used-book stores, balancing the Bible with *The*

Golden Bough, Uncle Tom's Cabin with *Gone with the Wind*. He felt somewhat sheepish for shopping at the literary equivalent of a Salvation Army counter for so elegant a girl as Kyra, but he had decided to buy her the Polinski Creation, and he had to save money somewhere.

Once on a book-buying expedition he splurged, getting her a brand-new Pelican edition of Shakespeare and a copy of Bulfinch's *Mythology*. On the flyleaf of the latter, he wrote, "Kyra, read about Merope on page 186. That is you. T.B."

Evenings he spent mostly in the bar, nursing a drink and talking woods lore with a bartender who was a summer outdoorsman and who seemed particularly entertained by Breedlove's tales of the Quinault Indians. On Wednesday he called Abe Cohen, who assured him the hearing would "probably be sometime this week."

"The week's half gone and they haven't brought her back. Aren't they dragging their feet?"

"Not as much as usual. If they held the hearing in mid-June, it'd be setting a track record."

On Thursday morning he was awakened by Kyra tweaking his toes beneath the covers and calling, " 'Up, lad; thews that lie and cumber sunlit pallets never thrive.' "

He jackknifed to a sitting position to see her seated cross-legged at the foot of his bed, wearing navy-blue slacks and a white sailor's tunic unbuttoned at the neck to reveal a golden tan. She had pulled the drapes, and sunlight flooded the room.

"Who's been quoting Housman to you?"

"A cute little bluejacket in Diego."

"What were you doing in San Diego?"

"The Navy is training porpoises for undersea rescue operations and wanted me to analyze their language with my acoustic converter."

So here had been the reason for Slade's exultation; he had instantly spotted a use for the device that would gain Kyra the Navy's vote.

"Were you able to talk with the dolphins?"

"Oh, yes. They have a simple language, mostly sailor talk, 'Ahoy, there. . . . Man overboard. . . . Watch out for the doggamned propellers!' I didn't eat on the plane, Breedlove, so we could eat together, and I've ordered breakfast sent up."

"Thank you. That's a beautiful tan. Your complexion would let you pass for any ordinary, shapely, indescribably charming earth woman."

"I got lots of sun. That's a fantastic collection of books in the living room, and I'll kiss you for comparing me to Merope as soon as you're shaved." She arched her neck and looked up at the mirror above his bed. "What an odd place for a mirror!" Then she looked at him, almost accusingly, and said, "Breedlove, you belong to a weird species. Now, get shaved and dressed. Breakfast will be here in fifteen minutes."

He emerged into the living room only a few moments before a maid wheeled a serving table in and unfolded the leaf table. She was about Kyra's age and size. Her coppery skin, twin-plaited black hair, and the slogging motion of feet accustomed to mocassins told him she was Indian, but there was about her too a tantalizing familiarity. He studied her covertly until a memory returned to him of a little girl, five years ago, on the Quinault Indian Reservation, the sister of the youth who had acted as Breedlove's guide.

"Fawn Davies! How did you get here?"

She was pleased that he recognized her.

"I was going to beauty school," she told him, "and yesterday a man came in and hired me for this job. When I get here each morning, Mr. Slade wants you and me to exchange a few remarks in the language of my people."

"Why does the chief warrior wish this?" he asked her in the Quinault dialect.

"He fears a warrior greater than he from beyond the sunset who might come to take Kyra wearing my face," Fawn answered in her tongue.

"Can you imagine," he turned to Kyra, "that Slade's afraid some Oriental disguised as Fawn might slip into these quarters and kidnap you?"

"Fear is Ben's stock in trade," she said. "When he can't find it, he invents it."

Over breakfast she described her excursion to San Diego, where she had been taken out to sea in a Navy barge to swim with trained dolphins. "They have a terrific sense of humor and really love one another—or any other mammal that gets in loving distance."

Her skittering, breathless narrative was interrupted by three quick raps on the door. Slade entered, carrying a briefcase. In Kyra's presence the security chief's manner was courtly. He inquired about her breakfast with the interest of a chef inquiring about his own culinary creation and asked if her new quarters met with her approval.

"Our rooms are lovely, but you've taken my horizon and given me two potted palms."

"You'll not have to tolerate them long, ma'am. Your hearing is tomorrow at ten, and you've won the Navy vote with the dolphin caper. The commissioner's name is Hunsaker. He has the power to veto your request, but he won't, because the committee's going to okay it and Hunsaker's too cautious to assume sole responsibility for the committee's action. He'll forward the approval to the President, who can okay it or hand it back to the Joint Committee on Atomic Energy, but he should approve it. You may get a 'No' vote from Norcross, who commands the

North American Air Defense. He once bragged that an acorn couldn't fall in his air space without showing on his radar. Now that you've landed a spaceship undetected, the scrambled eggs he used to wear on his hat are on his face; but if you can charm him into a 'Yes' vote, it'll make the President's approval easier. Your permit should be signed by Tuesday, and you should be on your way by Wednesday."

Listening to the quiet confidence in Slade's words, Breedlove felt no elation. Instead he felt sad and morose over Kyra's imminent departure. He was not alone in his dejection.

Three tentative raps sounded on the door, and Kyra called, "Come in, Little Richard."

Turpin entered, greeted the group, and Kyra said, "Pull up a chair while I pour you coffee. Ben tells me I'll be leaving Wednesday."

"I wish you would stay with us," Turpin said. "The world has need of you."

"Now for the best news of all," Slade said, opening his briefcase and speaking directly to Kyra. "To get a seat at the petition hearing, the State Department has designated you a 'head of state.' That status entitles you to a credit card issued by State. The cover story is that you and Breedlove are newlyweds in town on your honeymoon. You'll have the freedom of the city under covert surveillance, which means you'll be guarded unobtrusively. As your husband, Breedlove will carry the credit card, but you'll have control of the purchases, and whatever you buy will be a gift to you from the people of the United States."

It was a subtle ploy to cement Kyra's allegiance to the country, Breedlove felt, but it was nevertheless generous.

"We're off to Mason's, Breedlove," Kyra said, "to buy you know what."

"For you, Breedlove, there's one proviso," Slade began, shuffling through his papers, when Laudermilk entered

147

without knocking and said, "Good morning, folks. This cat's come to look at the queen."

"Take a seat on the sofa, Gravy," Kyra said, "and pour yourself a cup of coffee."

Slade had taken a document from his papers and began to read: " 'At all time the head of state's escort will observe appropriate behavior in the presence of the visiting dignitary, showing proper deference to the emissary's status—' "

"That means no hanky-panky, Breedlove." Laudermilk interjected.

" '—and at all times his manner shall be friendly, helpful, cheerful, and reserved.' "

With a ceremonial bow Slade handed Breedlove the credit card. "You're also entitled to sit on Kyra's left at the hearing tomorrow, but sit is all. The pleading will be handled by Abe Cohen. Here's another prop for the cover story." He took two wedding bands from the briefcase. Breedlove's was the larger and heavier of the two rings. "You can place the ring on Kyra's finger, but I'll kiss the bride."

"I'll put the ring on her finger, but the articles of protocol apply to you also."

Breedlove slipped the ring on her finger. She held it out admiringly and said, "Now, Breedlove, we can go shopping, and Saturday you can take me to the lake in the mountains."

"Splendid. We'll drive up."

"No, I'll fly you up in a helicopter," Laudermilk said. "Where Kyra goes, we all go. Breedlove, you're the official eunuch."

Laudermilk was jocular, but Breedlove's expendability was given official weight by Slade, who unfolded a map of the city on the coffee table to plot Kyra's shopping tour. If Kyra was threatened by an armed assailant at any point on the tour, Slade explained, Breedlove, as her closest guard, was to interpose his body between the assailant's weapon and Kyra. "Security is a split-second business. In the time it takes the hostile to waste you, we can liquidate him before he hits Kyra."

Mason's, the only Seattle store offering the Polinski Creation, opened at ten. Breedlove and Kyra would arrive at the store at 10:37 in an unmarked green sedan driven by a former member of the Green Beret. After she had finished shopping, the three other members of her bodyguard would join her for lunch at the Mandarin Palace. With its wide selection of vegetables, Chinese food should appeal to her, and the atmosphere would give her some idea of the varied life styles on earth.

Afterward, at Kyra's suggestion, they would go to a bookstore to augment the library Breedlove had selected for her. She wanted more scientific volumes. After the afternoon's shopping Breedlove suggested dinner at Pierre's, overlooking Puget Sound. At a French restaurant that featured old-fashioned cheek-to-cheek dancing, he felt he could review for her the recent history of social dancing and broaden her knowledge of world cuisine. Slade postponed the visit to Pierre's until Friday night. Abe Cohen was coming by the motel this evening to interview Kyra for tomorrow's hearing.

After plotting the tour, Slade left for the command room on the first floor to instruct the security guard on the day's activities. Kyra excused herself to go to her room and dress. As she walked from the room, Breedlove noticed that Turpin's gaze followed her and focused on her hair, while Laudermilk's gaze followed her and focused on the sway of her hips.

"I'd die for that woman," Turpin said.

"I'd rather live for her," Laudermilk said, "and be her man for all seasons, particularly the early summer season."

Obviously Kyra had won the hearts of her bodyguard,

Breedlove told himself. Turpin's admiration verged on idolatry, possibly because he was religious and it was his nature to worship something, and Kyra responded to his adoration with gentle sensitivity. After she learned of his practice of saying grace before each meal, Breedlove discovered, Kyra had taught Turpin the Lord's Prayer in Kanabian, and with that gesture she had earned his fealty. Laudermilk's attraction to her was more pragmatic.

An atmosphere of wealth hung over the exclusive dress department at Mason's. A uniformed guard stood at the entrance. No dresses hung on racks in the plushly carpeted area. All the garments were fitted on manikins, and even the manikins were patrician; here Breedlove saw his first dummy with gray hair. Nowhere could he see a price tag.

He and Kyra were the only customers in the showroom. As they wandered among the displays, a woman wearing a panache of dignity glided up. About thirty, she was trim and poised, with well-groomed hair framing an aristocratic face.

"Good morning. I'm Annette Duchamps. I'd be happy to serve you." Her softly modulated voice carried a trace of a French accent.

"My name's Breedlove. This is my wife, Kyra. You advertised a Polinski Creation."

"Indeed. A masterpiece from a master designer and the only one offered in the Pacific Northwest. If you and Kyra would be seated"—she waved them toward an intimate settee near the window—"it will only take me a moment to bring the item from our humidity-controlled storage room."

When they sat their knees touched and Kyra said, "Remove your knee, Breedlove."

"Why?"

"Protocol." She laughed and stroked his leg. "I can fondle you, but you can't touch me."

"What are you going to do with all your clothes?" he asked as she gave his knee a final pat.

"Matty can have them, all except the Polinski Creation. I plan to take it and my Bulfinch as keepsakes of earth."

Annette returned, bearing the garment in her arms.

"Our model will be here shortly to demonstrate the features of the Polinski Creation, but first I want you to feel its fabric. The skirt is made from genuine Irish linen reinforced with starched damask to give it crispness, buoyancy, and a sparkling Bopeep effect. The jacket is lined with silk to offer the ultimate in caressing intimacy, yet as you can see, Kyra, it manages to capture that casual, nonchalant flair."

Annette was giving a prepared lecture much as he gave to park audiences, but he had never had such an attentive listener. Fingering the material, Kyra nodded agreement. Beside her Breedlove felt the poignancy of the moment grow almost unbearable. She who looked at the dress with such feminine longing would wear it no more than three times in the setting it was designed for. It would strengthen her affinity for a planet she had grown to love and must soon be leaving.

She was an airy Moses given only a glimpse of the Promised Land. Soon an iron door would clang shut, and she would have to resume an awesome hegira across a void that might reach to infinity and still deny her a home. At the moment his compassion would have made him willing to cry to her, "Stay," and, like Faust, exchange man's destiny for Kyra's knowledge and beauty, but she was not

151

Mephistopheles and did not wish to barter for his soul.

From no selfish motive, he decided, he would not let the dress be a gift to her from the people of the United States. He wanted it to come from Thomas Breedlove, from one man to one woman as a meaningful gift of love, and he would buy the dress for her. He would like to get the price down, but up or down he intended to pay the bill.

With long, jerky strides a model strode from the fitting area, pacing and swirling before them. About Kyra's size, she wore a platinum wig and green contact lenses. The make-up was an impressive bit of stage business which no doubt upped the price of the garment, but the performance created a paradox. While the model paraded before them in an exclusive Polinski Creation, Kyra held a duplicate of the garment on her lap.

"Notice the lilt and swirl of the skirt, assertive yet effervescent, and the casual drape of the jacket revealing the peekaboo V of the blouse—"

"Hold it, Annette," Breedlove interrupted. "You said this was an exclusive creation, and I can see two of them before me. If I'm laying out over seven hundred dollars for a yard or so of cloth, I don't want my wife to be meeting herself when she walks down the street."

"Mr. Breedlove, I said it's the only one of its kind sold in the Pacific Northwest. If Kyra buys it, only her size will be selected. The remaining dresses will be held for six months and remaindered by our outlets in Fresno and Tucson. Kyra will never see anyone in Seattle wearing a duplicate of this dress, I assure you."

"But they're identical. They must be machine-made, so they can't be all that exclusive."

"It's the pattern that is exclusive, and the dresses are not made by machines. They are handsewn by seamstresses in Warsaw."

"What if there's a defect in workmanship?"

152

"The value of the garment would actually increase. A defective Polinski Creation is a collector's item. . . . Notice the snugness of the waistline, Kyra. The hugging effect gives one the feeling of being loved. Kyra, this dress is you!"

With a dramatic gesture she leaned down and lifted the dress from Kyra's lap. Involuntarily Kyra's hands grasped the garment before she reluctantly let it trail from her hands. Annette was not taking it from her. She was merely holding it at arm's length, tantalizing Kyra with its nearness as the model wheeled and strutted on the floor.

"Enough, Mona," Annette called to the Kyra-like model, who wheeled and strode from the showroom.

Speaking now to Breedlove, the saleswoman said, "I'll leave you alone with the Polinski Creation. I realize it is a family investment and that such matters should be discussed privately." She laid the dress on a pattern table.

Her work done fully and well, Annette turned and followed the model through a curtained doorway. Kyra rose and walked to the table to finger the skirt. She turned to Breedlove. "I must say you're taking our cover story seriously. From the way you were eyeballing the lady over the price of the dress—"

"I wasn't acting, Kyra. I'm buying you the dress."

"Never! I've learned about money since I first saw the ad, and I'm not letting you squander your wages on me. Besides, I have the autographed Bulfinch."

"The book was a gift of friendship."

"What greater gift is there?"

"A gift of love," he blurted out. "I'll have a long time to make up the deficit in my savings, but how long will I have you? Another five days. I don't want this to be from the people of the United States, people who don't even know you. I want it to be from me. Then, long after you're the reigning queen of some beautiful planet, you'll wear it and remember the man of earth who loved you."

"Breedlove, goddamn it, you've touched me!" Her eyes misted over. "You make me feel like an earth woman, and I like the feeling, so why do I want to cry? Hug me."

He put his arms around her and she began to weep against his chest, and the tears amazed her. Probing her own mystification, she mumbled into his coat lapel, "I want you to know I'm crying because I feel loved and wanted and not because you're buying me that gorgeous little number on the table."

"You are a woman and you are loved and wanted and it makes no difference whether you came from another planet or fell out of a coconut tree, there'll never be another woman on earth like you. You've given me something very dear by being here. If I should live to be one hundred, I'll remember your radiance and be happy, and if I die remembering you, I'll die contented."

"Hush, Breedlove. You aren't helping me stop crying one bit."

He too was beginning to weep. Something was amiss in his emotional machinery. He had not wept since he was a child, and a weeping man was mawkish.

"Your crying's not helping me either, so go try on the damned dress."

She looked up to see his misting eyes and said, "I'm off, Breedlove. Somebody's got to command this ship."

Wrenching herself from him, she clutched the dress and ran sobbing into the fitting room. Assailed by a throat-tightening sadness, he turned to the window and looked down into the street, seeing it as hazy and blurred. Struggling against his inner turmoil, gulping, focusing his vision, he fought for and regained composure before the elegant and composed Annette walked out to rejoin him, smiling.

"Kyra's being fitted for the alterations. As soon as she's pinned up, she'll be out to model for you. Don't be disturbed if she seems upset. Young brides usually react

154

that way when their husbands buy them a Polinski Creation. She'll need accessories for the dress. I'll give you my card to take to Mr. Landon at the jewelry counter, first floor near the entrance, and you tell him you've bought the Polinski Creation. He'll find just the right diamond to match the dress.''

Accepting her card, he realized that he was being touted and that she would get a finder's fee from the man at the jewelry counter, but she had earned her commissions. She had solved a problem of conscience for him. Since he was buying the dress, the people of the United States could buy Kyra a diamond.

"When will the dress be ready?"

"Monday."

"Impossible, Annette. My wife has to attend a very important reception tomorrow morning. That's why I'm buying the dress—and the diamond."

Annette's face fell. "Mr. Breedlove, by working a seamstress overtime, I might get the dress ready by Saturday, but tomorrow is impossible."

He knew then that Saturday was the earliest he could expect delivery, as otherwise it meant the loss of Annette's commission. He could set the dancing date at Pierre's back to Saturday night and they could spend Sunday and Monday at the lake, but Kyra would be disappointed. She had wanted to charm General Norcross with the dress.

"If it's the best you can do, I suppose I'll have to be satisfied, but do me a favor, Annette. When Kyra comes out, say to her, 'Kyra, you're the height of fashion.' "

"Certainly, Mr. Breedlove, for she will be indeed."

She was. Striding out, imitating the long, mechanical steps of the model who had imitated her, Kyra whirled and posed before them. Annette voiced the enchanted phrase while Breedlove stood mute. From nothing more than a line drawing in a magazine, found on a farm near Spokane, a woman from another planet had selected a garment from an alien culture that seemed specifically designed for her. It enhanced the lilt of her personality while framing her beauty in the perfect frame.

Stricken dumb, Breedlove reached into his wallet and handed Annette his own credit card as a gong sounded somewhere in the dressing area.

"I have an emergency call," Annette whispered, taking his card and moving swiftly toward the doorway.

Flushed with happiness, Kyra swirled before him and curtsied. "I haven't heard a peep out of you, Breedlove."

"I'm speechless. The dress does something for you, and you do something for it, and the two of you keep reinforcing the loveliness of each other until you go beyond the limits of describable beauty."

"You keep talking like that and I'll have to sing you back to sanity. Do you think it will make General Norcross vote 'Yes'?"

"I hate to tell you this, Kyra, but Norcross won't get to see it. The alterations won't be ready before Saturday."

"Then we'll change our date at Pierre's to Saturday night, and you can swirl me around in my Polinski Creation. Did you hear Annette tell me I was the height of fashion?"

Not waiting for an answer, she whirled before a full-length mirror to admire herself. Annette returned, her face wreathed in smiles.

"Mr. Breedlove, I've good news. My call was from Major Laudermilk, a very dear friend of mine. He wanted me to give his good friend Kyra Breedlove special treatment, so I will personally do the alterations and the dress will be delivered to your motel this evening."

"Now, isn't that just like Gravy?" Kyra said. "Always trying to butter me up."

Kyra's remark brought from the dignified saleswoman a sidelong, animated, and knowing smile, the smile of a

French coquette who shares a delicious secret with another woman. Breedlove stood beside them dumbfounded. The only way Laudermilk could have known of the problem was by overhearing Breedlove's conversation with Annette. That meant, too, the skillful lover had listened to his inept protestation of affection for Kyra.

The unreal world of Kyra's palace guard, Wynken, Blynken and Nod, had intruded too far on his privacy. Slade had him bugged. Somewhere on his person, in his belt buckle, the tip of his shoelace, a microphone was hidden.

No. Not there. Here.

Neither Kyra nor Annette saw him when he slipped the wedding ring from his finger, but either might have heard the loud clunk it made when it hit the bottom of the waste basket had they not both been totally engrossed by Kyra's Polinski Creation.

Chapter Eleven

———————— ❋ ————————

At the hearing in the Federal Building, Commissioner Hunsaker sat at the head of the table. On his left were representatives of the Army, Navy, Air Force, State Department, and Immigration. Of the three military men jointly representing the Department of Defense, only General Norcross was in uniform. With iron gray hair and steely blue eyes, he cut an impressive figure, and he wore more ribbons than Laudermilk. To Hunsaker's right sat Breedlove, Kyra, Abe Cohen, an HEW representative, and a man from the President's Scientific Advisory Committee. In chairs lining the wall behind Breedlove sat advisers to the men at the table and Kyra's bodyguard.

Around the table everyone appeared to be relaxed, but Breedlove sensed a tension in the group. Part of the unease might have emanated from the commissioner himself, a small man with bushy eyebrows and a retiring, almost apologetic manner. Hunsaker made the opening statement.

"Gentlemen and gentlewoman, if I occasionally forget

the rules of order at this hearing, forgive me. Ordinarily the petitions I consider concern only power plants or radiology labs. I have never faced such an august group before and never in its history has the Atomic Energy Commission been petitioned by such a charming and, I might add, stylishly dressed petitioner with such an unusual request."

His compliment brought silent shouts of agreement to the eyes of the men at the table.

"This morning," Hunsaker continued, "Miss Kyra Lavaslatta, a citizen of no earthly realm, as duly attested, comes before this committee with a request for eighteen ounces of enriched uranium to be used in certain unspecified processes which will permit her space vehicle, now marooned somewhere in the state of Idaho, to lift off from our planet and continue on its journey in search of a habitable planet for Miss Lavaslatta and her companions. I have read the depositions and documents relating to the petition and recommend it be approved and forwarded to the President for immediate action. I am aware that any unilateral action taken by the United States in behalf of a nonresident alien for the extraterritorial use of nuclear fuel would violate the terms of the Nonproliferation Treaty, but I am positive an ex post facto explanation to the signatory powers would be concurred in by them, since I have been informed by Health, Education and Welfare that if our visitor is held beyond June twenty-first, an instinctual response of her species to the sun's declination will compel Kyra to seek asylum on earth. Looking at the young lady, my impulse is to say 'Welcome,' but I understand her retention here would have grave consequences for mankind and that it is her wish to go. Although I urge haste, procedure must be followed, and any dissenting voice must be heard before my request can be acted upon. Comes now for the petitioner, her attorney, Mr. Abraham Cohen. . . . Mr. Cohen."

Cohen did not stand. He began the plea in a casual, conversational manner as if appealing to a circle of old friends.

"Gentlemen, the being beside me is a potential national treasure more valuable than the gold in Fort Knox, but the unfortunate legal fact is that she does not belong to this country, this planet, or to this era. You see your future before you; it's beautiful, it's logical, and it's different from what men might yearn for, but it is a thousand years hence, and we must find it for ourselves, not only for moral but for practical reasons. Kyra Lavaslatta knows she holds our world and our future in her hands, but in her kindness she wishes to leave our planet and leave our future for us. We must let her go."

He paused momentarily, looked at the faces around him, and continued: "Our time is running out. An Israeli agent, since deceased, discovered her presence amongst us. Other nations, unaware of what we have learned from Kyra and fearing what we have learned, might also discover her presence and seek to seize for themselves this treasure who belongs to no nation. If this should happen, the forces gathering for the task might prove irresistible. If it has already occurred, each hour she remains among us increases her peril and our own.

"Biological reasons of which I am not authorized to speak outweigh all other arguments for granting her request, but there are other more apparent and urgent reasons why she should not be detained. The mere outlines of her knowledge might prove as dangerous to nations as matches to children who have not learned the perils of fire, and detailed knowledge could be elicited from her by unscrupulous men.

"There are dissidents in our world, large groups of people with valid and often justifiable grievances who might make this just person the symbol and focus of their discontent.

There are religious sects which would transform this being of grace and wisdom into a cult goddess worshipped against her will. Although I am Jewish, the thought even occurred to me when speaking with Kyra last night that you Christians might have been right all along, that your Messiah does live and has now returned. Would it not be fitting for Him to come back in the guise of a supplicant, a woman meek and good, asking only for a spoonful of uranium?''

"Amen," Turpin said softly from behind Breedlove.

"I thought of these things," Cohen continued, "and with my thoughts came a question: Gentlemen, are you ready for the Second Coming? And the Jewish observer in me, standing aside, detached, answered, 'No, gentlemen, you Christians are not ready.' ''

After a pause for the laughter that greeted his observation, Cohen shifted his arguments. "Let us turn now to positive reasons for granting Kyra her spoonful of uranium other than the simple reason that she asked for it. What would we get in return? It is our nature to ask that question, and I answer: we have our rewards already. We have learned from her visit that extraterrestrial life does exist. Merely by coming, she has expanded our knowledge of the universe in a manner that we could not have accomplished by emptying our treasuries for space exploration. We have learned that the patterns of evolution are universal and benign, that space is not occupied by the monsters of fantasists but by a nobler species of beings, gracious, merciful, and, in this instance, beautiful. For most of us, I suspect, she brings particular gifts. For me as a lawyer she has given the opportunity to establish a precedent in the yet unformulated laws of space, a precedent which asserts that compassion and not piracy shall rule the seas of space as it now rules the seas of earth.

"But more than all she has given she now offers, our

humanity for a spoonful of uranium. If we deny her request we deny our humanity. If we grant her request we grant ourselves humanity. Gentlemen, I ask you, can we refuse such a bargain? Shall we reject this exchange Kyra offers? I think not."

Cohen was finished. In the long silence following his words, each man at the table seemed in confrontation with himself or possibly in communion with the better angels of his nature. So exquisitely balanced were the practical and abstract appeals of Cohen's arguments that Breedlove was certain he had captured the minds of all his listeners.

"Do I hear a dissenting opinion?" Hunsaker asked in a tone that implied he expected none.

Two hands went up. Breedlove was half surprised to see that one belonged to Norcross and wholly surprised to see that the other belonged to the man from the State Department. Slade had said that State was in the bag.

Norcross noticed the other hand, leaned over, and called graciously down the table, "The military is happy to yield to the gentleman from the civilian establishment."

"Commissioner, I have reservations about the correctness of this procedure," the man from State said. "I'm not disagreeing that an ex post facto explanation of the committee's actions would not be acceptable to other treaty powers; in fact the arguments are so persuasive I think they would agree without question and act promptly. For that reason and to preserve our international reputation for honesty, I move the proceedings be suspended until the signatory powers are notified."

"Are you out of your pea-picking mind?"

Slade hurled the question at the speaker. Glancing behind him, Breedlove saw that Slade was not acting now, unless he could command his face to go pale with anger.

"Mr. Slade has tabled the question," Hunsaker announced.

There were wheels within wheels in the government, and Slade was apparently a very big wheel. Although he and the Texan had not been on friendly terms since the bugging incident, Breedlove felt a proprietary pride in Slade's command of the situation.

"I agree with Mr. Slade that this matter should be kept in the family," General Norcross said, "but I think the operative term at this hearing has already been voiced by the commissioner, and that term was 'unspecified processes.' No one wishes this charming young lady Godspeed on her journey more than I, and I'm willing to grant her request with one proviso, that she be escorted to her alleged space vehicle by selected technicians, who will determine if in fact the vehicle is present and mechanically ready for liftoff."

"What says our petitioner to the general's request?" Hunsaker asked.

"For the general's request," Kyra said, "the charming young lady has another general's answer, 'Nuts!'"

The urbane Norcross did not falter at the laughter.

"Dear lady, on this planet we have what is called 'quid pro quo.' On the record your space vehicle does not exist. We offer an ample quid, a rare and expensive metal, for a meager quo, proof that there is indeed a vehicle and that the uranium will be used to power it. Are we being unreasonable in asking for such proof?"

"You have it in Breedlove's testimony."

"Ma'am, I am not questioning the credibility of Ranger Breedlove, a gentleman who I am sure would not lie—under oath. But you must admit that the young man could have succumbed to the charm you evidence in such ample quantity. I have studied his reports in the file, and I notice he has evinced a strong admiration for those charms. Though you sit before us now dressed in the height of fashion, I cannot but remember that Breedlove first looked upon your beauty bare. You might have bewitched him. While we older men dream wistful dreams, young men see visions, and another name for a vision is a hallucination."

"Breedlove didn't fall in love with me at first sight. It took him a little time. He told you he saw inside my ship, and he's honest."

"We're all honest men, and it is my professional duty to register an honest doubt about the existence of a space vehicle which intruded into my air space without so much as rippling a radar. Dear lady, I have absolutely no doubt you descended from the heavens. Your unearthly charms tell me so. But traditionally angels arrive and depart on wings, and it is your unusual mode of transportation alone that I question. You will forgive an old soldier if he votes not against you but against the credibility of your vehicle, which is even more incredible than your incredible loveliness."

Two champion charmers had competed, and the general won, after a fashion. The vote was seven to one for granting the petition and forwarding it directly to the President. There was polite applause for Kyra when she stood to thank the committee, or to give it a full-length view of her dress. As well-wishers gathered around her to compliment her on her victory, Breedlove turned to Cohen.

"Congratulations, counselor. It was a cogent, powerful, and spontaneous plea you made."

"I was up all night getting the spontaneity, but it was useless . . . useless."

His voice trailed into silence. As he gathered his papers to place in his briefcase, his usual crisp movements were slow and uncertain.

"What makes you think it was useless?"

"Norcross is going back to Washington to persuade the Joint Chiefs to persuade the President to throw the petition back to the Joint Committee on Atomic Energy. They'll hold a hearing and you'll be subpoenaed."

"Why me?"

"You know where the vehicle is. He wants you under oath and testifying, figuring your patriotism and desire to save your own hide will force you to locate the vehicle. Then he'll get his technicians aboard to try and figure out how Kyra landed undetected."

"Where is that man's compassion?"

"Compassion is not his responsibility. The Norad air space is."

"How long will this delay Kyra's petition?"

"Another week or ten days if I can head off Norcross. Forever if I can't. But I foresaw the general's move and reserved a flight to Washington. Now the infighting begins."

Cohen was preoccupied. Slowly he buckled the straps of his briefcase as Breedlove, his mind in a turmoil, blurted out, "How did you know the Israeli agent Ajax was dead?"

"Slade told me last night when he and Turpin were briefing me on the religious and security angles to cover." He straightened, squared his shoulders, and stuck out his hand. "I'm off to Washington. If I lose this one we all lose, so pray to Jesus that I win."

He turned and strode from the hearing room. Listening to the determined fall of his footsteps, Breedlove was encouraged, but Cohen's parting request disturbed him. When a Jewish lawyer asked for a Christian's prayers, the situation had to be critical.

Remaining apart from the well-wishers around Kyra from the fear that his gloom might infect their joy, he overheard Slade suggest that they all take lunch at the Mandarin Palace again, to celebrate, and he heard Kyra agree. She liked Chinese food. This morning he had hoped to lunch with her without her attendants, but now he was glad he would not be alone with her, for she was intuitive and

165

would inquire about his pessimism. With others demanding her attention, the group would remain happily unaware of the impending crisis.

Still, the conversation might get strained. Yesterday he and Slade had argued heatedly over the ring Breedlove had tossed into the basket. It cost $12,000, Slade claimed. But the ring, which had been retrieved, was not the issue. Privacy was the issue. Breedlove had refused to let Slade "wire" him.

When Kyra finally managed to detach herself from the throng, Commissioner Hunsaker walked with them to the elevator, and Breedlove dropped back to give her charms operating room. He found himself walking beside Slade and without thinking said to him, "You didn't tell me Ajax was dead."

"You haven't been speaking to me."

"That's your fault."

"Breedlove, I'm buying lunch. Is it a truce?"

"If you'll tell me the truth about Ajax. Did you have him murdered?"

"We never murder anyone. We terminate them with extreme prejudice. Ajax died a natural death, and I'll prove it to you as soon as we get to the restaurant."

Kyra and her four guardsmen entered the Mandarin Palace from the parking lot. After they were assigned a booth, Slade sent Turpin out to get a newspaper. Without looking at the menu, Kyra said, "There are five of us, and if we all take number three we'll get almond chicken, egg foo yong, and Peking duck extra."

"Since I'm paying the bill," Slade said, "that's what I'll order, for everybody."

The waiter had taken their order and gone when Turpin

returned with a newspaper, which he had folded to a story on an inside page. He handed it to Breedlove and pointed to a mug shot with a caption headline:

PHILANTHROPIST SUCCUMBS TO HEART ATTACK

The photograph was of the man who had introduced himself to Breedlove as Abe Cohen; there was no mistaking the jowls and drooping eyes even in the light of the booth, but the story identified him as David Asherman. His list of charities was long, but it was the last paragraph that held Breedlove's attention.

> After attending a testimonial banquet given him by the Scout Masters of America last night, Mr. Asherman died in his sleep sometime this morning according to his physician.

He had died this morning, and Slade had told the real Abe Cohen of his death last night.

"Slade"—Breedlove's voice was harsh—"your men liquidated Asherman."

"Speaking of liquid," Kyra said, "I'm so thirsty I'm about to burst. Excuse me, gentlemen."

Breedlove was glad she had chosen this moment to go to the restroom. He preferred not to discuss the depravity of his species in her presence, particularly not that of her own inner circle. He himself had preferred to regard these men as nothing worse than actors in a farce whose only villain was their own paranoia, but now he saw that their playacting could have lethal consequences, that their superficially attractive camaraderie bound them in a fellowship of murderous criminals. They were truly out in the cold, outside the pale of human morality.

Slade sensed his disgust and spoke to him in consoling tones. "He would have died hereafter. Our man at his testimonial dinner was an expert in heart ailments and recognized terminal symptoms. But don't waste any sympathy on him, Breedlove. He could have murdered you without compunction, using only his feet as weapons."

"Tell that to your audience in the goober gallery. He was personally a warm and gentle person. He could have been apprehended and held incommunicado until after Kyra was gone."

"He could not have been apprehended under our legal system. His charities were his cover story. As far as his gentleness was concerned, Ajax was a deadly little bastard. He was a master of *shalom aliel*, a Hebrew martial art only the Cabalists know about, and they're not talking. Unlike judo and kung fu, *shalom aliel* is not a defensive martial art, and it is designed to be fatal. The Judeans developed it to use against armored Romans, who had one vulnerable point of attack. A quick kick to the scrotum doubles the victim forward in agony and a heel to the nape of his neck finishes him off. It's always a double-blow job, no more, no less, and your mild-mannered little man was a master of *shalom aliel*."

"Which translates from the Hebrew as 'peace forever,'" added the scholarly linguist, Laudermilk, "or, in the vernacular, 'Buddy, you've had it.'"

As Breedlove fell into a simmering silence, Slade took the paper, opened it to the headlines, and exclaimed, "Hello, what's this?"

Breedlove glanced over at the headlines:

SOVIET-ISRAEL ACCORD NEAR

"Listen to this," Slade said, reading. "'With the sudden release of two hundred and eighty long-delayed French Mystère jet fighters on order by the Israeli Air Force and hurried Russian-Israel discussions in the Kremlin, experts are predicting sudden and unusual developments in the Mideast.'"

"We didn't get to Ajax fast enough," Turpin exploded. "The dastard sold his intelligence on Kyra to the French and Russians."

Turpin's use of the strong expletive indicated that he was upset, and Breedlove, himself amazed by the headlines, was shaken by the knowledge that Kyra had indeed become a pawn in a vast, international power play. The farce these actors played in was suddenly becoming a realistic drama with overtones of tragedy, not for a pedestrian secret agent but for Kyra.

"What Moscow knows, Peking will discover," Laudermilk said.

"Huan Chung!"

The name burst from Slade's lips, and he went visibly pale. Turning to Breedlove, he said, "Go get Kyra and take her back to the motel. Go into the restroom if you have to, and drag her off the commode, but get her out the back way, and walk naturally. I'll be a few steps behind. Give your driver two words, 'Huan Chung.' Now move. Turpin, take the front door. Laudermilk, pass the word and cover me. Look for sudden movements. This *would* be a Chinese restaurant."

Impelled by the urgency in Slade's voice, Breedlove moved. Entering the rear corridor, he was relieved to see Kyra emerging from the ladies' room. Seeing him approach, she asked, "Do you have to go too, Breedlove?"

"We're both going—out the back door. Take my arm and walk along beside me, naturally. The others are coming."

"What's wrong?"

"I don't know for sure. It's something about an Israeli agent finding out about you and telling the Russians and French, maybe the Chinese."

When they exited into the parking, their driver was already pulling the car up to the rear exit. He opened the door and Breedlove helped Kyra in, saying, "Huan Chung."

"The major radioed ahead," the driver said, flipped down his sun visor, and laid a pistol concealed there on the seat beside him. It had a long barrel with a silencer. With a squeal of tires the car pulled away as Kyra asked, "Who is Huan Chung?"

"I think he's the Chinese secret agent Fawn mentioned. Slade seems to fear him most and thinks he's coming to get you."

"Breedlove, is this whole planet mad or is it only Ben?"

"I thought it was only Slade, but after the headlines I saw in the newspaper I'm not sure."

"Maybe Ben had a paper printed with the headlines. He's tricky."

It was an idea. As the driver stopped for a light, Breedlove glanced at a newspaper kiosk on the corner. Clipped to the side of the structure were several copies of the newspaper blazoned with the same headlines.

"Kyra, I'm afraid it's not Slade who is crazy."

The car radio confirmed the authenticity of the report, and there was no doubt about the anxiety it had aroused in Slade. When they arrived, sentries were patrolling the motel and grounds, and Turpin, who had raced ahead to inspect their quarters, was waiting when they entered. Only moments later Slade came in with Laudermilk and informed them he was setting Condition Able, the maximum security watch, for the motel.

Yet Slade's self-possession was such he had considerately ordered their lunch brought from the Mandarin Palace, and it arrived only twenty minutes behind them. But by the time they sat down to eat the atmosphere here was far grimmer than it had been in the restaurant. Two men in plain-clothes stood on Kyra's balcony holding automatic weapons at order arms. Across the patio two other armed men sat on the motel's roof. Of a sudden the motel had become a bastion in a state of siege, and Kyra was a prisoner in a stucco tower, with nothing but a view of the opposite wall and two imitation coconut palms.

Breedlove knew there would be no dancing tonight at Pierre's.

At lunch Kyra asked, "Ben, who is Huan Chung?"

"Little lady, he is no fit subject for polite conversation. I want to talk to you about your future on earth, which is going to be short. I'm getting you off this planet by next Friday or bust a gut."

"I trust you implicitly, Ben, but please don't injure your entrails."

Kyra's confidence dismayed Breedlove, remembering Cohen's conversation, but he did not wish to shadow her optimism, and besides, Slade might be right. In any event, Kyra's activities in the future, whether it was short or long, would be severely restricted. She would be confined to the motel, where all pretenses that it was a civilian establishment were being dropped. All employees, except room clerks, as a sop to the management, would be given temporary leaves and their places taken by security personnel.

Passwords would be used.

"Tonight's password is 'abracadabra,' " Slade said. "Huan Chung has trouble pronouncing an *r*. If the lights should go out some night and you're challenged, answer promptly. Tonight, for instance, if a challenge is given and the answer is 'ablacadabla,' any security guard will know it's Huan Chung and blast him back to the Celestial Kingdom with no questions asked."

Kyra would take her meals in the dining room in the company of her personal bodyguard. To help make Kyra's confinement easier, movies would be shown in the motel conference room. The motel was already equipped with a gym, a sauna, and the swimming pool. Kyra listened to the ground rules politely and attentively, but Breedlove sensed that she was displeased. He himself felt that she was being victimized by Slade's professional paranoia.

After lunch Laudermilk invited Kyra and Turpin to a game of three-handed rummy. With a toss of his head Slade signaled Breedlove to join him on the balcony. Outside, flanked by the two immobile guards, whose eyes alone moved, sweeping the patio and opposite rooftop, the two men talked.

"A flea couldn't hop across the pool area without my men spotting it," Slade said. "At night they'll have infrared snooperscopes, and I'm bringing in helicopters with heat-sensing devices that could spot a tomcat prowling a back-yard fence a mile away."

"Sounds airtight to me, Slade. My compliments."

Slade slowly shook his head. Speaking from the corner of his mouth, he kept his voice low. "Men are gathering from the corners of the earth who can crack this nut easily and make off with the kernel. Our big advantage is that Kyra's worth far more to them alive than dead. My guess is that all the intelligence Ajax got from you went to the French for the jets, but the Israelis may be feeding it piecemeal to the Russians to get more concessions. If the Russkies know about the people Kyra left on Jones Meadow, they might liquidate her and go after them, but they may not have enough information yet to know, as Norcross knows, that genetically Kyra's people are harmless without her."

Breedlove did not know it either. He was hearing confidential information from a man who suddenly seemed unaware of his low security rating. Apparently Slade was organizing his thoughts out loud, talking to himself from the corner of his mouth.

"With his amazing deductive powers Huan Chung won't

make that mistake. He'll deduce that Kyra's the key to the operation and come after her. Your love feast with Kyra yesterday morning at Mason's clued me into one of his possible methods. He might enter the patio in disguise, climb the palm tree—he's a human fly—concealing himself from the guards on the opposite roof by using the trunk. Along here he'd be beyond the peripheral vision of the balcony guards. He'd climb on up to the fronds, hang there till the time was ripe, drop to the balcony—he's a superb gymnast—dispatch the guards with karate chops—he's a karate master—and enter the apartment unseen.''

Slade was in error. True, the palm fronds would support a man's weight—they had steel spines—but no one could hang there undetected by the guards on the roof across the patio. But obviously Slade, thinking out loud, was merely weighing possibilities.

"Of course he has other approaches," Slade continued. "He could get into her room disguised as Fawn, and there you can help. When you greet Fawn each morning in the Quinault language, check her accent carefully. Now, I know how you feel about being bugged. My own opinion is that any man who is too jealous of his privacy is usually up to something he shouldn't be, but I am concerned about Kyra's privacy. The few days ahead are going to be trying on her, with Laudermilk casing her body and Turpin hell-bent to save her soul. They'll tear her to pieces if she can't get a little rest, so I'm going to lay the law down to them about their visiting privileges.''

Here Slade was showing depths of compassion Breedlove had not glimpsed before.

"I'll have to throw the burden of the Kyra watch onto you, Breedlove. As a favor to her, I'd like for you to carry a cigarette lighter, even though you don't smoke. This lighter is not a microphone. It's a beeper. I'll show you how it works.''

Slade pulled an ordinary cigarette lighter from his pocket and flicked its lever. It didn't light, but a klaxon blasted somewhere in the building and the riflemen on the opposite roof leaped to their feet. Slade flicked the lighter again and the klaxon sounded twice. The men across the patio settled back down.

"That was a drill. When you sound it, it'll not be a drill. If you hear a thump on the balcony followed by two quick thuds, don't look. Sound the beeper. If Fawn's accent sounds a little off, sound the beeper. We'll not criticize you for being too quick on the trigger. Out of respect for your privacy, and Kyra's, I'll keep the television monitors out of your quarters if you'll carry the beeper."

"Of course, Slade. I'll be glad to carry it."

"Good, and when you sound it, I'll know Huan Chung is here."

"Tell me, Slade, who is this Huan Chung?"

"Who is Huan Chung?" Slade repeated the question slowly, rhetorically, his shoulders slumping forward into his storyteller's stance. Breedlove detected a slight movement in the erstwhile immobile balcony guards. They were leaning forward to catch every word of Slade's story.

Chapter Twelve

———————— ✳ ————————

"Huan Chung," Slade's tale began, "happens to be the most fantastic character in the history of espionage. More insidious than Fu Manchu, a greater hypnotist than Doctor Lao, his symbol is the black lotus. He leaves the black lotus behind him as sort of a calling card, but it is part of his mystique never to use a cover name. Whenever he registers at a hotel, it's always as 'Mr. and Mrs. Huan Chung,' for reasons I'll soon make clear.

"His only known legitimate hobby is the practice of parlor magic, mostly sleight of hand or legerdemain, although he has perfected a less legitimate sleight of end or leger-de-derrière trick no other magician has ever duplicated. He has several other illicit hobbies, chief among them being to figure out new ways of dispatching his opponents. Mind you, I did not say 'his enemies.' Huan Chung kills with a creative flair, but there's nothing personal about his artistry.

"Huan Chung was born—dropped rather—by a Commie female during the Long March. Some say his father was

Chairman Mao, but he is the acknowledged son of no man. He was raised in a commune and at the age of six could recite the whole 'Little Red Book.' He's such a dedicated Commie he chews ginseng root so he can pee red.

"He's expert in every known method of killing a man, and there are several methods not yet published that he holds the copyright on. He has committed murder by suicide. In Hanoi once he hypnotized a French secret agent and had him commit hari-kari by autosuggestion on a stage before an audience. The fastidious little bastard was so confident of his powers as a hypnotist that he even provided a bowl for the Frenchman to disembowel himself into.

"An illusionist, he can merge into any background, emerge, strike, then fade away. He's master of the diabolical plot and a genius at sinister intrigue, but that which makes Huan Chung the world's greatest superspy is his mastery of the art of disguise. If you think Kyra is lovely, you should see Huan Chung gussied up as Mrs. Huan Chung. Kyra in her Polinski Creation is to Huan Chung in drag what Sammy Davis, Junior, is to Diahann Carroll.

"Back when I worked for the CIA, my man in Hong Kong once hired a Chinese stenographer, a petite, almond-eyed little babe built like a sandalwood outhouse. He fell in love with the Chinese doll and for three weeks the romance went along hot and heavy until the doll got the combination of his safe and made off with our Asian code books. In the safe where the code books had been, she left a memento, a black lotus.

"She was Huan Chung pulling his sleight-of-end trick. My man had been so diverted and beguiled between the sheets he never noticed that his Oriental nifty had balls. We had to lead him out of the cold by his hand. His career was ruined, but that did not bother him as much as his broken heart. He had fallen in love, and he never recovered from the fickleness and infidelity of Huan Chung, truly a master of disguise."

The tale ended in a look of awe on the teller's face, and Breedlove asked, "Aren't you laying it on a little thick, Slade?"

"No. Hyperbole is understatement when you speak of Huan Chung. . . . I want you to study these coconut trees, Breedlove. Count them. Notice their size and shape—"

"Wait a minute! You aren't telling me—"

"I'm telling you Huan Chung is a contortionist. He can coil himself in a ball and disguise himself as a coconut until he's ready to backflip onto the balcony. We'd better get in. I've got to break the news to the boys about their new visiting hours."

Inside, Kyra had rummied, and the laughter, general gaiety, and the sunlight flooding the room made for anything but a dismal scene, yet it seemed to Breedlove that the tendrils of a fog were coiling into the room, that it was growing darker and clammier. Huan Chung had cast his shadow before him.

"Alone at last," Kyra sighed as the door closed behind her bodyguard. "And not a minute too soon. I've got five hundred years of reading to catch up on."

She strode to a cabinet now crammed with books, chose one, and returned to the sofa. Glancing over, Breedlove saw it was *Gone with the Wind*. She became engrossed in the book immediately, but as an object. Slowly turning the pages, she fingered the texture of the paper and admired the typeface and page layout. He sometimes did the same before reading a book.

Glancing toward the balcony, he was reassured by the thick necks of the guards, but only momentarily. A shadow flitted across the balcony, and he flinched, fearing the fall of a coconut and two quick snaps of breaking necks. But it was only Slade's helicopter, now arriving overhead, which had passed before the sun.

"Breedlove, you're worried," she said, without looking up from the book. "What did Ben tell you on the balcony?"

"Just a story. Another one of his originals."

"About Huan Chung?"

"Yes."

"And what foo yong did Ben feed my Breedlove about Huan Chung?"

"Slade didn't tell you, probably because he felt it might frighten you to no purpose, and I have to agree."

"Oh, fiddle-de-dee! Y'all ought to know if I frightened easily I wouldn't be here. More likely Ben didn't tell me because he knows I know when he's exaggerating. Now, tell me his tale, with all the embellishments."

He told her the story, but he censored Slade's comparison of her beauty with that of Huan Chung. When he finished the tale, she lifted her eyes from the book and asked, "Who is Sammy Davis, Junior?"

He told her.

"Is he pretty, witty, and vivacious?"

"Well, he's witty and vivacious."

He saw a hurt look in her eyes and rushed to change the subject. "Ben was just using an extreme figure of speech. He likes to impress me with those little verbal tricks. But if you overheard that on the balcony, did you hear what Cohen said to me in the hearing room?"

"Yes, and I think Cohen was right. You shouldn't try to keep bad news from me. I need to know everything to take countermeasures."

"If you think Cohen was right, why did you give Slade a vote of confidence when he said he'd get you away by next Friday?"

"That was a countermeasure. Ben is a man of wiles and I

was ordering probabilities." She dropped her eyes back to the book but kept talking to him in a thoughtful vein. "Breedlove, I think Ben created Huan Chung in his own image out of some deep psychic need of his own or to give his men an ideal of perfection in the spy business to strive for. He created Huan Chung from the same need for legendary heroes that made lumberjacks escape their own workaday world with Paul Bunyan or railroad men with Casey Jones."

"You may be entirely right," he agreed, surprised by her observation. "Slade probably borrowed Huan Chung from Sax Rohmer, a writer who created an insiduous but wholly fictional Doctor Fu Manchu, another Oriental spymaster."

She nodded with the pleased, agreeing nod of a school-teacher complimenting her favorite student. "As many actors have, Ben has an identity problem, and Ben is an actor, perhaps the greatest natural actor since Richard Burbage, but unfortunately he studied dramatics with the CIA. So don't listen too attentively to everything he says. I wouldn't put it past him to try and frighten you, because he's afraid you might want to fly the coop with me some night and take me dancing at Pierre's. Believe me, I'd be willing, and it would be perfectly safe. If Huan Chung exists, he couldn't capture me. My evolutionary training would help me avoid the grasp of any man I don't want grabbing me. . . . By the way, did Slade tell you I wanted to cut back on our socializing?"

"He told me he was going to give you more privacy." ·

"Let him have the credit for the idea, but I don't want Laudermilk bursting into the room at all hours without knocking, and I'm not ready for deification by Little Richard. I declare, they do get tiresome, and if we can't go dancing at Pierre's tonight, I want to spend a quiet evening at home with nothing but the backs of our two riflemen for company. Unfortunately we have to make an appearance in the dining room. . . . Breedlove, were you ever on Peachtree Street in Atlanta?"

"No. I'm sorry."

Her reference was to *Gone with the Wind*. She wasn't leafing through it, she was reading it while carrying on a conversation with him, and now she lapsed into silence. Outside, the sound of laughter drifted up from the poolside, and he ignored the sounds, watching her face as she slowly turned the pages. He was seeing a mime show of sadness, mirth, and occasionally the misty-eyed yearnings of romance played out on her face. Fascinated at first by her expressiveness, he slowly began to feel like a voyeur.

Trying not to disturb her concentration, he arose and started from the room, intending to join in the merriment below, but without looking up, she asked, "Are you going down to quaff the nut-brown ale and old?"

"Yes. Care to join me?"

"No. I'm going to finish this terrific story and read *War and Peace*. Gravy recommended it."

Below, he found her three guardsmen at a poolside table and joined them. In the pool were several lithely muscled women. "You're allowing females on the premises," he said to Slade.

"They're all cooks and waitresses," Slade said, "but most of those dolls have earned black belts, so don't make any sudden moves in their direction."

"Speaking of dolls," Laudermilk said, "did I tell you about the fräulein I met in Dresden?"

As a storyteller, Breedlove discovered, Slade had a rival in Laudermilk, although the major's repertoire was limited to bedroom stories. Yet despite the graphic details they were told with a verve and enthusiasm that lifted them above the merely salacious and claimed even the polite attention of Turpin. In addition, Laudermilk's detached sense of wonder and artistic appreciation suggested a motivating impulse behind his amours as objective as that of a collector of any exotic erotica, such as Mayan fertility symbols. Some of his lectures were illustrated. He divided women into two categories, good and better, and the latter group he divided into squeezers, twisters, and snappers. The greatest of these were the snappers.

Next to his heart he carried a billfold with a plastic fold-out designed for credit cards but carrying photographs of girls, some so young and virginal-looking Breedlove found it difficult to imagine them involved in liaisons without creating statutory problems. The queen of Laudermilk's "pussy pantheon" was an Italian snapper with the face of an Eleonora Duse.

"Her professional name was Beatrice del Amores, but I called her 'the Living End.' She walked with the same twisting sway of Kyra—"

"Leave Kyra out of this, Laudermilk!" Turpin blurted in anger.

Slade and Laudermilk glance at the former FBI operative, who seemed suddenly ashamed of his outburst. He continued in a softer tone, "I don't want to sound strait-laced, Major, but Kyra's above this sort of talk."

With fatherly understanding Laudermilk nodded and continued in a sprightly, ruminative tone. "Talking about strait-laced people, I met this pious little thing down around Ben's country, a choir singer in the Midlands Baptist Tabernacle. She was reverent and modest but built like a Gothic cathedral with a flying buttress that would have made Christopher Wren envious. She had developed this pelvic movement she called 'the Born-Again Bounce,' and—"

"Dang it, Laudermilk. You're just pulling my leg."

So passed the lazy afternoon, the major regaling them with tales from his latter-day *Decameron* while the woman who could have given him an unbeatable record as a sexualist finished reading *Gone with the Wind* and commenced *War and Peace* before going down to dinner.

Though he was attentive to Laudermilk's tales, Slade's eyes kept flicking toward the entrances to the patio, toward the opposite roof, and once he craned his neck to look up at the coconuts on the tree under which they sat. It was then that Breedlove began to wonder again about Slade's sanity, wonder if his peculiar profession had so warped his sense of reality that he had come to believe his own yarns.

With the commencement of Kyra's restriction to the motel, Breedlove entered reluctantly a Cloud-Cuckoo-Land of secret agents he considered strictly for *The Birds*. However personable the men around Kyra might be, he was convinced their attitude was a product of aberrant minds, and to escape momentarily from their influence, to give Kyra solitude for her concentration, and to store up eyewitness accounts of the world outside to relate to her, he began to take walks through the surrounding neighborhood. Along the tree-lined sidewalks he saw nothing more Oriental than a Siamese cat, which he photographed for Kyra. The helicopter, whose maddening drone constantly overhead added its bit to their boredom inside, seemed to follow him in his walks, and he knew he could be under surveillance from the machine. It was not beyond Slade to suspect him of being a double agent—or Huan Chung in disguise.

Once he returned from a walk to find Kyra seated on the side of her bed, gazing wistfully at her favorite dress spread before her. In the pathos of the moment he would have risked the wrath of Slade and spirited her on an outing if they could have eluded the cordon around her stucco castle keep.

Forced into close and continuing proximity to Kyra, he felt his attitude toward her broadening and deepening, and the changes were not all from within. Subtle but profound alterations were occurring in her. The nimbus of femininity always around her grew more alluring, her movements more languid, her voice throatier; her girlish vivacity seemed to be mellowing into womanhood.

More pronounced than any physical change was her growing humanization, and that was superficially apparent to the entire security squad after she made a bikini-clad entrance into the pool at nine, Saturday morning, by plunging from her balcony railing directly into the water. Only a scattering of people watched her dive then, but Sunday at nine a larger group had gathered, and by Monday there was standing room only at the poolside. Balancing for a few extra seconds on the rail, she obviously enjoyed the calls and wolf whistles from below.

Fawn Davies, the displaced beauty-school student, took to spending almost an hour each evening brushing and styling Kyra's hair, for Kyra enjoyed the ministrations as fully as any woman of earth.

Breedlove had reason to believe her adaptation to human ways went deeper than the acquisition of feminine attitudes and to feel that a deeper dye of human longings and aspirations was staining her soul. On the first Sunday of her captivity, he directed her to Shakespeare, explaining that a knowledge of the author's works was the *sine qua non* to an understanding of English literature. Then he went for a walk until lunch, at which time she told him the Bulfinch helped her understand Shakespeare's allusions. By dinnertime she had read Shakespeare's complete works.

He had reservations about the amount of information

any speed reader retained, but it would have been presumptuous of him to quiz her. Although Shakespeare's archaisms were explained in footnotes, he felt she must have had difficulty with his concepts and the rich, compressed Elizabethan style. At dinner she proved he had erred.

Dinner was Kyra's mandatory public appearance each day at the center table in the interior dining room, surrounded by her bodyguard. Her appearance assured other security personnel, many of whom never saw her during the day, that their ward was alive and well. After Turpin had said grace over the meal, Breedlove remarked, "Gentlemen, we now have with us a Shakespearian scholar. Just before we came down, Kyra read the last line of his last sonnet."

"I wonder what the last line of the last sonnet is," Laudermilk said, and Kyra took the remark as a question.

" 'Love's fire heats water, water cools not love,' " she answered.

Emboldened by her eagerness and the accuracy of her response, Breedlove plucked one of his favorite lines from memory. "Complete this line, Kyra. 'On such a night did Dido—' "

"Oh, that's Lorenzo speaking to Jessica in *The Merchant of Venice*."

She straightened. Her shoulders leaned slightly forward. She spoke, and her voice, registering a bantering, masculine affection, caught all the flirtatious nuances of the lines as she recited:

> "In such a night
> Stood Dido with a willow in her hand
> Upon the wild sea banks, and waft her love
> To come again to Carthage."

Each man at the table had some literary background.

Slade wrote western romances. As an Army officer with little else to do, Laudermilk read extensively, and Turpin could quote the King James Bible at the drop of a fork. Breedlove spent long winters without television and had an English major's degree from college. The astonishment and pleasure of the four men showed in their eyes.

Measuring the effects of her artistry against her audience, Kyra gained confidence. Leaning back, arching playfully away from the man who had spoken the lines, she became a mocking Jessica, answering:

> "In such a night
> *Did young Lorenzo swear he loved her well,*
> *Stealing her soul with many vows of faith,*
> *And ne'er a true one."*

"Little lady," Slade said, "I'm inviting you to recite Shakespeare before the whole squad in the theater Monday night. You owe it to your talent to let the people see it."

"Why, Ben, I'd be right happy to do just that."

The next morning Breedlove selected her readings from the more familiar passages of the poet. Looking up from a book on molecular physics she was reading, Kyra noted his selections from the page numbers, but she did not review the lines. Her omission of a rehearsal, which indicated that she could recall the lines, made him aware that her intensive reading was truly an attempt to store in her memory banks all she could gather of the world's culture and science in order to take the library with her in her mind.

But no computer stood before a tough-minded audience of security people Monday night and brought to it the sadness and laughter her performance evoked. It was the shortest hour Breedlove had ever spent. Kyra's range of feelings and her ability to project those feelings astonished him as it did the others. She could not have made them feel

185

if she did not possess the feelings herself, and the realization of her transformation, her acquisition of a human heart, as it were, planted the seed of a purpose in his mind.

The memory of the evening helped to soften the news Slade brought to them on Tuesday: the President was still considering Kyra's petition. There would be no automatic approval.

"It's a budget problem," Slade explained. "The value of the uranium is too great for a state gift and too small to be included in any foreign-aid program."

"Is plutonium cheaper?" Kyra asked. "It would do as well."

"It's all restricted, and the price is academic anyhow. The uranium will be on its way by Wednesday. The Government Accounting Office is working out the kinks."

But on Wednesday the President referred Kyra's petition to the Joint Committee on Atomic Energy. Norcross had won the first round. A telephone call from Cohen brought the news to Kyra's suite before Slade came through the door, disappointed and chagrined over his error in prognostication. Although depressed by the rebuff, Kyra reacted with a sensible question, "When will the joint committee meet?"

"Not before next Wednesday. At the moment it doesn't have a quorum in Washington, but I think we're being given a runaround."

Wednesday would be June 9, less than two weeks before the summer solstice. If Cohen failed, Kyra would be marooned on earth. Breedlove had felt Kyra's fears at the prospect on the meadow, but the girl who had transmitted her anxieties to him then, by the touch of her hand, was different from the woman she had become. She no longer evinced the detached attitude toward suffering which had drawn the comment of his mother. Even the pity she felt for Slade in his chagrin was genuine, her consolation touched with sympathy.

"Don't be so downhearted, Ben. You're not responsible for that old committee, and I know you're doing everything you can for me—short of violating the law."

Reinforcing Breedlove's growing hope that Kyra might adapt to earth was his confidence that the government knew what it was doing. By now the President had all the facts he needed to make the correct decision, and Breedlove remembered Slade's remark that Kyra was no genetic threat to the earth apart from her tribe. Separate provisions could be made for them. If they had only a fraction of Kyra's adaptability, they could find a home on earth. Even Myra had been frightening only in a psychological sense, and she could learn to control her hostility. On earth, too, Crick would be able to find his longed-for playmates, and green hair was statistically only slightly more unusual than red.

He could almost convince himself to pull for General Norcross in the dispute being waged in Washington. Norcross had all the findings about Kyra at his disposal, and the general would never risk the security of the continent, much less the planet, unless he was very sure of what he was doing.

Such reasoning came easily to him when alone in the suite with Kyra, where he could hear the swish of her slacks as she passed, the tinkling notes of her laughter, and surreptitiously watch the halo the light formed around her hair as she sat reading. Conversationally she was delightful. Once in reading Gray's "Elegy," she took exception to the lines:

> *Full many a flower is born to blush unseen,*
> *And waste its sweetness on the desert air.*

"Breedlove, flowers are brazen hussies. They bloom. They don't blush. They wear bold colors when all other plants wear green and flaunt them to tempt every roaming, sex-mad bee."

Such an original fancy would have drawn him to any woman, and in Kyra it made him more aware of a beauty that was becoming more alluring with each passing day. The hips beneath her narrow waist seemed to grow more rounded, their sway more pronounced as she walked, and her bouncing breasts grew fuller. His behavior toward her was at all times proper. If anything, his was still Shelley's "desire of the moth for the star," but the gravitational pull of earth's committees was swinging the star closer, and Kyra had virtually promised herself to him if she should stay.

If she had to be on the planet when the transit of the sun swung southward, he wanted to be near her to comfort her when the seasonal terror he had glimpsed in the wardroom began. Then, when the summer storm had ebbed, he would make her a citizen of earth by marriage. As his wishes became his desires, he decided to plead his suit with Kyra honestly and openly, but he would have to transfer her from this penal atmosphere, the dining-room sycophants and hallway snoopers, into an atmosphere of candlelight and wine, in short, Pierre's.

But there were the guards who checked her bed at midnight, the anger of Slade if he was detected sneaking out with her, and there was the threat of Huan Chung, who might or might not be a figment of Slade's imagination. One night, as his fancies idly played with the idea of escape and the perils Kyra might face outside the walls, she looked over from a book she was reading and said, " 'Tis the eye of childhood that fears a painted devil.' "

"Why did you think of that?"

"I was remembering Lady Macbeth," she said. "Those

are her words. Now, there was a woman. It was she who said, 'We fail! But screw your courage to the sticking-place, and we'll not fail.' "

"Kyra, you can read my mind!"

"Not at all, dear Breedlove. I can read your facial expressions."

Chapter Thirteen

————————— ✳ —————————

He never broached his plans to Kyra, because he could devise no scheme for getting her out of the motel and, finally, because he did not have to. Set in motion by a telephone call from Abe Cohen, Friday afternoon, the parts of the plan fell together like a self-assembling jigsaw puzzle while Breedlove merely stood and watched. Cohen's call came at the end of the lawyer's day in Washington.

"The hearing's set for Friday the eighteenth. The committee's chairman is being called back from an African junket. Meanwhile the State Department's moving for an open session, and State has an argument. A secret session to grant a nonresident alien uranium would destroy U.S. integrity and jeopardize the Nonproliferation Treaty. I'm using a counterargument from HEW to get the President to sign, but he's wary of secret agreements, and the HEW argument is not as strong as I thought."

On news he would have considered catastrophic a week earlier, Breedlove hung up the telephone feeling elated. The eighteenth was only three days before the solstice, international agreements took priority over Kanabian biology, and this committee would never get Kyra off the ground. More immediately, Cohen's call gave Breedlove a reason to enter Kyra's bedroom, where Fawn was styling her hair.

Seated before her dresser mirror watching Fawn at work, Kyra looked up at Breedlove when he entered and said, "From the gleam in your eye, I'd say you're bringing bad news."

"Cohen called. The Joint Committee on Atomic Energy won't convene until the eighteenth."

" 'Tomorrow, and tomorrow, creeps in this petty pace,' " she intoned. "Well, Breedlove, it looks as if you're going to father a new breed of hybrids after all. . . . Doesn't Fawn have nimble fingers?"

"She comes from a long line of porcupine-quill pickers," he commented, surprised by Kyra's blitheness.

"With this hair style," Fawn said, "you'll look ravishing."

"But for whom?" Kyra asked, her gaiety gone. "Tinkers and Evers and Chance? I can hardly bear to face those plastic palm fronds another week, or Ben's tales, Gravy's leers, and Little Richard's adoration. Breedlove, why don't you spring me out of this joint and take me dancing at Pierre's?"

"I've been trying to figure a way to smuggle you out and get you back in time for Slade's bed check."

"It would be easy tomorrow night," Fawn volunteered. "On Saturday I punch out at eight p.m. You could slip Kyra's dress into the back of your car. I could bring Kyra a black wig and Coppertone for her skin, and she could walk out in my uniform as me."

"That's a terrific idea," Kyra said, "You could bring a platinum wig and make-up and take my place in bed. I'm sure Breedlove would slip you a few bucks for baby-sitting our guards. And I know I can get Ben off the premises Saturday evening. Would you take me, Breedlove?''

''Of course, but we'd be alone out there with no protection.''

''I don't need any protection, unless Huan Chung shows up in drag and you fall in love with him.''

No longer asking his advice or consent, they continued the planning, even considering such details as a table reservation at Pierre's, which Fawn would make from an outside telephone. Fawn was as excited as Kyra, and so cooperative Breedlove broke into the conversation with the remark, ''If this comes off, Kyra and I will name our first hybrid girl 'Fawn.' ''

If either heard his remark she ignored it.

Saturday morning Slade did not drop by the suite after breakfast, and Breedlove thought he knew why. Slade had broken the news of the committee's delay manfully enough at dinner, then sunk into a morose silence Kyra seemed to share. Now the twice-dishonored prophet refused to show himself in Kyra's suite. Instead he remained in the patio, alone, dressed in a swim suit, lounging in a deck chair and staring into space, a completely dejected man.

At breakfast Breedlove said to Kyra, ''Slade's down by the pool alone, sulking like Achilles in his tent.''

''I'll dive down and cheer him up, but I want you to stay here. I hope this weather holds for tonight. I can literally taste a pas de deux. I read this book on ballet, and I just love its expressions.''

''Treat me nice, and I might treat you to a pirouette.''

''I've never mistreated anyone in·my life, and I'm five thousand years old. But I fear I'm breaking my record this morning. I've got to be brutal with Ben to get him off the premises while we're making our escape."

"How do you propose to do that?"

"Mentally emasculate him. Crush him. Then give him a framework on which to rebuild his manhood. You see, Ben cares for me, but he cares more for himself as a daring, do-anything guy."

"And you're doing a good job of not telling me what you're going to tell him."

"You're too honest and law-abiding. You'd want me to stop and consider. Ben won't. He's a frustrated two-gun man straight out of the old West. He gave me autographed copies of his books and I read them. By his fantasies ye shall know him. Pass the toast. I need an excuse for more honey."

A few minutes after breakfast, lithe but voluptuous in her bikini, Kyra emerged from the bedroom and walked onto the balcony. Nodding to her guards stationed there, she leaned over and called down to Slade: "Good morning, Ben. Isn't the world bright and beautiful?"

"It's beginning to look a little better now."

"It's the beginning of such a joyous weekend, I'd like to share it with you. May I come down and join you?"

"You're what my doctor ordered."

"No, Ben, not me." The tenor of her voice changed. "What you need is a bandage for your busted gut. Remember the gut you were going to bust if I weren't off this planet by—when was it? Ah, yes. Yesterday. But, don't despair, you two-dollar pistol with a defective firing pin. I'll come down and mend you."

It was the most gratuitous act of public humiliation Breedlove had ever witnessed, and then she was plunging into the pool to slither toward him with the undulations she had learned from the dolphins. Breedlove looked out the window to see her emerge dripping from the pool to squat beside Slade and begin talking with an intent look on her face. Slowly Slade regained his composure as she talked. The lines of his jaw set. His face hardened, and he began to nod slowly, agreeing with the arcane argument that Breedlove had not been permitted to hear.

Suddenly Slade smiled, a smile of joy and release, nodded emphatically, and Kyra rose and kissed him on the forehead. Hand in hand they dove into the pool together to swim its length and back, and Breedlove drew back from the window amazed. As quickly as she had crushed Slade, Kyra had revitalized him.

That afternoon Slade left the motel shortly after Fawn arrived with the escape gear and word that she had reserved a window table at Pierre's for nine o'clock that evening.

"Talk with an English accent, Tommy, when you get there. To be sure you got good seats, I pretended I was your social secretary and reserved the table for you in the name of Lord and Lady Greystoke."

"But, Fawn, that's Tarzan and Jane."

"I thought the name sounded too aristocratic for me to invent. But it doesn't matter. It's a French restaurant."

It was a balmy evening. Stars glittered in a cloudless sky. A breeze lapped the waters of the sound and rustled the pines which scented the point on which Pierre's stood. Walking beside Kyra from the valet parking station to the rustic entrance of the restaurant, Breedlove felt joy swelling within him. "Your hair shimmers in the starlight."

"Wait'll you see it by candlelight."

They entered to be greeted by a headwaiter whose eyes blew kisses at the beautifully gowned, beautifully coiffured, beautifully poised, and beautiful Kyra. He did not ask for their name, but merely bowed and said, "This way, m'lady."

He led them across the empty dance floor through suddenly hushed voices that resumed as they passed. He caught comments on Kyra's dress from the women and comments on her figure from the men, and he knew that Kyra with her acute hearing heard more. He could tell from the sway of her hips, for he had grown good at reading her movements, that she was delighted to be in this environment.

They were seated at a corner table with view windows opening on the sound and its wooded shoreline. Gazing around her enchanted, Kyra settled into the chair, and the waiter handed them menus. Breedlove ordered martinis, and the waiter bowed out with a "*Merci*, m'lord."

"French again," Kyra said, glancing at her menu. "We should have brought Gravy along to translate."

"Please, Kyra. Let me enjoy my dinner."

So the evening began in banter, and Breedlove planned to keep it thus for a while, to ease gradually into more serious matters. Over the drink he spoke in generalities of the radiance of her smile, of the lights in her eyes, and how her simplest movements were imbued with a grace unknown in earth women.

"Breedlove, I've smote the living liar! Oh, look . . ."

Lights glittering, the night boat for Victoria glided by, casting its lambency on the waters. In silence they watched the receding ship until Kyra, with a tremor in her voice, said, "How fleeting and beautiful the varied sights of earth."

The longing in her voice threw him off his timing. Impulsively he grasped her hand and said, "Stay here, Kyra, with me."

The orchestra was filing toward the bandstand as she

said, "If I were a woman of earth, nothing would please me more than to stay with you to the end of my days."

"Would you be willing to marry me?"

"If I were of earth and feeling as I feel now, if you asked, we would leave tonight for your cabin, and after you were able to walk again, we'd hurry to the preacher and I'd make an honest man of you. But for now, let's dance."

He led her onto the floor. While jitterbugging in the family's living room, he had discovered her lightness. In these more measured steps he learned of her rhythm. Her body flowed with the music and almost pulsated with the percussion instruments. Through the entire set her head nestled on his shoulder; they danced in silence. Apotheosized by her grace, he feared words might break the spell.

After the swirling finale they returned to the table to find a plate of hors d'oeuvres. Even here they ate in silence until he finally said, "You do dance divinely."

"For all your mass, Breedlove, you're good too."

They ordered the meal and he ordered wine, but the conversation went slowly in the euphoria that followed their dance. But his euphoria helped ease him into the areas of conversation he wanted to explore.

"When I first saw you, I wanted very much to help you in what seemed an impossible task. You captured my heart as a charming, bright, but dependent little girl. In the past week my feelings toward you have been changing. They seem to be broadening . . . deepening . . ."

He struggled for the most accurate and least offensive word.

" 'Ripening'?" she suggested.

" 'Maturing.' I've begun to look at you, well, less as a girl and more as a woman."

"I've known of the feelings growing in your heart, and they please me. I love the way you peek at me when you think I'm not looking, the way your eyes follow me when I pass, and the way the swish of my slacks sends you."

"There's no need telling you anything. You know it all already."

"But I like to hear you say it. Besides, I'm not guiltless. I've been showering with my door open, hoping you'd peek."

"Have you been tempting me, you Jezebel?"

"My season's coming on. If I can't get any uranium out of this planet, I want to get something."

"If you're stranded here you have a prime piece of merchandise right on your counter. Every man who lays eyes on you falls in love with you after his fashion, but I think I can offer you a quality of desire no other man can offer. I would make no demands on you. I'd only want to be with you, to nurse you when you're sick, to provide for you, to protect you when you're threatened. I told you I'm no great lover, but I—"

"Methinks you protest too much about loving." She held a palm to him for silence. "Who are you to judge whether you're a lover or not? Leave that to your loved one. I'm your loved one, and I say you're the greatest lover on earth for me."

"How can you say that when I've never made love to you?"

"Are you talking about love, or about copulation, earth style?"

"Well, I wouldn't put it so bluntly, but I suppose I am talking about copulation, in a way. After all, it's a function of love."

"Well, I declare. If you're worried about your ability to give me pleasure as compared with some sex hero as you imagine Gravy to be, forget it. In the art of fornication as practiced on Kanab, probably neither of you could do as well as Crick, and he can't function yet. As far as your capacity to manufacture sperm is concerned, I'm sure you're adequate. You haven't been castrated, have you?"

"I wouldn't be talking like this if I were," he protested. "I'm talking about my love for you as a woman, and on earth sex is a part of the relationship. It gives a man and woman in love a way to express tenderness toward each other on a continuing basis."

"But it's a rather brief pleasure, isn't it?"

"Yes, but it has symbolic value. It testifies to the union of a man with a woman and excludes others from their union."

"On a planet with the variety earth offers, doesn't that exclusion get tedious?"

"In some marriages, yes. But if a man and woman truly love each other, the act of love becomes an expression of their intimacy, a sharing and an exploration."

"How much exploring can you do in such a limited area?" she asked, rhetorically, he hoped. "From the way your psychologists explained the mechanics to me, it's less a sharing than a borrowing and lending or a transfer."

"But the sensation is shared," he said, beginning to feel like a swimmer going under for the third time.

"Breedlove, are you telling me you'd take on all my problems for a tremor in the loins?"

"Kyra, you've got to be kidding. I know from the charge you put in your readings of Shakespeare you understand the concept."

"Yes." She nodded, sipping her wine meditatively. "Shakespeare got explicit on the subject. 'The expense of spirit in a waste of shame is lust in action,' and 'Shun the heaven that leads men to this hell.' I'd say he covered the subject pretty damned thoroughly."

Breedlove went under. "Then, I take it your answer is No."

"What was your question?"

He remembered then he had not asked the question, and he said, "Oh, hell. Forget it."

The waiter had brought their salad, and he turned his attention to the plate. But she would not let him be.

"Ben Bolt, you're frowning at sweet Alice. You know I'd do anything for you. If it's fornication you want, ask the waiter to clear the table."

"It isn't being done on tables. Not this year. With you I'd want a relationship that's dignified and permanent."

"If it's mating you're after, wait a few days, but it's not very dignified and never permanent Kanabian style. The consummation annuls the ceremony, and we she-things from Kanab don't go in for multiple small tremors. We hold back and let go with one big sensation to end all sensations, until the next summer."

She was laughing openly now, and the music was beginning. Smiling at her glee, he led her onto the floor, where all misunderstandings were forgotten in the keen aesthetic joy of movement. Dinner was served when they returned, and he hoped the meal would take the alcoholic glow from her mind. In the next conversational session he wanted to move straight to the subject.

Their main dish was a ragout prepared from a secret recipe handed down from Louis XIV, but for all the attention Breedlove paid it, it could have been corned beef hash. When he dabbed the last bit of sauce from his lips and laid his napkin aside, he assumed the mind-set of a businessman proposing a deal.

"I want to pose a hypothetical situation in detail, and I want you to listen carefully. Assume that you're grounded on earth and have to live among humans. Assume you choose the United States as your country of residence. Your easiest route to citizenship is through marriage. Suppose we married under the conditions you lay down, valid intimacies once a year, invalid intimacies whenever the table is cleared. Assume you had children by me as you say you can. You'd need a husband. Genetically, not all of our children would be capable of living off sunlight and vegetation. They would have to be housed, fed and clothed, educated and cared for. The function of the husband on earth is to provide for the family. Obviously our green-haired children would be different from other children, but all great men are different. Our children would stride the earth as princes of the realm, their green hair marking them as the sons of Kyra. As their mother you could be proud of their accomplishments, but as their father I would love them for themselves, even the ones who couldn't get their names in a telephone book."

He had her attention now, and he did not wish to lose it. "But above all, there is you. You've been too long a-roaming. It's time you quit playing the stray hound of heaven, sniffing the spoors of space for an oxygen planet, because you've found one, Kyra. You've come home, to me."

He lost the mind-set of a businessman when he saw the tears threatening her eyes. With a feeling of inner urgency he shifted to a more humorous tone. "I know you're responsible for the people on the meadow, but they too could find a home on earth. Flurea could easily get a job as a women's track coach in college. The big-breasted girls could make good money as topless waitresses in San Francisco, and they'd all find mates."

"Even Myra?" she asked.

"She'd make an ideal wife for some Yankee farmer who's trying to protect his acres from summer campers. You and I could raise Crick. There's enough ground around the cabin to grow his vegetables."

"A quarter acre of prime alfalfa ought to do it." She laughed, recovering now.

"After Crick's grown, if he's as potent as you say he is, we'll send him to Hollywood, where such things are appreciated, or to Texas, where they wouldn't be noticed."

"Oh, that," she said. "I was only trying to make a point, that there's not enough difference between men to point an admiring finger at. Our men have better manners on Kanab. With them it's a survival mechanism. But you would have been cherished on Kanab. I fell in love with you the first morning when you addressed me as 'ma'am.' And Crick would have no trouble adjusting to earth. The others would. Some are neuters and function only in relation to me. If you mated with me, Breedlove, you'd have a large family before you even said 'I do,' and you'd have to join us on the meadow. Our children would need the controlled environment the spaceship can provide. In fact, it's only a modified form of the ships we used on Kanab in our migrations."

"Oh, I could accept those terms," he said. "The ship's in commuting distance to my office. But we'd have to do something about Myra."

"She's neuter. If I had you around for protection, I could terminate Myra—hypothetically, of course."

"Then, hypothetically, you can accept my proposal of marriage?"

"This is not hypothetical, Breedlove. If I'm here this summer, you'll be the first to have my hand in marriage, if it's my hand you're after. But the music's playing."

Once more they danced, the orchestra playing lilting airs that reinforced his happiness. She had accepted his proposal if only on a contingency basis, but that contingency might materialize. At the finale of the set he whirled her into a pirouette that sent the hem of her skirt flying.

Because it was past eleven, he ordered after-dinner drinks and settled his account. Now they sat holding hands, and he had never known anyone who was so remote and enchanting yet with whom he felt so intimate and open. For the most part they were silent, waiting for the music to begin, when the orchestra returned for their final dance of the night. Finally, only to hear her voice, he said, "The situation may be hypothetical but the devotion is real. To me you're the equal of Guinevere, Deirdre, Helen, or any legendary beauty. You have of late a luminosity, an effulgence, like a halo of light."

"The luminosity is nature's way of making me attractive. As young earth girls are loaded with hormones to make their cheeks glow and eyes sparkle, my hormonal attraction is reinforced by stored sunlight." She smiled at a fancy that struck her. "You might say my sparkle is amplified by the stimulated emission of radiation. . . . But would you love me after my sunlight has turned inward to nourish other life? Will you love me when I'm pregnant as you love me when I'm lithe?"

"I'd be your most devoted midwife," he promised.

"If I didn't believe that," she said, "I would reject even your hypothetical proposal, but, dear Breedlove, hypothesis is all we have. I shall be leaving the earth by Tuesday."

"How do you figure that?"

"Ben promised me."

"Slade's not God!"

"Ben doesn't know that," she said, "and I'm certainly not going to be the one to tell him."

"You can't believe everything Slade says," he protested. "Look at his fable of Huan Chung. Where has that insidious Chinese been all evening?"

"I don't have complete faith in all Ben says," she admitted. "But I can extrapolate from past acts and arrange probabilities."

That she could do, he admitted. The brief appearance of the model at Mason's, imitating Kyra with a platinum wig and green eye lenses, had given her the idea that permitted them to abscond so easily from the motel. No doubt in her reading she had hit upon some other simple scheme for obtaining enriched uranium. Whatever the plan she had imparted to Slade this morning, it had given him a new lease on life and had, perhaps coincidentally, got rid of him for the evening, thus clearing the way for her escape scheme. Kyra's plots, he thought, interlocked like the pieces of—well—a Chinese puzzle, and he was sure she would not even consider a plan that did not offer a strong chance of success. By next Tuesday, he admitted to himself, she could indeed be lifting off from earth.

With the admission he felt a sinking sensation in the pit of his stomach, felt his spirits descending toward despair, and he blurted, "Kyra, I don't want to let you go!"

"It is I who must let you go, my best beloved, and I confess that it will be painful. I am a woman, but I have evolved from processes older than earth. I am a space seeder, the ultimate life bringer. Your race has the potential to join mine when your sun dies, but you are not ready yet. Still, my memories of earth and of you will be held sacred, and when the day comes, as surely it must, when your sons' sons must flee the wrack of once-beautiful earth, it is my hope that some may encounter in the far reaches of the universe brothers named Breedlove and sisters called Fawn."

"I'd rather have the woman and forgo the memorials."

"Don't press your offers too freely, Breedlove. Being what I am—and where and when—I might accept, and the pain of knowing you would sear my life. Leave earth I must, and if I'm to live in the legends of men I'd rather live as a Helen or an Isolde, not as Medusa."

Her remark carried nuances that cried for interpretation, but he was beyond nuances. "Could you take me with you? Could I survive?"

203

His sincerity caused her to smile, although her expression remained grave. "Probably you could endure outside your space-time continuum, but the probability is not for me to arrange. God knows, I'd like to roam the fields of heaven with gentle Breedlove by my side, but you belong to the forests of earth as I belonged to the woodlands of Kanab. The spaceways call me. My destiny is there. We are not sure of ever finding a habitation. We know only that if one awaits us it must be found. Could I exile my beloved into the darkness, the cold, and the vast uncertainty? Never! Yet, I can promise you this: before I leave earth I will let you know in all its intimacy and glory the love that only a Queen of Kanab may grant."

She intoned the promise with the solemnity of a proclamation, and as soon as the edict was issued the laughing girl had returned. "Now the music's playing, Breedlove, and I've saved the last dance for you."

As she had lifted a dejected Slade by the poolside, she lifted Breedlove's sadness with her promise. Leading her again onto the floor, he whirled her into a waltz, and they moved as lightly together as falling leaves. From his joy in her company and the tenderness he felt for her, he knew by any earthly definition he had found his love, and others on earth agreed. When the music ended and he escorted her from the restaurant, strangers smiled at them as they passed.

Outside, the stars seemed more glittering and less remote. Hand in hand they strolled toward the valet station, where Breedlove handed his claim ticket to the dispatcher, who called it over a public address system, and while they waited he and Kyra stood with arms around each other's waist. To a casual observer they might have been any boy and girl of earth engaging in the immemorial rites of spring, and Breedlove was so thrilled by her nearness he was almost pleased when he saw the valet bringing up the wrong car from the parking lot. As the driver leaped out to open the door, Breedlove turned to the dispatcher to inform him of the error, but the dispatcher had moved closer and was standing behind Breedlove, pressing a hard object into his ribs.

"That's a piece in your ribs, Breedlove. Don't reach for your beeper."

The smiling attendant, wearing a red jacket with a gold P embroidered on each lapel, continued to hold the door open and continued to smile as he said, "Step inside, Kyra, or we splatter your boyfriend's guts all over your Polinski Creation."

These men were not Oriental, but they knew that whatever powers Kyra might summon to her defense were immobilized by the threat to Breedlove.

Chapter Fourteen

————— ✳ —————

They knew his name and Kyra's and knew of her affection for the dress, but some things the men did not know. They did not know that Breedlove had a woodsman's skills and powers of observation. In the split second his attention shifted from Kyra to the man at the car door, he noticed the man held no weapon. Obviously the two considered him the key to Kyra's capture, a hostage to command her obedience. They did not know that with Kyra threatened any hostage became dispensable. They could not know that Breedlove could strip a tree of dead limbs by guiding a heavy-headed ax with the flick of one wrist, or that the beeper they feared had been left on his bedroom dresser, or that he was ticklish around the ribs and quick to anger at any invasion of his person or privacy. Lastly they did not know the isolated life he led permitted him to see few movies and that he did not know what a "piece" was. If the man had said "pistol," events might have gone differently, but as it was they moved so fast that witnesses later remembered the events in segments and pieced them together.

In irritation Breedlove's ax-handling hand chopped down against the wrist of the man who held the "piece." He heard the man's wrist snap and saw the pistol fly through the air, land on the pavement, and spin under a car parked ten yards away. He turned to Kyra, but she was gone, darting with the speed of dancing light among the parked cars and well out of harm's way. Glancing back to the man he had struck, Breedlove saw he was fleeing toward the street exit, holding his injured wrist.

Wheeling to contend with the man still holding the door, Breedlove heard a sound from behind like a stifled cough, and the man's head snapped back. Brain matter spurted from the back of the man's head and streaked the roof of the car. He slumped against the vehicle, slid down the side, and crumpled into a sitting position, his knees buckling and spreading apart, his head lolling downward.

Breedlove looked in the direction of the sound and saw Turpin step from behind a pine tree, holding a pistol with an elongated barrel in both hands and sighting it on the figure fleeing down the sidewalk. Again the weapon coughed. Twenty yards away the man stumbled, fell forward to the pavement, and slid a few feet on his face, still holding his wrist. He lay still.

Slade stepped from the shadows, holstered his pistol, and lighted a cigarette, and Turpin turned toward him, calling, "You see that, Ben? Twenty yards, a moving target, and just one shot."

"Typical of the FBI," Slade said, "shooting unarmed civilians in the back."

Then it had been Slade, Breedlove deduced, who had shot the unarmed civilian by the car in the face, and the deduction was borne out by Turpin, who turned to the older man and said, "Ben, I want credit for *both* of them. You've got enough notches on your gun."

"Then fire your pistol again, Turpin," Slade said. "You can't claim two with one shot."

In an absurd but stately ritual Turpin moved to the edge of the walkway and fired his pistol into the grass of the lawn. Exaltation showed on his face. At the same time Slade sauntered over to look down on the body by the car with a proprietary air. Dead, the man looked very young, Breedlove thought. Seated beside the car, knees spread, his wrists resting on his kneecaps, he seemed to be in deep thought. Had it not been for the hole in the back of his head, he might have looked up to speak to the man who killed him. A dark stain from his voided bladder spread over the crotch of his trousers.

"Who were they?" Breedlove asked.

"Corsicans. A French restaurant's an ideal cover for them."

"How did everyone know we were here?"

As if noticing him for the first time, Slade looked over at Breedlove, and the Texan's voice was edged with contempt. "When Lord Greystoke puts in a reservation at a French restaurant, the waiter gets suspicious. When Lord Greystoke pays the dinner check with a credit card issued to Thomas Breedlove on a coded State Department number, the number and location of the credit card gets to the credit center, fast."

Even so, Slade had moved quickly, and Breedlove wondered if he should thank the security man, decided any effusive statement of gratitude would be inappropriate in view of Slade's contempt and the bodies lying about, and started toward the parking lot to look for Kyra, but Slade called him back. "Stay where you are, Breedlove. You've done enough damage for one night. We'll find Kyra."

"I don't want her seeing this mess, and I don't want her here when the police come."

"She can't miss seeing the guy on the sidewalk. The police won't be here. Ten minutes after we're gone, the stiffs will be on their way to Corsica as a professional courtesy. Give Turpin your car keys. He'll bring your car. . . . Turpin, snoop around and listen for a thumping in a trunk. They stashed the parking attendants somewhere."

Turpin had taken the keys and gone when a green sedan pulled up on the inoffensive side of the parked car. Laudermilk was driving and Kyra was slumped in the rear seat. Breedlove got in and she huddled against him, her body trembling. He held her head against his shoulder and shielded her eyes from the form on the sidewalk as they drove by.

On the highway driving homeward, she straightened and leaned toward Slade, seated in front beside Laudermilk, and said, "Ben, I don't want you firing Fawn. I persuaded her to help us."

"So Fawn's the blonde in your bed." Slade looked back. "Lady, you know it's academic now whether she's fired or stays hired. Breedlove's the one I'd like to terminate—with extreme prejudice."

"He was just giving me a farewell party," Kyra said.

Slade fixed Breedlove with a hard, unwavering stare, and Breedlove dropped his eyes. He deserved the hostility. All along he had doubted Slade's credibility, and now Slade's fantasies had converged with reality.

Slade's voice lashed him. "I've got some good things and bad things to say about you, mister. First the good things: you've got the arms of a gibbon and the caution of a gorilla. Now, the bad things: as a security agent you'll never win the Allen Dulles Award, and that was the most harebrained caper I've ever heard of, although I reckon I should compliment you for not taking Kyra to a Chinese joint. Actually I ought to put you under protective custody, but I won't, because you've got me at a Mexican stand-off. I need your help. Tonight I'm putting in television monitors to cover every inch of that apartment, including the johns, and you'll have more bugs in there than a flat in Harlem."

Slade turned his gaze forward and sat in stony silence as Laudermilk steered onto the freeway. Breedlove was perplexed by Slade's reference to a Mexican stand-off. He had not consciously maneuvered the Texan into an impasse. And why was the firing or hiring of Fawn now academic?

His perplexity deepened when they pulled into the motel parking lot and Turpin's voice sounded in the car's radio, "Little Dick to Big Ben. I released the penned rabbits. The meat has been shipped. Delay conference until I get there."

"Wilco," Slade answered.

It was past midnight. Any conference at this hour would have to be a crisis meeting. Apparently some crash program was afoot to get Kyra off the planet, which would account for her confidence at dinner. Kyra's meeting with Slade at the pool this morning was probably the genesis of the late conference. Breedlove was beginning to feel like a puppet.

They entered the lobby and were moving toward the elevator when an agitated night clerk called from the check-out desk, "Mr. Slade, may I show you something?"

Slade went to the desk, where the night clerk opened the register and pointed. Slade's jaw tightened, his face set, his eyes narrowed, then inexplicably he grinned. Turning back to the group, he strode up and gave Breedlove a complimentary slap on the back.

"Son, you didn't intend it that way, but you've pulled off the security coup of the century. While you were out dancing with the dolly, Huan Chung hit the motel and found zilch. Mr. and Mrs. Huan Chung checked out of the bridal suite at midnight with no baggage."

Slade was elated and Breedlove was shaken, not by Kyra's narrow escape but by the implications of Huan Chung's visit. Kyra's theory had been wrong. The insidious Chinese was not Slade's creation. The center pole of Breedlove's lodge snapped, bringing his sense of reality crashing around him. First the incident at Pierre's, and now this. The insane world of Ben Slade was real.

"Don't look so horrified, Breedlove," Slade said. His tone was now convivial and consoling. "Signing the register is one of the fillips that make the little bastard famous. It's as much his calling card as a black lotus. He'll coil and strike again, but the next time he strikes, our fair visitor will be hauling it past Uranus." Slade paused for dramatic effect, lowered his voice, and said, "Tomorrow, we're springing Kyra."

Slade's consolation was the worst he could have offered Breedlove, and his casual air of triumph did little to mitigate Breedlove's sudden horror at the emptiness awaiting the woman he loved and the emptiness she would leave behind her.

"Does Washington know?"

"No, but I've got assurances from the highest sources that any successful attempt to rid the President of this hot potato without his knowledge will be appreciated."

"Those words sound familiar," Breedlove said as they stepped from the elevator.

Inside the suite Slade stalked to the balcony and told the two guards, "All right, you bums, you can knock off and go home. The woman you've been guarding all evening has been out painting the town."

Entering the room, the two guards looked at Kyra in amazement, and one hung back to apologize. "When we relieved the watch she was asleep in bed."

"Out!" Slade snapped.

"Aren't you being a little harsh, Ben?" Kyra asked. "After all, Fawn fooled you too."

"My anger was a put-on," Slade said. "I want their dismissal on the record for their own protection, and I want them out of hearing distance when we start talking. You'd better awaken your decoy and get her out too."

Kyra went into the bedroom to awaken Fawn and called, "Ben, come here!"

Panic in her voice brought Slade quickly to her side. Glancing into the bedroom, he doubled up with laughter, slapping his knees in appreciation of the comic scene inside. Behind Slade, Laudermilk glanced in and grinned. Turning to Breedlove, he said, "Huan Chung kidnapped the wrong woman."

It was no laughing matter to Breedlove. Fawn Davies was a friend and the sister of a friend. He walked to the door and looked in. Where Fawn had lain, the bedcovers were folded back to leave an expanse of white sheet. Centering the whiteness, so sinister it filled the room with its evil, lay a black-petaled lotus blossom.

Slowly he walked into the room, leaned over the bed, and picked up the bizarre flower. Apparently Fawn had offered no resistance. Nothing in the room indicated a struggle. Even the pillows were fluffed and neatly in place. Only the grotesque flower testified to the crime.

Actually it was not a black lotus, Breedlove noticed. It was a magnolia blossom whose stem had been dipped in ink, and the bloom had darkened itself through osmosis. But its menace as a symbol was not lessened, and Fawn Davies was gone.

He turned to Kyra, standing distraught at the foot of the bed. "If you're willing to take me with you off this crazy, mixed-up planet, I'm willing to go."

"What will they do to Fawn?" Kyra asked dully.

"Nothing." The emphatic answer came from Slade in

the doorway. "By now she's on Air China's midnight flight from Vancouver to Peking. He gave her a whiff of zombie gas to make her obedient to his commands. As soon as she's alert enough to answer his questions, he'll discover his error and she'll be on a return flight to Seattle, but by then she will have given us the breathing space we need. She'll never remember seeing him. He'll hypnotize her, give her posthypnotic suggestions, and when she steps off the plane Monday, she'll have a detailed memory of a weekend in Seattle."

"Huan Chung must have read *The Manchurian Candidate*," Breedlove commented.

"You might say he ghosted the book," Slade agreed. "It was based on facts he put into the CIA files."

"She'll be safe," Laudermilk said. "We never kill anyone but ourselves."

Breedlove wanted to believe them. Fawn Davies was on his conscience, as she was no doubt on Kyra's. He glanced toward Kyra, who nodded reassuringly, and her nod did more to relieve his anxiety than their assurances.

Slade slapped his hands together, rubbed his palms, and said, "Let's get the show on the road, boys. Graves, go down to my office and bring up the floor plans. Breedlove, help me set up the conference table."

Laudermilk left. Breedlove tossed the black magnolia blossom into Kyra's waste basket and turned to join Slade, when Kyra spoke: "Ben, Breedlove's tired and should be in bed. I've had him out dancing all night."

"If it concerns you, Kyra, I want in," Breedlove said.

"We're planning a bag job on a hospital," Slade said to him, "to heist enough radioactive cobalt to fuel Kyra's ship, and she's afraid if you know too much you can be indicted for conspiracy after she's gone. I told her this morning the conspiracy laws won't apply unless we're caught in the act. If we succeed, the caper becomes a part of Project Fair

Visitor and will be cloaked by national security."

"I've heard that song before," Breedlove said, thinking this could be a conspiracy directed at Kyra. "What assurance has Kyra that you're not setting her up for a jail cell to simplify your own security problem?"

"I'm Kyra's assurance," Dick Turpin said from the doorway. He had entered the suite unobserved. "Three of us will be going into the hospital, and if only one comes out it will be Kyra."

"But why are you taking Kyra in?"

"We're heisting the core from a cobalt-ray machine in the Seattle General Hospital's radiology lab," Turpin said, "and we need her to carry the bag with the nuclear shield. She can handle the cobalt, and a bag's less conspicuous when a woman carries it."

"There's little danger of our being apprehended," Slade said. "We're not Cuban patriots. We've been trained to make surreptitious entries. We'll be organized and we'll have the advantage of surprise. Who'd expect anyone to heist the core from a cobalt-ray machine?"

"Will cobalt do the job?" Breedlove asked Kyra.

"Better than uranium," she answered. "I researched the problem. I've been a nuclear physicist since Thursday."

"Then this is your plan?"

"It was my idea. The plan was set up by the Three Musketeers."

Meanwhile Laudermilk had returned and unrolled a set of plans onto the extended dining table. Breedlove moved over and looked down at the architectural drawing of a complex warren of corridors and compartments marked by dotted lines made with colored felt pencils. He glanced at the caption in the lower right corner of the drawing: BASEMENT FLOOR PLAN—SEATTLE GENERAL HOSPITAL.

"Where did this come from?"

"I stopped in at the Hall of Records this afternoon,"

Slade said, "and did a little one-man bag job on it."

Never having served in a war, Breedlove had never participated in a tactical planning session before where the high courage of each participant was taken for granted, where the risks were foreseen and planned for with such cold detachment and each perilous step outlined in detail. They seemed to have covered all the facets of a "hit" that would certainly be the most spectacular burglary in the history of breaking and entering. On Sunday the radiology laboratory of the hospital would be closed, and it would be guarded by a single security guard. Wearing a dark suit and carrying a briefcase, Slade would approach the basement clinic in company with Kyra and Turpin.

"Anyone walking down a hospital corridor with a brief-case and wearing a suit is assumed to be a doctor. Little Richard will wear a green smock and Kyra a nurse's uniform with a cape to conceal her figure from the interns on Sunday duty," Slade explained to Breedlove. "Dismantling the machine's simple if you have the right tools, which I'll carry in the briefcase. Actually the theft won't hold up the clinic's operation more than an hour Monday morning. The hospital will simply requisition another core."

Apparently Slade had even considered the moral aspects of the burglary. He continued briefing Breedlove, his voice carrying the peculiar élan of a man of action functioning in a role he liked best.

"After the hit you'll escort Kyra back to her ship, and she *must* be delivered. Once the core is in the spaceship, the heist goes under a security blanket and we're all home free. After Kyra's aloft, call Peterson on your walkie-talkie and report, 'The admiral is on the high seas.' I'll relay the word to Washington, and the book on Kyra will be closed—for the next one hundred years. Afterwards we'll all be recognized as heroes, posthumously."

No deviation from the motel's security schedule would occur until after dinner Sunday evening. Then Breedlove would take his hired car back to the rental agency, and at 8:32 he would stand on the sidewalk before the agency, where he would be picked up by Turpin, who would be driving a car stolen from the commuter parking area at the airport.

Breedlove would drive Turpin to the hospital and return to the motel, where he would find Kyra waiting on the sidewalk in a nurse's uniform. She would be under the covert surveillance of Laudermilk while waiting. "In the vernacular," Laudermilk commented, "I'll be crouched in the shrubbery, prepared to waste any masher who tries too hard to pick up Kyra."

Breedlove would drive her to the hospital, which she would enter alone, meet her confederates in the cafeteria, and from there they would descend to the basement clinic. After the cobalt was lifted, all four would drive to the airport, where Breedlove would park the car in the slot from which it had been stolen and board the eleven-thirty flight to Spokane.

"From the Seattle airport on she'll be your responsibility," Slade told Breedlove, "and you'll be unarmed, since you can't get past the air passengers' checkpoint carrying metal. We'll reserve a Jeep for you at the rental agency in Spokane. Now show me your route to Jones Meadow."

On a road map Breedlove pointed out the shortest way to the area which avoided the ranger station: along Route 2 to Priest River, due north through the Kaniksu Forest, then east along an old sawmill road over the mountains and into the meadow from the west. It would be wrong, they agreed, to implicate Peterson before the plot was an accomplished fact, and the regulations-conscious chief ranger might conceivably imperil the mission before Kyra's liftoff.

Breedlove's estimated time of arrival at the space vehicle was nine Monday morning.

Each man on the strike force was assigned the task that best matched his skills, and Laudermilk's role, though the least risky, impressed Breedlove most. On early Sunday afternoon the major was to date a nurse he had met at the Navy clinic, a woman whose proportions were similar to Kyra's, and persuade her to lend him her uniform, cape, and identity papers to be used in Kyra's cover. Laudermilk was to bring the uniform to Kyra's suite and take over the interior guard duties from Breedlove while Breedlove drove downtown to return his rented car and pick up the new one from Turpin.

It was two in the morning before the conference broke up, and each participant knew precisely what he was to be doing tomorrow, at precisely what time. Exhausted by an evening of joy and tenderness, violence and sudden death, the kidnapping of a friend and the planning of a burglary, Breedlove went immediately to bed and quickly to sleep to arise to a bright Sunday morning, which was nonetheless gloomy because of Kyra's imminent departure.

At breakfast Kyra comforted him with aphorisms: "Leave-takings are always sad, Breedlove, because life's great beauty lies in its ephemerality. Else we'd prefer wax flowers to real roses." And, "Never envy the romantic hero, Breedlove, because he is the paragon of the average, seeking the happiest means to please both Polly and Patty."

After breakfast, telling Breedlove she wanted to bid her guardsmen good-bye, Kyra called Turpin on the house phone and invited him to meet her at the poolside. Then, wearing her bikini, she dove from the balcony for the last time. Breedlove took the Sunday paper onto the balcony, now divested of guards, but he could not read. His gaze kept drifting to Turpin and Kyra, below and across the pool, who were lounging in adjacent patio chairs. Turpin leaned toward her and listened to her last words to him with reverence. After a quarter-hour she touched her fingers to his lips in some private ritual of farewell, and Turpin arose and left her.

Apparently he carried a summons to Laudermilk, who came in turn for his final private meeting with Kyra, and the major's usual exuberance had been replaced by an air of gravity. Unlike Turpin, Laudermilk talked more than he listened, and the always gracious Kyra was attentive to his words. Finally she put her fingers to his lips, and Laudermilk arose and left her.

Slade came last, bringing with him a restlessness and unease, but his disquiet left him as he talked with her, and he was smiling at the end of his audience. After Slade arose and left her, the strange devotionals were over, and Breedlove wondered what each man in his turn had heard her say.

"I have bidden them all a formal farewell" was all the information Kyra volunteered when she returned, "but I'm saving my farewell to you for tomorrow on the meadow."

Her promise lightened the gloom of the day and made Sunday's long prospect brighter. Expectancy softened the Sunday *tristesse* that habitually came to him at twilight, and Kyra's last dinner arrived in an atmosphere of sorrow touched with joy. Not a man at the table wanted to see her go, but the goal they had all worked for was soon to be achieved. Characteristically Turpin put the dinner in a religious context. From this Last Supper, he averred, would come no Crucifixion. Kyra would go straight to the Ascension, for this time the disciples would confound the Pharisees. But the ever-cautious Breedlove wondered if a Judas sat at the table.

None of the tension Breedlove expected pervaded a group intent on committing a crime that very evening whose scope and novelty would put it on the front pages of the world's newspapers. Though the monolithic pile of the Seattle General Hospital loomed large in Breedlove's thoughts, his companions seemed intent only on Kyra.

Slade was optimistic about Kyra's chances of finding a home. "The Rand Corporation estimates six hundred million habitable planets in the Milky Way alone, and that's in spitting distance for you."

"If there's any real estate out there," Kyra promised, "I'll find it."

Although he made an effort to fall in with the mood at the table, Breedlove felt a growing apprehension about the burglarizing of the radiology laboratory. Why had Slade insisted on Kyra entering the basement of the building? Because the exits from it were limited? This afternoon Laudermilk had successfully charmed the panties, bra, and uniform off a Navy nurse for Kyra's use; why had he not charmed the nurse into going all the way and doing the job for Kyra? It was true that Kyra might have more savvy about handling the cobalt and getting the core into the sphere, but Turpin would have done it for her with his bare hands. Why hadn't Slade recruited one of his black-belt holders from the kitchen or scullery to play the feminine role in this caper?

Even apart from Kyra, for every reason Breedlove could summon to justify these three men's actions in taking part in an illegal scheme, he could think of a better reason why they shouldn't. All three were government agents and sensitive to their careers, which were being jeopardized by this act. On the other hand, they were intelligent game players who could spot the promotional advantages that would accrue from the betrayal of their own kind.

Kyra sensed his trepidations. After dinner they sat on the balcony alone together, waiting for Laudermilk to bring in Kyra's uniform and to take over the interior watch on her while Breedlove delivered his car to the rental agency. It was then Kyra remarked, "Don't worry about anything, Breedlove. Once I have the cobalt in the bag, it's mine. You know I can outrun anyone on earth, and I have you to rely on."

She spoke the truth. He had seen her darting among the parked cars after he had broken the Corsican's wrist. And she had Turpin too. His loyalty to her was maniacal. If Slade was trying to get her jailed to make his security tasks easier, he would not be around long enough to guard her. Turpin would see to that.

At eight o'clock Laudermilk arrived to relieve the watch, bringing Kyra's uniform freshly pressed and starched. Before taking his suitcase to the car, Breedlove stood looking around him, trying to remember the room as it was now with the books, the bookcase, and with Kyra seated on the sofa, reading, with the light throwing a halo around her hair.

Laudermilk interrupted his reveries.

"Wear these when you're driving the hot car," he said, handing Breedlove a pair of silk gloves. "You won't leave prints."

Breedlove pocketed the gloves, lifted his suitcase, and left the room.

An overcast had rolled in from the ocean by the time he had driven into downtown Seattle. The low-hanging clouds sopped up the city lights, and the few pedestrians abroad on the Sunday-night sidewalks scurried from streetlamp to streetlamp. He parked behind the rental agency, took his bags into the office, and settled his account. At 8:32 he stood outside on the sidewalk with his bags and wearing his silk gloves. At 8:32 a dark-colored sedan pulled up at the curb, and Turpin swung around from the driver's side.

"Throw your bags in the back seat. You drive."

As Breedlove complied, Turpin took a small walkie-talkie

from his coat pocket, extended its antenna, and spoke into it, saying, "Checkpoint able, all clear."

Breedlove was under the wheel when Turpin took his seat, closed the door, and handed the ranger an envelope. "Your tickets, confirmed, on the eleven-thirty flight to Spokane. The car belongs to a man who's spending the weekend in San Francisco."

As he pulled away from the curb, Breedlove said to the one agent who had his complete confidence, "Dick, there are elements to this plan I don't like. Technically, you know, we're committing treason."

"Technically Christ was a criminal."

"But Christ had no earthly ambitions."

Turpin caught the thrust of his remarks and said, "Don't worry about Slade. Kyra and I discussed that matter this morning, and all possibilities have been provided for."

So the possibility of betrayal had occurred to Kyra early, and she had been ordering probabilities since this morning. Suddenly invigorated, Breedlove dropped Turpin off at the hospital with a cheerful "Good luck." Caught up now in the spirit of the enterprise, he was eager for the night's adventure, with an eagerness that mildly alarmed him; he was beginning to enjoy his temporary job as an undercover agent.

Everything was moving with precision. Very probably the car he drove would never be reported as stolen. At most its owner might think that someone had siphoned his gas tank. Laudermilk had got the uniform and identification for Kyra with no trouble, and the first checkpoint had been passed on schedule. He reached checkpoint baker exactly on schedule. At 9:02 he turned the corner at the intersection near the motel and saw Kyra under the streetlamp, looking pert and efficient in her cape and nurse's cap. Somewhere in the shrubbery behind her Laudermilk crouched with his pistol at the ready.

Breedlove pulled up, threw open the door, and called, "May I give you a lift, ma'am?"

"Ma'am" was a code word to reassure the watcher in the bushes. Slade had figured no masher would use that term of address. Kyra slid into the seat beside him, and he continued the charade with a "Where to, ma'am?"

But for Kyra the fun and games were over—he could tell from the insistence in her voice.

"Move fast, Breedlove. Go directly to the airport. Slade's setting a trap for me. The hospital's swarming with police, and there's nothing Turpin can do about it but kill Slade and I don't want that to happen—for Little Richard's sake."

She was talking fast, without equivocations, and he knew she was telling the truth. What a comment this, he thought with a sinking heart, on the loyalty and trustworthiness of human beings. "How'd you find this out?"

"Gravy told me. Ben enlisted his aid, figuring an Army career man due for promotion in two weeks wouldn't jeopardize his job with treason, but it wasn't really Ben's fault. His pride was hurt. He found out that my petition was going to be rejected after all his promises, and that your government was going to keep me from my people on the meadow. Your biologists knew I was helpless without them. Slade was leading us to the hospital's morgue, not its radiology lab, and karate experts would have been there waiting for Little Richard. We'll have time to get on the ten o'clock flight to Spokane before Ben is alerted to the fact that I'm not coming at all. Gravy bought our tickets. We'll be traveling first class as Mr. and Mrs. Paige, spelled with an *i*."

"I can get you back to the meadow, but where do you go from there?"

"Straight up. I have the cobalt in my bag. Gravy's girl friend, the Navy nurse, was a radiology technician at the clinic, and she requisitioned the cobalt this afternoon and gave it to Gravy. It was that easy! Gravy said the only person to get sacked for his bag job was the bag he had to sack to get the cobalt.''

As she spoke she squirmed out of the cape and took off the nurse's bonnet. Beneath the cape she was wearing the Polinski Creation.

Chapter Fifteen

————— ✳ —————

From the Seattle airport the jet rose above the murk and climbed into starlight, rustling eastward. Breedlove ordered the free martinis that came with their seats, saying, "Figuring the surcharge for first-class fares, these drinks cost Laudermilk twenty dollars apiece."

Sprawled on the seat beside him, Kyra said sleepily, "He always wanted to give me something to remember him by. Maybe this is it." She stretched and yawned. "I'll remember him, and all the men of earth, with kindness."

"Even Slade?"

"Particularly Ben. He was almost hysterical with relief when he found that Fawn instead of me had been kidnapped. . . . Maybe Fawn and I overdid the Huan Chung business."

"What Huan Chung business?"

Fixing him with a lazy smile, she said, "Fawn wasn't kidnapped. She slipped away for a weekend on the Quinault Reservation. It was she who signed Huan Chung's name to the register while the night clerk was gone to the men's room. I wanted to impress Ben with the danger to me to reinforce the appeal I had made to him earlier."

"You fooled me," Breedlove admitted. "Up to then I thought Huan Chung was only one of Slade's fantasies."

"Maybe it was, up to then. After that, we had Ben believing in his own creation. . . . Aren't the stars beautiful? Just think, tomorrow I'll be out there among them."

Her comment carried no note of anxiety, only wonder. Seemingly indifferent to the fate awaiting her, she leaned her head against his shoulder and fell instantly to sleep. It seemed to Breedlove her head had lain there only a minute before the cabin began to creak from decompression and the warning light began to flash. He fastened her seat belt without awakening her and heard the clunk of distending landing gear. She continued to sleep as they touched down and taxied toward the terminal, and in her profound sleep the luminosity seemed drained from her. When the jets ceased to rumble and the cabin doors were opened, she awakened torpidly to his repeated urgings.

No one opposed their entrance into the waiting room, where he went immediately to a telephone booth and called his father. He had decided not to attempt to rent a vehicle at the airport. By now Slade would realize that they were gone and would begin to make his moves to apprehend them. There would have to be no easily obtained description of the vehicle Breedlove was driving.

His father answered the phone, and Breedlove explained his situation in general terms, asked his father to have the farm Jeep gassed and waiting, and requested that his mother lay out one of his ranger uniforms. It was a short call, and Kyra waited outside the booth, slouched drowsily against a wall, the bag hanging nonchalantly from her shoulder. When he told her his family would be waiting to greet her, she smiled wanly. In the bright light of the waiting room her face looked chalky, and as she walked beside him to the luggage counter he noticed her usually bouncing stride had become languid and flowing.

Apprehensive and tense himself, it occurred to him that her apathy might be feigned to steady him, as a general might feign confidence to strengthen the morale of his soldiers. Certainly nothing about the semideserted Sunday-night airport looked sinister, but there had been nothing suspicious-looking, he reminded himself, outside Pierre's restaurant when the Corsicans struck.

He lugged his suitcase to the taxi stand and tapped on the windshield of a cab to awaken its driver. As the cabbie was stowing Breedlove's suitcase in the car's trunk, the public announcement speaker rasped, "Will Ranger Thomas Breedlove take a personal and urgent telephone call in the manager's office. . . . Will Ranger Thomas Breedlove . . ."

The squawk box kept repeating the announcement in mechanical desperation as the cab pulled away and headed for the highway. Slade was acting out of character, Breedlove thought; he had committed a gross violation of security procedures by letting his quarry know that the chase had begun.

In the interval of her absence the strangeness of Kyra's arrival on earth had been absorbed by Breedlove's family, but the wonder of her had grown in the telling. When she came again into the Breedlove living room, she came as an embodied myth. The welcome she received was touched with awe but with genuine devotion the greater part of it, and in the presence of the Breedloves she bestirred herself from her languor. She gave Breedlove's mother the diamond she had bought in Seattle and told them, with an assurance that Breedlove questioned, that Slade would

send them her books, for Breedlove, and her clothes for
Matty.

Since she needed something to carry the cobalt in, she
exchanged Matty's denim book satchel for her shoulder
bag, because Matty was still undecided about what career
she should follow.

"Go to college and study chemistry," Kyra counseled
her, "then analyze the fabric in this shoulder bag and you'll
make a killing in textiles."

None of the Breedloves hesitated in accepting her gifts.
They knew of her destination, and her beneficence was too
queenly to affront with hollow protestations. They went
with her and Breedlove, now back in uniform, to the front
porch to stand in the porchlight and wave good-bye. As
they got into the Jeep, the telephone rang, and Mr. Breedlove went to answer it.

"Get moving," Kyra commanded. "That's Ben calling."

Breedlove gunned the Jeep in response to the urgency in
her voice even as he wondered why Slade should call his
home. Did the Texan expect his father to arrest him? . . . As
he swung onto the road, heading north, Breedlove saw his
father emerge from the house, waving for them to return,
but he pressed the accelerator to the floorboard. Darkness
whipped by them in a sibilance of wind past the windshield as the Jeep rocketed forward.

As he drove, Breedlove began a cat-and-mouse game in
his mind, figuring and countering the probable moves of
his pursuers, as Kyra, beside him, fell asleep in a sitting
position. Without compromising the secrecy surrounding
Kyra, Slade could enlist the aid of the State Highway Patrol
by making Breedlove the object of his search. Slade by now
had learned from his father that he was wearing his
ranger's uniform and driving a Jeep, and Slade's orders
would be to pick him up and hold his companion for
questioning. The patrolmen on Route 2 between Spokane

and Newport would be alerted and the bridge over the Pend Oreille blocked.

But at the junction Breedlove swung northwest on Route 395 to Deer Park, then drove due east past sleeping farms and rejoined Route 2 near Milan, thus avoiding a major segment of a highway he took to be dangerous. A few miles north, he took 6B due north, bypassing Newport, and joined Route 6 on the west bank of the Pend Oreille. Even with his early start the longer route would prevent him from reaching the meadow until after sunrise, but no one would expect him to enter the Selkirk area from the north.

At 2:00 a.m. he crossed the river at Metaline Falls and took the gravel road across the mountains, breathing easier as he swung from the pavement to head east, now at fifty miles an hour. Despite the jouncing, Kyra still dozed erect beside him. At 3:30 he circled Helmer Mountain and edged into Canada along a five-mile stretch of road. When the road became macadam he was back in the States and a few miles west of Porthill, Idaho, but three miles from Porthill he swung south onto an old sawmill road, with Kyra still asleep beside him.

A chuckhole made him reach over to steady her and she awakened, muttering, "I feel dawn coming."

"It is," he said. "But we should be in Jones Meadow in another hour."

Constantly shifting gears and maneuvering, he drove the vehicle on a climbing, twisting course along the overgrown road, and the trees beside the trail reflected the increasing altitude, growing stunted, then twisted, then sparse. Pale gray was tingeing the east as the vehicle jolted toward Sawyer's Summit, and when they trundled over the shale near the crest, the dawn of a cloudless day was breaking.

Kyra awakened, saying, "Look at the glorious morning 'flatter the mountain-tops with sovereign eye'!"

"Yes," he agreed, "and I need all the light I can get. It's

easy to lose your bearings on this lunar landscape."

Craning above the windshield, she ranged her ears in the manner of a blind person and said, "Go that way," pointing. "Myra has set the howler going."

"To guide you home?"

"No. To lure Crick home. He has run away. Well, you can have him, Breedlove, if you can catch him, because I'm leaving without him."

"That's a cold way of dismissing the boy," Breedlove complained.

"He's only a male we don't need any more. He likes it here, and he's incapable of altering life on earth. He's intelligent, and he'll learn your language quickly, I'm sure. Look around for him next winter. If a cold snap hits he'll hibernate, and it should be easy to spot his green hair against the snow."

Nothing she said about the lost boy was unkind, but her detachment, if he chose to be hypercritical, might indicate she was fast losing her acquired human traits even as she seemed to be losing her human coloration. Perhaps it was a survival mechanism, this objectivity, or perhaps fatigue from the long night drive had altered his own sensibilities. After all, he couldn't expect her to rend her hair and pound her breasts in lamentation over a child who had found what he sought, sanctuary on a friendly planet. Still, he thought it inappropriate that she should forget Crick altogether and call his attention to a flowering plant struggling from a crack in a granite wall with a "Look, Breedlove! How pretty."

Below the rocky saddleback he crossed a swath of meadow, rolled over underbrush, and canted onto a pack trail wide enough for his vehicle. At six o'clock, in bright morning light, he drove onto Jones Meadow. The turf was dry now and as closely cropped as a fresh-mown lawn except for tufts of wire grass her people had left him for scouring his pans. He wheeled the Jeep to a stop in the bend of the creek a hundred yards downstream from the willow.

She was safe. No jet planes whined through the sky. No helicopters hovered over the surrounding peaks. Across the creek in the aspen grove the invisible needle of her space vehicle towered above them. Gazing around him at the peaceful scene, Breedlove felt the strong impression that he and Kyra had fled from pursuers existing only in their imagination.

She swung from the Jeep and leaned against the fender to remove her shoes, then to his mild astonishment she continued to undress, slipping out of her dress, unstrapping her bra, and folding the garments on the seat beside him. Finally, naked in the sunlight, she stood beside the vehicle in which he sat, transfixed, and apologized, "You know, Breedlove, I've been around you human beings for so long I feel self-conscious about undressing in front of you."

"We've made you lose your innocence."

"If I ever had any"—she smiled—"I'd be losing it from the way you're looking at me now.... I'm sorry I can't invite you in. With Crick gone the mood inside will be foul. It'll take me only a few minutes to hook in the cobalt and wash this goop out of my hair. I'd like to tell you good-bye as I was when we met and on the mound where I found you. We'll have time together while the steam pressure builds in the propulsion unit. All I'm taking from earth is the Bulfinch and Polinski. You can take my shoes and undergarments to Matty, or keep them, or donate them to a museum."

She put the folded dress into the satchel, turned, and was gone, fording the creek in long bounds. Without glancing back, she disappeared into the aspen grove, leaving her undergarments, hosiery, and shoes on the seat beside him. He drove the vehicle upstream, parked it beneath a cluster of alder bushes, and walked to the mound. Arms folded across his chest, Breedlove stood looking out over the scene and thinking.

Away from Kyra, his mind began to function with its usual clarity, and he found himself wondering why Slade had telephoned him, first at the airport and then at home. The calls had been such gross violations of security procedures they did not fit Slade—unless they were the spontaneous reactions of an innocent man. Besides, if Slade had wanted Kyra in jail, he would have needed no byzantine hospital bag job to entrap her on a conspiracy charge; he could have simply placed her in a jail cell on his own authority. Slade was a melodramatic actor and fantasist, but he was no cretin. And if he had been cooperating with authorities who wanted Kyra kept away from her people, the skies above the meadow would be crowded with helicopters from the Air Force, waiting to sight his Jeep.

Something had gone askew in Seattle, he decided, and if it wasn't Ben Slade it would have to be Thomas Breedlove. A horseback theorist might assume he had been manipulated—by one who artfully understood every human being's basic need for a Huan Chung.

Yet he could not bring himself to accuse Kyra of supplying his imagination with a handy villain to spur him in their flight, despite elements that pointed to her doing so. There would have been no need for Slade to pursue them if he truly wanted to assist Kyra off the planet—especially after he discovered that Laudermilk had furnished her with the cobalt—and obviously there had been no massive pursuit. Slade knew their destination and their estimated time of arrival, although Breedlove had made better time than he expected in racing from the imagined pursuit.

He had never questioned Kyra's assertion that they *were* being pursued. From the moment she entered the car in

Seattle he had responded to her anxieties as a programmed automaton, but in the beginning at least her fears had seemed real. Only later had she grown apathetic, and her torpor could have been an emotional reaction to released tensions. Obviously she believed Laudermilk, but what if Laudermilk had lied to her? The idea seemed far-fetched; the major had no reason to slander his comrade Slade.

Hunkered down, chewing a blade of grass, cogitating, he saw Kyra emerge from the creek near the willow, drifting as lightly as a sunbeam over the close-cropped grass. He remained crouched as if impaled on the vision of her beauty and renewed strangeness, for her skin was again birch silver and her hair green. In her unadorned simplicity she was as self-complete as a flower or a tree, and it occurred to him that he was looking upon the ideal beauty men had sought since the beginning of human imagination.

As she moved toward him she gathered the sunlight and became an embodied radiance, feminine and sensuous yet so ethereal she might have swum in air. Nearing the mound, she flung herself into a pirouette, swirling on tiptoe, spine arched, head back, arms extended, displaying the harmonies of her form in exuberant glee. Sunbeams swirled around her, and she began to sing in the liltings of her own language a song as blithe as darting swallows and gamboling colts.

Even at the distance her magic touched his imagination, creating the overpowering ambience of quintessential springs yearning toward fruited summers. He stood, feeling as vital and as fresh as one awakening to his first morning in some Edenic forest. Near him, she ceased the swirling and singing and walked toward him, smiling and regal, her hands extended for him to take.

"Now, Breedlove, I must take leave of my dearest votary. Kneel."

It was a queen commanding him, and he obeyed, kneeling before her as a knight swearing fealty, and again he felt her weird duality as a living presence and as a legend. She placed his hands lightly on her hips and placed her palms on his temples, tilting his face toward hers as she drew him closer. She smelled of violets.

"Come with me, Breedlove. Follow. Follow."

Looking into her eyes, he saw through them into a universe of pellucid green light. The light drew him into a vast hemisphere centered by the whorl of a sun, and he felt himself levitating to her. "Come, my best beloved, follow, follow."

Ascending faster in tightening spirals, his psyche rose through the green empyrean toward the distant sun. He was undergoing a transfiguration, becoming a soaring phallic angel, God's ultimate drone. The dichotomies of his flesh and spirit were merging into one consummate whole, the parallel lines of his nature meeting in a green interior space. Plunging upward toward creation's fiery womb, he failed to hear the humming in the sky as the park's helicopter cleared Hallman's Peak.

At that moment he touched the perimeter of the sun. Into its dazzling core his psyche plunged. Sheathed in Kyra's radiance, knowing creation's keenest quivering thrust, of a sudden he held summer in his hands. It bathed him in its eternal glow. If death had claimed him then, he would have died replete, but a melodramatic voice, amplified by the crowd-control speaker on Peterson's helicopter—Slade's voice—blasting over the meadow and rumbling among the hills, shattered the moment's sublimity.

"GET AWAY FROM THAT SHE-THING, BREEDLOVE! IT'S THE HARLOT OF EDEN. IT'S LILITH."

Kyra dropped her hands from his temples to glance upward, and with the breaking of her touch the spell was broken. Gone was the pale green empyrean and the splen-

233

did sun. She stepped back, gave the Kanabian curtsy, and with a dancer's whirl, turned away from him; smiling back over her shoulder at him, she was queen no longer, but the bright, gleeful girl he had first met on the meadow.

"I've got to get the hell out of here, Breedlove. As you say on earth, 'Business before pleasure.' "

Laughing, she sped from him across the meadow with the flashing, sunbeam speed no man could equal, and the helicopter swung around and down to herd her toward the aspen grove. With four bounds she cleared the creek at an angle, dashing toward the trees. Her last gesture to humankind was to wave the helicopter away, pointing toward the invisible spaceship towering above the forest.

At the helicopter's controls, Peterson remembered and understood her gesture, and Peterson's voice over the loudspeaker was the last human voice she heard, saying, "Good luck, Kyra, and happy hunting."

Peterson veered the machine and circled back toward the mound, settling toward the grass a few yards from where Breedlove stood, arms folded, watching the last flash of silver and green vanish amid the aspen boles. Peterson was right. She was not Lilith, not Merope, but Kyra.

What had happened to him on the mound, Breedlove decided, was simple yet inexpressibly complex. She had opened a door. He had stepped through it to gain an understanding of immortality with a mortal's finite mind. For a moment only they had shared a love, but now he knew, as she had always known, that love was eternal, for in that moment he had shared the immortal love of an angel.

Running at a crouch from underneath the rotor blades, Slade made for the mound as the vanes whirred into silence.

"Where's her vehicle?"

Breedlove pointed toward the aspens. "Over there."

"She killed Laudermilk last night," Slade said. "She

234

emasculated him root and branch. He died of ecstasy, shock, and blood loss, in that order.''

''She didn't kill him,'' Breedlove contradicted. ''He killed himself.''

Slade looked at him sharply and said, ''That's what Turpin said, but Turpin claimed it was divine retribution for Laudermilk's carnal ways.''

Breedlove looked toward the helicopter, saw only Peterson emerging, and asked, ''Where's Turpin?''

''He had to go back into Seattle General, for psychiatric observation. He thinks that through Kyra he's walked and talked with God.''

Peterson walked onto the mound, his hand extended to Breedlove, and said, ''Welcome back, Tom.''

''Thanks, Pete. I'm ready to resume duty.''

''Good. Your first assignment is to get that Jeep out of the wilderness area. What's holding up the girl?''

''She's building up steam for liftoff,'' Breedlove said.

''That's only part of what she's doing,'' Slade said. ''She's also strapping herself to that slant board, bottom up, and hooking a lot of wires to her lower abdomen.''

Slade's remark suggested an interesting and involved theory, another of the Texan's specialties, but at the moment Breedlove was not encouraging any dramatic monologue from Slade. The three men stood quietly, looking toward the aspen grove and waiting.

They did not wait long. Although they were mentally prepared for what they would see, when it came, shaking the earth with a seismic roll, the sight was mind wrenching.

First the noise, an instantaneous crack and roll of thunder as if the safety valve on a Titan's boiler had burst, not with a hiss of steam but a roar like Niagara's. Billowing from the aspen grove, compressed by its invisible weight, a white cloud of condensing steam rolled across the meadow, and even in his awe Breedlove understood why Kyra wanted him on the mound, to keep him beyond the perimeter of the scalding blast. He saw the aspen tops bend from the blast, clacking outward in frenzy. From the center of the grove, slowly at first, a truncated column of steam arose. Then it extended upward in a whiplash of motion whose G forces would have crushed any human occupant of the ship that rode the column, and Kyra ascended.

Terrifying but beautiful, the column of pristine white hurled itself into the cloudless sky, arcing above them from the earth's rotation and conveying a sense of arctic chill to the expanse of blue. In silence the three men stood gazing up at the attenuated white cloud as the warm rain of its condensation drifted against their faces. Silently Breedlove formed a prayer to the God of Exiles to see Kyra to a haven.

Slade broke the silence, saying, "So ends, let us hope, Project Fair Visitor. But remember, gentlemen, it still remains top secret. The world's not ready for this one."

"You don't have to worry about *me* telling anyone," Peterson said, and perceptive as usual, Slade understood the chief ranger's emphasis.

"Kyra got you off the hook on your little-green-man report. We used it to authenticate our records. . . . If you don't mind, Chief, I'd like a private word with your boy here before we leave him to his Jeep."

Peterson nodded and walked back to the helicopter, and Breedlove turned to Slade. "Did you come here to stop Kyra?"

"Not to stop her. To warn you. I had lost one of my boys, and I didn't want to lose another. Not that I grieve much for Laudermilk. His number was up anyhow, and Kyra gave him what all military men want—a glorious death."

"What happened to Laudermilk?"

"Breedlove, I'll tell you true. I reckon you figured me for project chief, and I knew the whole picture. Laudermilk didn't. On a need-to-know basis, Kyra's anatomy was no concern of his. Theoretically she was off-limits to him because his orders were specific, no hanky-panky, but Kyra was all woman. She had more Fallopian tubes than a telephone exchange has cables, with multiple clusters of quick-ovulating wombs designed to produce embryos only. As far as that went, she was safe enough, but with Kyra what went up did not necessarily have to come down. To insure the fertilization of her multiple womb system she had a vagina like a snapping turtle. Of course some of the medical boys gossiped about Kyra's 'snapper,' some nurses overheard, and Laudermilk got the rumors from the nurse he dated. Putting two and two together, he came up with five. He figured Kyra was a snapper like the stars in his fold-out gallery."

Slade shook his head sadly and continued: "Thinking like that, Laudermilk wasn't about to be stopped by an order. He heisted the cobalt from the Navy clinic and used it to dicker with Kyra. No doubt he supported his offer with some tale of treachery on my part. He wanted to bring her here, reasoning as you did that I wouldn't follow, but she didn't want to come with him, apparently. For that task, she wanted you. It wasn't that she didn't like Laudermilk, it was that she didn't trust him.

"What Laudermilk didn't know—hell, you didn't know it and you'd been inside—was that Kyra's spaceship was a beehive. Doctor Upton, the entomologist, figured it out. The ship was a brooder. The pipes carried the embryos from the queen bee to the brooder cells, where they were nurtured through the fetal stages. The slanted gravity couch was designed to use G forces to ram home the seminal charge through the network of womb ducts. Our computers verified the ship's layout, and the computers were verified last Saturday by a green-haired male juvenile picked up by the sheriff of Shoshone County. The boy had defected because he did not want to play the role of sacrificial lamb in Kyra's operation.

"Meanwhile, back in Seattle, along comes Laudermilk offering Kyra instant cobalt on the spot for a price, probably backing it up with a tale to make Kyra believe she is trapped. He knows she's got to go. He knows she's going. But Laudermilk's got his record to think about, and Kyra is his chance for immortality in the hall of records. So he persuaded her, never knowing that she was the queen bee and that the drone that couples with the queen bee loses his coupling gear. I've got the strong idea that if Peterson and I had got here five minutes later, you'd be stretched out here with the same grin on your face that Laudermilk had when he expired. Anyhow, Laudermilk set a record that'll never be touched, but too bad it's classified top secret. He'll never even get to enjoy it posthumously."

Breedlove listened, neither believing nor disbelieving Slade's story. At most points it agreed with the facts he possessed. Laudermilk had bought the first-class tickets for himself and Kyra, no doubt hoping for a second session on the meadow, and he had concocted the tale of Slade's treachery. But there was a logical flaw in Slade's telling of the tale.

"I have a low-grade security clearance," Breedlove reminded him. "If what you say is true, and if the project is still top secret, why are you telling me all this?"

"I'm clearing you for the total picture for a reason. There's a possibility that Laudermilk's advances were not accepted under duress. He might have been her first choice as a drone, because she knew that once the colony was ready to swarm it would have to settle. Earth was the only habitable planet she had found, and it was populated. If she has to settle on an inhabited planet, she'll need a warrior brood, and Laudermilk was a warrior.

"We figure there's a good chance she won't leave the

solar system, that she'll hang out there in orbit waiting for her brood to develop. The hive has a capacity for an estimated 21,000 babies, and she's packed with enough spermatozoa to cull all but the green-haired males. With the forced-growth methods she uses in her beehive, she can return in a decade with an army of guerrillas, more mobile and agile than cheetahs, which could live off grass and sunlight. What can we do against such an army, blowing up power plants it doesn't need and fighting with weapons we never dreamed of?"

It was a rhetorical question, and Slade paused for dramatic effect. In the pause it occurred to Breedlove that if Kyra carried the seeds of man she would have no need to consider swarming times or incubation periods, since she was even now moving into frames of relativity where light and matter and time merged into one timeless whole.

"Plenty!" Slade answered his own question. Then, forty miles from the nearest hamburger stand, he leaned closer to Breedlove and began to speak from the corner of his mouth to keep from being overheard. ". . . *If* we know when and where she lands. You'll be the one to help us there, old buddy, because you'll know. Kyra was a queen, but she was also one hell of a woman, and she had the hots for you. All the psycho-emotional compatibility charts said so. When her swarm settles, she'll contact you because she's a baby farm and has to keep the crops coming. She'll want you for her next drone."

"How would she get in contact with me?"

Slade looked at him in amazement and exclaimed, "Hell, she'd call you on the nearest telephone—dial you collect! You'd be happy to pay the charges. But when you get that call, son, you call me pronto. Call any government bureau, tell them you're Tom Breedlove and you want to speak to Ben Slade. Don't hang up. No matter where I am in the world, I'll be on the phone in five minutes."

"I'll believe she's coming back when I hear her voice."

"You'd better start believing now, son, and when it happens you'll call me, won't you?"

There was a plea in Slade's request that Breedlove's humanity would not let him deny. Slade was the perennial spook whose professional task was to create conspiracies to guard against, but a deeper, more personal concern fretted behind his words.

"Of course I'll call you, Ben." Breedlove extended his hand to seal the promise. "Kyra would be heartbroken if you were absent from her welcoming committee, and she'll need a general for her army who's familiar with earth's terrain. Now, fly away. I want to be alone."

Slade held the hand for a moment, slapped Breedlove's shoulder in unvoiced gratitude, turned and strode toward the helicopter. Reluctant to move from the mound on which he stood, Breedlove watched the helicopter lift off, threw it a wave of his arm, and stood looking down at the willow aslant the creek, remembering that Kyra's name had meant "the far-wandering willow." In the sunlight the tree had the same shimmering quality as the girl.

She had been a quick learner. From the model at Mason's she learned the ruse for escaping from the motel. From the tale of Huan Chung she had learned how to make Ben Slade happy. And she had been generous. Beyond her general gift to humankind in her promise of an evolutionary progress toward transcendentalism, she had given each of her acolytes a special gift—Slade a continuing conspiracy, Laudermilk an unbreakable romantic record, Turpin a different and no doubt happier reality—but she had given most to Thomas Breedlove.

From the psycho-emotional charts and compatibility analysis the learned philosophers had decreed that she loved him, but what she had revealed to him on the mound was beyond documentation. Contrary to Slade's belief, there had been a consummation, and it had been more than a union. She had lifted him to heights unachieved by artists or poets and opened to his imagination the furthermost horizons of an ideal beauty, when with her radiant body she had touched his mind.

On this spot, with her time running out, she had bequeathed him one moment of grace in the fulfillment of their devotion, and the memory of her grace would provide him a quiet harbor through the vicissitudes of his remaining days. It was enough, and it was all he would ever have of her, for he knew that Kyra would not come again to Carthage.

A selection of books published by Penguin is listed on the following pages.

For a complete list of books available from Penguin in the United States, write to Dept. DG, Penguin Books, 299 Murray Hill Parkway, East Rutherford, New Jersey 07073.

For a complete list of books available from Penguin in Canada, write to Penguin Books Canada Limited, 2801 John Street, Markham, Ontario L3R 1B4.

If you live in the British Isles, write to Dept. EP, Penguin Books Ltd, Harmondsworth, Middlesex.

Science Fiction from Penguin by John Boyd

THE LAST STARSHIP FROM EARTH

Mathematicians must not write poetry—above all, they must not marry poets, decrees the state. But Haldane IV, mathematician, and Helix, poet, are in love. They are also puzzled, for they have been studying the long-hidden poetry of Fairweather I, acknowledged as the greatest mathematician since Einstein. As they explore further, the danger for them grows; the state has eyes and ears everywhere. Will they find, before it is too late, the real meaning of the following words by Fairweather I? "That he who loses wins the race,/That parallel lines all meet in space." "Terrific . . . it belongs on the same shelf with *1984* and *Brave New World*"—Robert A. Heinlein.

THE POLLINATORS OF EDEN

The coldly beautiful Dr. Freda Caron has waited too long for her fiancé, Paul Theaston, to return from Flora, the flower planet. Determined to learn what has happened, she begins a study of plants from Flora, and slowly she is warmed by her communion with them. Eventually she makes the trip from Earth to Flora for further research and to see Paul. What she finds is the secret of the flower planet, but in her initiation she too becomes a pollinator of Eden.

THE RAKEHELLS OF HEAVEN

In the future there will be colonial imperialism—in space! Two space scouts, John Adams and Kevin O'Hara, are sent to explore a distant world called Harlech. The Interplanetary Colonial Authority prohibits human colonization and control of those planets whose inhabitants closely resemble *Homo sapiens*, as the Harlechians do. Thus, relations with their women are strictly forbidden. But such rules were not made for Red O'Hara. From the Adams-O'Hara Probe, only John Adams returns. . . .

Fiction from Penguin by Lionel Davidson

THE NIGHT OF WENCESLAS

Young Nicholas Whistler is trapped. "Invited" to Prague on what seems to be an innocent business trip, he finds himself caught between the secret police . . . and the amorous clutches of the statuesque Vlasta. This first book established Lionel Davidson as a brilliant new novelist of action and adventure.

MAKING GOOD AGAIN

In Germany to settle a claim for reparation, lawyer James Raison is plunged into the old conflict between Jew and Nazi. His trip becomes more dangerous as the legal aspects of the case become more complicated, and at the same time he has to cope with his affair with Elke and his involvement with her fascist aunt Magda. *Making Good Again* is not only the story of a complicated and exciting search for the true identity of the claimant but also the story of a search that is going on in the minds of the English, German, and Jewish lawyers who are involved—a search to discover and understand the philosophy of the Nazi.

THE ROSE OF TIBET

Charles Houston had slipped illegally into Tibet to find his missing brother, only to be imprisoned in the forbidden Yamdring monastery. Now he has to get out of Tibet—quickly—for the invading Chinese army (and the cruel Himalayan winter) are right behind him. . . . Wrote Daphne du Maurier: "Is Lionel Davidson today's Rider Haggard? His novel has all the excitement of *She* and *King Solomon's Mines*."

THE SCIENCE FICTION OF EDGAR ALLAN POE

Edited by Harold Beaver

Presented together for the first time, and including the celebrated "Eureka," the sixteen stories in this volume reveal Edgar Allan Poe as both apocalyptic prophet and pioneer of science fiction. Through this new speculative fiction he sought to be the comprehensive theorist and seer of an age dominated by electromagnetism, and which witnessed the intensive exploitation of mechanical inventions and a parallel boom in all forms of transcendentalism. His tales of galvanism, mesmerism, time travel, resurrection of the dead, and demonic possession are marked by a bravado of thought, an imaginative sweep, and a sheer effrontery that is breathtaking. Together with a general Introduction and a select chronology of post-Newtonian science in the century preceding "Eureka," each of the tales in this edition carries an individual critique and full annotation.